HEARTS never LIE

BOOKS BY RACHEL BRANTON

Finding Home Series
Take Me Home
All That I Love
Then I Found You

Lily's House Series
House Without Lies
Tell Me No Lies
Your Eyes Don't Lie
Hearts Never Lie
Broken Lies
Cowboys Can't Lie

Noble Hearts
Royal Quest
Royal Dance

Picture Books
I Don't Want To Eat
Bugs
I Don't Want to Have
Hot Toes

UNDER THE NAME TEYLA BRANTON

Unbounded Series
The Change
The Cure
The Escape
The Reckoning
The Takeover

Unbounded Novellas
Ava's Revenge
Mortal Brother
Lethal Engagement
Set Ablaze

Imprints Series
Touch of Rain
On The Hunt
Upstaged
Under Fire
Blinded

Colony Six Series
Sketches

Other
Times Nine

HEARTS never LIE

RACHEL BRANTON

WHITE
STAR
PRESS

This is a work of fiction, and the views expressed herein are the sole responsibility of the author. Likewise, certain characters, places, and incidents are the product of the author's imagination, and any resemblance to actual persons, living or dead, or actual events or locales, is entirely coincidental.

Hearts Never Lie (Lily's House Book 4)

Published by White Star Press
P.O. Box 353
American Fork, Utah 84003

Copyright © 2017 by Nunes Entertainment, LLC
Cover design copyright © 2016 White Star Press

Printed in the United States of America
ISBN: 978-1-939203-88-5
Year of first printing: 2017

ZOEY'S
PLACE

I placed the bowl of chopped vegetables and bread in front of the swollen raccoon. It had been three days since the wounded animal had tried to bite me when I came to feed her in the quarantine building, and I had to admit my attachment to her was growing. I couldn't wait until Betsy, as I'd named her, delivered her babies. Homeowners had discovered her in their chimney a week earlier, her leg chewed and one eye missing after an apparent encounter with their neighbor's dog. Like many of the animals at Safe Haven Exotic Wildlife Sanctuary, coming here was her last chance.

A branch on a newly planted sapling banged loudly against the quarantine's solitary window, startling both me and the raccoon.

"It's okay girl," I murmured, darting a glance at the window. For mid-afternoon, it was growing dark, and I wondered if we were in for another microburst. I hoped not because Tuesday was fasting day for the big cats, the one day the sanctuary was closed to the public, and a storm would interfere with all the work we had to get done before the visitors returned.

I reached out to soothe Betsy as I would many of our other raccoons, but she stopped eating, cringing away from my hand. "Sorry girl," I muttered. I'd worked here a month and should remember that wild animals, even the most playful, didn't like being touched while they were eating. I eased back to give her room and came slowly to my feet.

"How's she doing?"

I jumped a little, my heart speeding into high gear, before turning around to see Stephen Carey's tall, lean figure outside the cage. He was wearing a leather bomber jacket, hands in the pockets as if he was cold, his short, brown hair standing slightly on end in the front.

"Sorry if I scared you, Zoey." He rubbed a hand through his hair, smoothing it down.

"That's okay." I glanced at the window. If anything, it was getting darker out there. "Looks like a storm."

He nodded. "Bad one, according to the forecast. A storm warning's been issued over half of Arizona, so I sent the volunteers home. We'll need to round up everyone else and secure the animals."

His aunt and uncle owned the sanctuary, and Stephen was the manager, which meant he had to deal with ordering food, public relations, keeping the books, and fundraising while the rest of us focused on the animals that came to us from all over the world. I thought we had the better end of the deal.

I ducked out of the cage door and shut it carefully behind me. Stephen watched, and I was all too aware of his stare. Last week we'd gone to see a movie together with a couple of the other sanctuary employees, and we'd had a great time. Stephen was smart, intelligent, and good looking. It wasn't anything like an official date, but ever since the movie, I'd thought about asking him out to show my interest. Yet something inside held me back. Would he even be interested if he knew the truth about my life and where I'd come from?

I pushed the thoughts away. Stephen and I were friends, and I wasn't going to let the past dictate my actions with him—or anyone else.

A movement caught my eye, but this time I wasn't startled as Declan Walker eased into view around the far end of the narrow corridor. One moment he wasn't there and the next he was, as though he had been there all along, or that we'd been expecting him. He moved with the same grace as our big cats—unhurried, powerful, and . . . natural. And just like when I watched the big cats, my heart leapt at the sight of him. He wore jeans topped by a jacket made of sturdy canvas, a bit of white wool lining showing where it opened at the neck. His slightly long, curly blond hair was messy, as if the wind had enjoyed playing in it.

Nodding a greeting, he squatted down in the narrow corridor next to the cage, studying Betsy. "She'll be dropping those kits any day now."

"How can you tell?" The raccoon didn't look any different to me than she had last week when she'd arrived, except for the healing wounds.

Declan angled his head upward, his gray-blue eyes wandering somberly over my face as if considering my statement—or perhaps wondering if I really wanted to know. I did.

"She's finished eating," he said. "Let's go in and I'll show you."

"What about securing the animals?" Stephen asked.

Declan's gaze shifted to him. "Your aunt and uncle and a couple of the others are heading out to the big cats. Ewan went for the alpaca and llamas. Kitcat's got the goats and bears. Blake's taking the wolves and coyotes. We'll check Betsy here, then divide the rest of the animals between the three of us. We'll be finished long before your uncle's back."

With nearly two dozen tigers and a half dozen other big cats to secure, I could believe that.

At Declan's reassuring words, the tension seeped from Stephen's stance. I'd noticed over the past month that Declan had the same kind of calming influence on the animals. "Ah, good," Stephen said. "Thanks for taking care of all that."

"Yep." Declan slipped inside Betsy's cage before I heard it unlatch. He moved toward the raccoon slowly, keeping low to the ground. She watched him advance, her eyes unblinking, but didn't cringe from his presence like she did most everyone except me, since I was the one who fed her.

I went back inside the enclosure after him, moving with not quite as much grace but just as slowly so I didn't startle her. To my amazement, Betsy allowed him to touch her stomach. I didn't really blame her—all the animals responded to him that way. And women. My solitary late-night study sessions certainly had as much to do with learning facts to impress him as they did with my love for the animals.

"See how tight this is?" Declan said. "You can feel the size of the babies. Go on, try it."

I touched her neck first, working my way down to her stomach, my hand brushing his as he pulled away. Gently, I explored the bulges under the raccoon's fur, all too aware of Declan's eyes on my face. We'd had many such experiences together, but for reasons I didn't want to examine too closely, being this close to him had started to make me feel uncomfortable.

Not that it really mattered, because apart from our work and training sessions, he kept too busy to exchange much casual chitchat. He hadn't even come to the movie with us last week because we'd been finishing up a habitat for a new tiger, and he'd wanted to make sure the place was ready for transfer the next day.

"Don't most raccoons give birth in late spring?" Stephen asked from outside the enclosure. "It's barely April. She's early."

Declan looked over at him, one of his shoulders lifting in a half shrug. "It happens." To me he added, "You feel it? At least four kits is my guess. Seem to be full term."

One of the babies wriggled against my touch before pushing back into the mass. I could imagine the curled form was about four or five inches long, but it was hard to tell. Betsy's stomach did seem to be stretched to the limit. "I'll have to take your word for it," I said.

Declan knew a lot about animals—even Josh Carey, Stephen's uncle, had turned over much of his beloved tigers' care to him—but I wondered how Declan could know this much about raccoon babies. Here at the sanctuary, our animals rarely had offspring. At first I was surprised that they neutered males when they were placed in habitats with females, but now it made a lot of sense. The point was to give abused or displaced wild animals the opportunity to live out their lives in comfort, not create more animals who could never return to the wild. We weren't a zoo, and living in captivity was never best for a wild animal.

"She'll be more relaxed once she's out of quarantine and with the other raccoons," Declan added. "By the way, Betsy's a good name for her."

I grinned. "I think it fits. Anyway, it was nice of everyone to let me name her."

"Hey, you won the coin toss fair and square." This from Stephen, who I suspected had rigged the game in my favor.

Together, Declan and I moved to the cage door, ducking outside and following Stephen down the quarantine's corridor. Stephen paused at the main quarantine door, which rattled slightly with the intermittent gusts of wind outside. "Let's divvy up the rest of the animals," he said. "I'll take the monkey house and the birds."

"I'll check the raccoons and the small cats," I put in hurriedly.

Declan gave a soft groan. "Guess that leaves me the apes."

Stephen held his hand to his heart and blinked dramatically. "That's because Gretta will do *anything* for you." He sniffed and pretended to wipe away a tear. "Ten years that gorilla's known me, and she still hates my guts."

"And mine," I agreed.

As far as apes went, the chimpanzees and orangutans weren't bad, but no one enjoyed coaxing any of our gorillas from their habitats and into their more secure feeding quarters. They were too independent, not to mention huge. Give me the cute little raccoons any time—and even the bobcat was more predictable. But Gretta, the oldest of the gorillas, seemed to consider Declan her mate and would do anything he asked.

Declan grinned and rolled his eyes. "Maybe I need to take a bath more often."

"Uh, I've been meaning to talk to you about that," I said, striving to keep a serious face. "But don't worry. If you don't return, we'll come looking for you."

Declan's grin became a laugh. "Thanks. Call me on the walkie if you have any trouble with Bob." His hand touched the two-way radio on his belt before zipping up his coat.

"Ah yes, Bob." The old bobcat didn't adjust well to new situations. I dragged the zipper up on my own jacket. Normally, I never used more than a long-sleeved shirt in April, but this morning I'd been glad the jacket I kept in my truck during the winter was still there.

Declan opened the quarantine door, and it was nearly pulled from his hand with a sudden blast of wind. He waited for us to emerge, then shut it carefully and headed off with a purposeful stride.

Stephen hesitated, leaning closer to me. "I had a great time last week. We should all do it again."

Warmth filled me, and I hoped my brown skin, a legacy from my Latina mother, would mask the tell-tale color that was probably seeping into my face. "Yeah, we should. It was fun." Maybe I wouldn't have to be the one to ask him out first. But why didn't I feel as excited at his attention as I'd expected?

He nodded and started away from the quarantine—only to stumble across a sharp-faced stranger in a black suit. The newcomer was as tall as Stephen but far thinner, and his eyes were too close together. He leaned into the wind, as if afraid of losing his footing. His mouth opened, but whatever he said was torn away by a gust, so I couldn't make it out.

Even standing close to him, Stephen had to yell to make himself heard, "I'm Stephen Carey."

More words I couldn't hear, and then Stephen walked back to me, his dark eyes gleaming with a challenge I knew wasn't directed at me. "It's Baxter Ross, that *attorney*." He spoke the word like a curse.

Before I'd come to work at Safe Haven, Stephen's uncle had filed a lawsuit against a local man in the community for using the content of the Carey's website to create a fake wildlife rescue site. The man had ended up bilking over a million from unwary donors. To add insult to injury, he'd sneaked into the sanctuary early one morning and hopped in with an aging Bengal tiger to make a video clip for his site.

"Seriously? Now?" I almost wished Cuddles had bitten the trespasser harder, instead of only giving him a playful warning. Of course that might have given this attorney grounds for a countersuit.

Stephen shot an annoyed glance at Ross. "We had an appointment, but I didn't think he'd still come with the storm. Our attorney texted and said he was canceling the meeting. This guy probably showed up hoping he could take advantage of our attorney not being here."

"Go deal with him," I said. "I'll check the monkeys and birds." There wasn't much to do with the birds except to make sure the aviary and flying enclosures were secure, but I'd want to double check that the herons and ostriches, who were in regular field enclosures, made it into their wooden shelters so they'd be protected from flying objects.

"Don't go easy on him," I added.

Stephen smiled with an anticipation I couldn't understand. This attorney had been dragging out the case for over a year now, and the quotes he'd shared with the press were at best intentionally misleading, and at worst outright lies. "Believe me, I have no intention of doing that."

He stalked toward the attorney, waving at him to follow. Well, better Stephen than me. I'd already had enough experience with attorneys to last a lifetime. I started into the wind as a tumbleweed passed. My long hair whipped around my face and my nose filled with dust. Pulling up my hood, I ran.

At the aviary, even the humid interior felt nice after being choked with dust. The place was locked down and food had been brought in but hadn't been placed in the feeders yet, as if someone had dropped the buckets mid-job. Probably when they got the call to check on the big cats. I took a few moments to dole out the food.

My phone buzzed in the pocket of my jeans. Still hefting the final bucket in one hand, I peeked at the caller ID and answered. "Hey, sis."

"Everything okay there?" Bianca asked. "You sound out of breath."

Using my knee to assist, I managed to dump the food without getting too much on the floor. "We're just having a bit of wind, so we're locking down the animals, but it should pass soon. Everything's great. Sorry I missed our call yesterday."

Bianca laughed. "You don't have to check up on me every day, you know."

At twenty-two, she was only a year younger than I was, but I'd been taking care of her since our mother died, years before Lily Perez became our guardian and we went to live at what would eventually become known as Lily's House. Keeping track of Bianca wasn't a habit I was likely to break any time soon. She was my best friend, not just a sister, and I missed her terribly. I'd almost passed up this job at the sanctuary because it meant leaving her in Phoenix. "You get that batch of pottery finished?"

"Oh, yes." Bianca practically breathed the words with her excitement. "I can't wait to show you my new stuff."

"I'm still planning on driving to Phoenix this weekend, so I'll see it all then." So far, I'd made the three-and-a-half-hour trip south to see my sister every weekend.

"Well, I have a big surprise for you! You're going to love it." She paused. "At least I hope so."

"I'm sure I will. How are you liking your new roommate?"

"She's good." Bianca's voice sounded a little forced.

"What aren't you telling me?" Since we'd aged out of the foster care system, we'd lived together in an apartment in Phoenix with some of our foster sisters from Lily's House— except for the past month that I'd been in Kingman, of course. Knowing the others were keeping an eye out for Bianca was the only way I'd been able to leave her, and I was still hoping she'd take me up on my offer to share my rented house here after she graduated from college this month.

"Nothing. She's fine. I'm just on my way somewhere right now, and traffic is being stupid."

"Oh, I see." I wasn't exactly buying her story, but a

storm *was* coming and I didn't want her out in it. Phoenix wasn't far enough away to be missed completely. "Well, I'm hanging up then so you can concentrate. Call me after you get wherever you're going. I should have the animals squared away soon."

"Okay, but did Betsy have her babies yet?"

"Nope. Not yet. Should be soon, though. I'll let you know."

"You love it there, don't you?" Bianca said. "I can hear it every time we talk. You finally found your place."

My place, meaning a calling in life, like the one Bianca had felt from the moment she'd picked up a piece of clay at our high school. She'd been confident that I'd find something I could be as passionate about, but it never happened, not even through four years of college and bachelor degrees in biology and chemistry.

By the time I'd finished three months at the research firm where I'd been hired after college, I was beginning to believe a "place" wasn't something most ordinary folks like me ever found. Six months later, I'd quit the firm.

This job at the sanctuary had been a fluke, and I'd intended it as a short term venture until I figured out where I really wanted to end up. Yet after only the first day, it was clear why my future had eluded me before. Who would have thought working with exotic animals was an option, much less a calling? But I belonged at the sanctuary as I'd never belonged anywhere else, except for maybe Lily's House.

"You were right," I conceded. "Now concentrate on driving. We'll talk later."

As we hung up, a faint rumbling came from outside the aviary, and several birds let out loud *ca-caws* in answer.

I was glad the aviary was built to withstand a hurricane because too many of our birds were maimed or wounded and wouldn't be safe out in this storm.

Ducking into the wind once more, I hurried past our large flight enclosures, where our non-tropical birds had already taken refuge in their wooden structures. Beyond the flight enclosures, I found the ostriches already in their shelters as well, but I had to entice the emu in. By the time I'd finished locking her down, my eyes stung with grit and I was wishing I had goggles.

Now for the monkeys, who were never very cooperative unless bribery was involved. I went inside and rattled the food dishes to attract their attention, and they came hurtling inside. Unfortunately, with the volunteer staff sent home and the rest of us securing the sanctuary, there was no food yet, and might not be any until much later, and they weren't shy about squealing their discontent and banging on the bars as I locked them in.

"Sorry guys." Once the five shelters were secure, I hurried on to the raccoon habitat, where we'd release Betsy after her quarantine was over. The raccoons were already inside their underground structures, huddled together for comfort. "That's it. Smart little creatures." Raccoons were good at self-preservation.

Only the small cats were left. The air was positively dark now, and I held the front of my jacket over my mouth to avoid breathing in the dust. This was bad—really bad. A sense of dread filled me. I hoped Bianca had arrived at her destination, or that the storm wasn't as bad in Phoenix.

The small cats were inside their underground dens,

except Bob, who was prowling along the fence, letting out irritable roars that made shivers crawl down my spine. Going inside each enclosure, I pulled down and locked the wood doors over the other dens while contemplating how to get the bobcat inside his.

Even as I watched, a large piece of wood sailed past, slamming into the fence near Bob, scaring him further. I needed to secure him before he was hit by something, but with how worked up he was, enticing him to safety was going to be a challenge. Like many of our wild animals, Bob had been rescued from a Vegas animal act, and he was accustomed to being around people. On a normal day, I wouldn't be averse to going inside and calling him to me for a nice scratch—but only a crazy person would jump inside his habitat before he'd eaten, especially when he was this upset.

I was debating whether or not I had time to go for a tranquilizer gun when Declan appeared, his hair wild from the wind, curling in every direction. He looked like a powerful Norse God, stepping out of the storm to come to my aid. Without argument, he was one of the most ruggedly attractive men I'd ever met, and for the slightest instant, I forgot to breathe.

Grinning widely, he tossed me a small sack, and something heavy squished in my hands as I caught it. At least it wouldn't be me Bob would take a bite out of today.

"Gee, thanks." My heart beat oddly in a way that had nothing to do with the storm but everything with Declan's presence.

"I figured temperamental Bob wouldn't go eas—"

Declan froze in mid-utterance as he stared at something over my shoulder.

"What are you—" I turned to see the entire horizon painted a dark gray, a maelstrom of . . . something heading in our direction. "Is that dirt?" I'd lived in Arizona all my life, and I'd never witnessed a sight so massive and utterly terrifying.

Declan nodded. "I think so. We'd better hurry."

The tasty slab of raw USDA Choice Beef was exactly the enticement the bobcat needed. With relief, I locked Bob safely inside and hurried to join Declan.

"We'll have to board the gift shop windows," he said, his voice hurried and tight.

"There are some two-by-fours in the quarantine."

Declan nodded. "It's a start."

We ran together, fighting the ever-increasing wind. As we rounded the quarantine building, our hands brushed and heat spread up my arm. What was going on with me? I angled farther away so it wouldn't happen again.

The wind ripped the quarantine door from my grasp as I opened it, but fortunately Declan managed to prevent it from banging open. It took both of us to shut the door behind us. We quickly loaded up with the wood and staggered back into the storm. The entire way back to the gift shop, I fought not to lose my load, clutching it against the aggressive blasts of wind.

Inside the gift shop, we found Stephen and the attorney

arguing. ". . . over a million dollars to feed our animals every year," Stephen was saying. "Not only did your client directly interfere with our ability to operate, but he endangered one of our tigers."

"Well, you've certainly publicized the occurrence enough," Ross retorted. "That should have more than made up the little you lost." The attorney turned to us as we approached. "Wouldn't you agree?"

Declan rolled his eyes. "People have donated to money toward the lawsuit to help the animals and because what your client did was wrong, not to lessen his responsibility. It makes no difference how much we've raised. No jury in the world is going to buy the sob story you're trying to spin. We're the victims here. All the rest is so much hot air."

"You've vilified my client," spluttered the attorney.

Stephen snorted. "It's true we've told everyone what happened, and we're proud of the support people have shown. However, your client's actions are the only thing that have vilified him. For the record, we officially reject your settlement offer of an apology."

Ross's face flushed and his thin nostrils flared. "You should talk to your attorney first."

"I don't need to talk to my attorney," Stephen said. "He works for me, and if he were here, he'd tell you the same thing. Now if you can't make it home, you're welcome to hang out in our breakroom while we finish securing the place."

Ross stalked toward the door, reaching past me for the handle, but he froze as he stared out the window, swearing under his breath. The angry wall of dirt had nearly arrived.

"Come on," Declan said to Stephen. "Grab the toolbox."

Stephen nodded. "I wonder why the others aren't back yet to help. Hope they're okay. Wish now I hadn't sent all the volunteers home." He snapped his fingers at the attorney, who was still gazing blankly out the window. "You, Ross! Snap out of it. If that dirt breaks the windows in here, it's not going to be pretty. Empty some of those boxes behind the counter. We can nail them over the windows when we run out of wood."

We left Ross emptying a box of plush tigers and went back outside. The air was already much thicker with dirt, and I pushed my face into my arm as I struggled against the wind with my load of wood. A shingle that had been ripped from a roof somewhere flew past, barely missing my head.

Declan and I held the wood in place as Stephen used the nail gun. After a minute, I grabbed it from him. "Let me do that." For someone who'd practically grown up at the sanctuary building habitats, he didn't seem to know how to drive a decent nail.

Stephen grimaced as I rapidly fired the nails into the wood. "Those'll be tough to get out. We'll have to repaint. Again."

Oh, so damaging the new paint was his problem, not driving the nails. Good thing I didn't have such reservations.

"Can't be helped," Declan said.

"I'll help you repaint," I added.

We only had enough wood for the two largest windows, and Stephen went inside for the flattened cardboard boxes as I fired in the last few nails. He returned in less than a minute. The storm was in full fury now, and my cheeks felt raw with the pounding grit in the air.

As we pushed toward the next window, I gaped at a tree

trunk coming our way, bouncing end over end like a stick some giant had thrown to his dog. "Look out!" I screamed, but the wind tore the words away. I watched helplessly as the tree hurtled toward Stephen.

Then Declan was there, shoving him out of the way. Too late. A sickening crack, and the tree connected with Stephen's right leg. Both men sprawled to the ground and the cardboard boxes caught the wind and flipped away. I'd barely reached the men when a second loud crash told me the tree had found another target: the quarantine. Through the storm, I could barely see part of it jutting from a huge hole in the side of the structure.

Oh, no, Betsy! Her cage was in the front middle of the building—right where the tree had hit. I felt sick at the idea of what might have happened to her. But there was nothing I could do about it now, not before making sure Stephen was all right.

"Help me get him inside!" Declan shouted.

Setting the safety and looping my arm through the handle of the nail gun, I grabbed one of Stephen's arms and helped drag him into the gift shop, where we both had to release him to get the door closed. After shutting out the howling wind, I knelt down next to Stephen. "Are you okay?" I asked.

His face was ashen beneath a thick layer of dust. "It's just my leg. Better get the windows from the inside as best you can. Too dangerous out there."

Declan was already grabbing more boxes, and dumping contents the gift shop workers hadn't yet had time to unload after the last shipment several days ago. I lifted the nail gun and went to work. At least this way we could stop some of the dust from entering, even if the windows broke. Not to mention protect ourselves from flying glass. That is, *if* the cardboard held, which was an unknown at this point. Another tree trunk would probably sail right through both the glass and the cardboard.

That made me worry about even more Betsy and her unborn babies out in the quarantine. Was she all right?

When the remaining two windows were as secure as we could make them, we also covered the window in the adjoining breakroom. "That should do it," Declan said.

"Just don't stand too close to the windows," I muttered.

"Right." Declan led the way back to Stephen, who still sprawled in the gift shop near the door. He was pale, and his forehead furrowed with pain, but he wasn't moaning and there was no blood leaking through his pants, which I took as a good sign.

"Help me get him to the breakroom," Declan said to Ross.

The attorney glanced down at his suit and then back at us, his bottom lip curled. "He's covered in dirt."

Seriously? What a jerk. "I'll help." I squatted down like Declan and grabbed one of Stephen's arms, draping it over my neck.

"Lift on three," Declan said.

Somehow we got Stephen up and half dragged, half carried him through the gift shop aisles to the door at the back and into to the employee breakroom.

"You're strong for such a little thing," Stephen said, biting back a groan as we reached the couch.

There had been a time when no one would have called me little, and I should be happy about his comment, but instead I felt partially exposed. "You learn to pull your weight where I grew up," I said, keeping my tone casual.

I glanced over at Declan to see him watching me intently. I wondered if he could somehow see past my current exterior to the frightened, abused, overweight orphan I'd once been. "What?" I said.

He grinned. "Your hair."

I touched it gingerly, to find it matted and filthy, as though I'd let it dry on its own after mudwrestling. I combed it with my fingers for a few seconds before giving up.

"I think it looks kind of sexy," Stephen said.

I rolled my eyes but didn't comment because he was breathing oddly. "Better find him some painkillers," I told Declan as I pushed Stephen to lie down on the couch. "Hold still," I added to Stephen. "I need to check out your leg."

Gingerly, I began touching his leg, working slowly from his ankle up to his knee, where he gasped and tried to jerk away—only to groan with the additional pain the movement caused.

"Your leg might be broken, but I can't feel any protruding bones or anything out of place, so you're probably not in immediate danger."

"He might have internal bleeding," Declan said. "We'd better keep a close eye on him just in case."

Stephen groaned loudly. "I'm fine. Just get me a pill. Then let's try to call the others on the walkies."

"Got ibuprofen right here." Declan grabbed a bottle from the first aid kit on the counter by the sink and began searching through the cupboard for a glass.

With everything under control here, my thoughts

returned to Betsy. "I'll be right back." Leaving Declan to watch Stephen, I went out to the main gift shop area where Ross was still standing, as useless as ever.

He perked up when he saw me. "You got any drinks here?"

"There's a vending machine outside." I smiled with false sweetness, jerking my head toward the door.

He gave me a sour glare that almost made me laugh. Striding to the fridge in the corner, he pulled out a can of soda. "So, do you like working for this outfit? Are you happy here? You must hear a lot of scuttlebutt. Bet you know all the ways they take advantage of their workers and how much money they waste."

"What I know," I told him, "is if you were any kind of an attorney, you'd stop egging your client on and advise him to take responsibility." I held up my hands in mock discovery. "Oh, wait. Then the case would be over and you wouldn't be able to bill him attorney fees." I turned from him, making my way to the door, where I stopped for a parting shot. "Look, you aren't fooling anyone except your client, who's probably stupid enough to believe he's got you fooled instead."

In three seconds flat, Ross's face turned from I'm-your-best-buddy-so-tell-me-your-secrets to I'm-going-to-murder-you-and-hide-your-body. It was rather gratifying to watch. He opened his mouth, but I turned from him and eased the door open a crack, grasping it firmly so the wind wouldn't yank it from me.

"Are you crazy?" Ross said. "Shut th—"

I slipped through the crack and out into the wind. It was

a bad idea. I knew it from the minute I stepped into the swirling dust. I could no longer see more than a foot in front of my face. How could I tell if another tree or something equally big was coming toward me?

No, I'd be fine. The quarantine was just a short distance away, and I had to know if Betsy was all right. If her enclosure had been penetrated when the tree hit the quarantine, as I suspected, she and her babies would be in serious danger. I'd already delayed long enough.

Launching myself blindly in the direction of the quarantine, I fervently began to hope I didn't get turned around, or maybe I'd end up with Bob after all. Thankfully, I was able to catch sight of the building's edge before I'd completely passed it. When I opened the door, the wind ripped it off its hinges, the corner slamming on the ground and splintering before the entire door cartwheeled out of sight.

Oops.

Gritting my teeth, I went inside. Dust and dirt swirled around the interior of the quarantine, but with the flashlight from my pocket, the visibility was considerably better than directly in the storm. As I'd suspected, the tree trunk had sailed partially into Betsy's cage and was now wedged firmly in the wire.

My heart fell to my stomach, where it sat like a lump of undigested food. "No," I murmured. I almost didn't want to look, but I had to know if Betsy was hurt and if there was anything I could do to help her.

I forced my feet to continue forward, gripping the flash-light far too tightly. I was tempted to call out, but the wind made hearing impossible. Easing around the tree trunk, I was encouraged when I didn't see the raccoon flattened on the bottom of the cage. In fact, I didn't see her in the cage at all. That was odd.

Further inspection showed a gap in the wire to one side of the tree trunk that might be large enough to have let the pregnant raccoon through. Great. That meant Betsy could be almost anywhere by now. I hoped her sense of preserva-tion meant that she hadn't gone outside, or we might never find her again. Even if she survived the storm, her babies most likely wouldn't.

I started at one end of the corridor, working slowly, searching every possible cubbyhole. Dirty tears stung my eyes. I probably should have moved her into the breakroom when the storm hit, but how was I to know it would be so bad?

Wait. Were those raccoon eyes? I crawled past the tree, edging closer to a barrel in the corner that contained metal scraps and pieces of wood destined for the garbage. The eyes had disappeared, but under my flashlight, I could see Betsy's fur. Relief shuddered through me. She was okay. Now what to do with her?

I was still several feet away when she attacked, launching herself at me as if I'd come hunting her. Razor-sharp teeth bit into my left wrist, piercing me again and again until I snatched my arm away. Pain clouded my vision.

She hurtled past me, but not until I saw that she was bleeding from a fresh wound. No. That wasn't blood from a wound, she was giving birth—or starting to. Immediately, I forgave Betsy for the bite, though my wrist throbbed horribly.

Betsy didn't dart out the open door as I'd expected, but into one of the other enclosures. I crawled back under the tree, one-handed, my hair whipping around in the wind. The entire building shook, as if threatening to blow apart. I slammed the cage shut and looked around for something I could use to protect her better.

My eyes felt full of grit and sand, and something wet dripped down my hurt hand. No choice but to press on. Betsy's rabies test results wouldn't be in for a couple more days, but there was no use worrying about that at the moment.

Past where we'd found the wood, I saw crates and blankets that might be of use, but what to do with them? Maybe I could put one of the crates inside the cage and she could hole up inside it and be okay, even with the wind and no help. How long until the storm passed, and we could get back to her? I'd heard of storms lasting several days, but surely that wasn't common.

The decision was made for me when I noticed the gaping

hole in the roof over the new cage. Too easy for her to get out. "Okay," I said, wrapping the blanket around my hurt arm until no skin showed. She shouldn't be able to bite through it now. Opening the cage, I slowly pushed in the crate and another blanket.

Oh, she isn't going to be happy about this, I thought, as I crawled inside.

Something told me I was crazy for going into the enclosure at all, but I was determined to save her. Quickly, I tossed the blanket over the raccoon, expecting her to go wild. Instead, she held perfectly still. It was a little matter to set the crate over the lump she made, pushing the edges of the blanket inside, so she wouldn't feel squished.

Then it was back out of the cage for a flat-edge shovel to gently push under the crate and the raccoon, followed by the almost impossible feat of making sure she stayed inside as I carefully and slowly tipped the crate right side up and placed the other blanket over the top. Before I could congratulate myself, I realized that with the pregnant raccoon in the crate, it was too unwieldy for me to get far with my hurt wrist, especially in that wind.

Great, now what?

"Zoey?" came a faint voice. I turned toward the door and there was Declan, looking again like a mythical Norse god. "I thought I'd find you here." He had to yell at me to make himself heard.

I waved the flashlight. "Help me with this crate."

He ducked inside the enclosure, his eyes straying to where Betsy had been when we'd left her earlier. "Oh, no."

"She's fine." I pointed at the crate. "But we can't leave her here."

"Right." He peeked inside. "Looks cozy enough."

"I'm pretty sure she's in labor."

He glanced around as the quarantine building shook. "This place looks like it's going to tear apart at any moment."

Together we pushed and pulled the crate out of the cage, where Declan was able to heft it. He leaned over and yelled in my ear, "Help me keep the edges of the blanket down, at least until we get to the gift shop door. If she jumps out, we'll never catch her."

I nodded, holding back a wince as I pushed down with my sore wrist. Together, we plunged into the storm. Dirt filled my nose and throat, choking me. Pebbles stung my cheeks. Each step seemed to take a lifetime.

I was beginning to think we'd passed by the gift shop altogether when my back slammed into it. Slowly, I slid along the building until we reached the door. I eased it open, catching the door between my knees, struggling to hold it steady.

Declan passed through. "Help her with the door," he growled at Ross.

The attorney did his first useful thing of the day—or maybe his entire life—and helped me pull the door closed. I sighed with relief.

"You're bleeding," Ross said.

Declan looked at me, but I shook my head. "Later. Let's get her into the breakroom closet." He nodded and led the way. Ross followed us like a pet dog.

Stephen was waiting for our return and listening to the radio broadcaster talk about the storm. While I'd been gone, someone—probably Declan—had wrapped a cardboard box around his leg and knee, securing it in place with rags.

The closet was the perfect place for the raccoon, the space dark and almost quiet after the wind outside. "Is she going to need help with the delivery?" I asked.

Declan shook his head. "No. At least I hope not. Let's give her a moment to calm down and we'll bring her some water and anything else we can find."

As I came out of the closet, Stephen's eyes fell on my bloodied hand. "What happened?"

I pulled back my jacket sleeve a few inches. "I startled Betsy. She was scared."

"Wait. There is a wild animal in that crate?" Ross asked. "You seriously aren't keeping it in here with us." His eyes strayed to a rack of guns displayed in a locked cabinet on the back wall. "You need to put it down. There's no telling who else it will hurt."

Everyone ignored him.

"Let's take a look." Declan helped me remove my jacket and began pushing up my sleeve, his hands gentle. I reached out to stop him from pushing it too high. I didn't want him to see what I kept hidden from the world.

"Oh, wow," he said. "That looks nasty. You're going to have a few scars."

If he only knew. Scars were the least of my worries.

My stomach was tied in knots, and I had to force myself to relax as Declan started across the room for the first aid kit. Could I stop him from guessing my secret? It would depend on how far up the bite marks went. I lifted my sleeve and found only one set of teeth marks that went too high. I pushed and held down the material of my long-sleeved tee to stop the flow of blood. I'd bandage that one myself later.

"Sorry about that," Stephen said from the couch.

I settled at one of the break tables. "Not your fault. She was really scared. I think she's in labor."

Stephen made a face. "Lousy time for it. You did good bringing her here. We were worried about you, though, when we realized you'd gone."

"I should have told you. I wasn't thinking."

"You mean, you didn't want us to stop you," Declan said, slapping the first aid kit onto the table and sliding into the seat next to me.

I stifled a laugh. "Okay, maybe a little."

At the other table, Ross gave a loud sigh and mumbled something under his breath.

Declan glanced in his direction. "You got something to say? Because you know where the door is, if you have a problem with us." Declan held Ross's stare until finally the attorney shook his head and looked away. The man wasn't bad, so long as he kept his mouth shut.

Declan began cleaning my cuts, his touch gentle yet surprisingly thorough. Heat suffused me, radiating out from his fingers like some kind of electricity. I couldn't tear my gaze from his face. He glanced up just then and caught me staring, but he didn't look away and neither did I. His eyes held mine for a long, silent moment as something passed between us.

I swallowed hard, my throat feeling dry and painful—and yet wonderful at the same time. Was this why I'd felt uncomfortable around him lately? Had I recognized this feeling hovering around us . . . poised for discovery? Discovery—and possible rejection?

I wet my lips, and he followed the motion before finally dropping his gaze to my wrist, his eyes unreadable. "Thirsty?" he asked, the slightest hitch in his voice.

"Yeah," I managed to say.

"Almost finished."

But I didn't want him to stop touching me. Not ever. As he wrapped tape around the gauze, I studied his face: square jaw, tanned cheeks, wide set gray-blue eyes, blond lashes now caked in dust. Lips that compelled me and made me wonder what it would be like to . . .

Before I remembered to stop him, he was pushing up my sleeve, revealing not only the final teeth marks, but also the two-inch scars. The self-inflicted ones, long healed, their patterns precise and unmistakable, numerous thin lines all in a row. I started to pull away, but it was too late. He'd seen them, and even if he might not understand this second, it wouldn't take him long.

I couldn't even look at him now. A moment before I was wondering what it would be like to kiss him; now I doubted I would ever have the chance to find out.

4

Lily's sister, Tessa, who was also my therapist, said I'd have moments like this when I would regret my past so entirely it would seem impossible to move on. "But remember that's a lie," she'd told me. "Because however much you hate your past, you *have* overcome it."

She was right. I'd survived and I'd kept Bianca safe. Whatever else happened in my life, I had that knowledge.

"Little sting," Declan said as he swabbed the teeth marks with alcohol, acting as if he hadn't seen the scars at all. "Betsy hasn't shown any signs of rabies since we brought her in, and the dog who attacked her didn't have it, but we won't know for sure—"

"For two more days," I finished. "I know."

"Lena may want you to get the shots anyway," Stephen said, referring to his aunt. "She's a worrier."

I made a face. "I hear the shots are awful. I think I can wait out the few days to be sure. They'll still be effective then." Rabies could be deadly, but getting treatment was more of a pressing serious matter than a dire emergency.

Declan nodded and placed the final bandage. "That's what I'd do. Whatever you decide, we can't do anything about it until the storm stops. There, all finished."

With relief, I pulled down my sleeve. What did he think of me now? I didn't dare meet his eyes again to see if there was any hint of his reaction to my scars now that he'd had a little time to think about it. Thankfully, he arose and went to the closet, squatting down and placing his cheek against the door, listening.

I went to the bathroom to see if I could get the grit from my eyes. I looked even worse than I'd thought, my dark hair matted like a character from a horror movie. Leaning over the sink, I rubbed my good hand over my scalp and watched the dirt fall. What I needed was a good shower, and though we had one here, it would be difficult with one hand and nothing to change into. After rinsing the best I could in the sink, I blotted my hair with a towel, flipped my head upside down, and brushed through the wet strands with a brush I found in a drawer. Washing my face one-handed was every bit as much of a challenge, but by the time I'd finished, at least the sandpaper feeling was gone—along with every bit of makeup I'd put on that morning.

When I emerged from the bathroom, feeling only slightly more human, Declan was still crouched by the closet door. He motioned to me. "She climbed out of the crate. I think it's time to give her water."

"We'll have to use the plastic bowls. I have some vegetables left over from lunch. She'll need the strength."

"Good idea."

Declan went for the bowls, while I fished out my veggies

from the fridge. The numerous food containers inside reminded me of the other employees. "Any word from the others?" I asked Stephen.

"Yeah, they couldn't make it back. They're taking refuge in the shed."

"That's good they made it there." We used the shed to store tools we used more frequently for the big cats. There was a breakroom and water there as well, for those who didn't want to come all the way into the gift shop, though the place wasn't nearly as nice as this breakroom. Sometimes Declan and the others would sleep there when they didn't want to leave a new animal overnight.

Declan pulled on thick gloves before easing the closet door open. Smart move with how upset Betsy had been. Nothing rushed out at us, so he placed the bowl inside, followed by another with my baby carrots and broccoli pieces, plus a few nuts I'd added for protein.

"Got a flashlight?" Declan asked.

I fished it from the pocket of my jacket and handed it to him. He flicked it around the closet. "There she is, behind the boots."

"Looks like she dragged over one of the blankets. Is that normal?"

"She's trying to make a nest. Listen." We both paused, scarcely breathing.

"I don't hear anything."

"No babies yet, then." He rose, changing the position of the flashlight. "Ah, but you're right about her being in labor. Notice how fast she's breathing? I'd say we're going to see a baby in the next few minutes. Hopefully. Otherwise she might need help."

"We'd have to sedate her." That would require a return trip the quarantine to get the drugs—provided the building was still standing.

Declan frowned and shut the door with the barest of clicks. "She'll be okay."

I hoped he was right.

The lights flickered twice before plunging us into darkness.

"There're some emergency lights in the cupboard." Stephen said, his face partially illuminated by the screen of his cell phone. "And a radio."

Declan was already moving, so I stayed where I was until the first battery-powered lantern turned on. Then I retrieved the radio, seeing with relief a pile of extra batteries. We'd have to thank Lena, the worrier, later.

Stephen awkwardly adjusted his position on the couch. "Hopefully, the radio will tell us what's going on if cell service goes down."

Declan broke out some granola bars, and we ate in a silence only broken by the radio broadcasters arguing whether or not this was the worst storm they'd ever seen. They were talking about rain, and I lifted the edge of the cardboard to look out. Everything was dark, more like midnight than five o'clock, but sure enough, though the sound of the wind hadn't changed, there were raindrops now on the window.

"They're right. It's raining," I said. "Maybe that means it'll be over soon."

"I hope so, or with how violent it is out there, we could have flooding." This from Declan.

That worried me. "Not here, right?"

"I think we're high enough to be okay, and so are the animal enclosures, but the roads coming in and out—I've seen them covered in several feet of water before."

I shivered involuntarily, thinking of my sister. "I wonder if the storm's this bad everywhere." Had she gotten home or somewhere safe before the worst had hit?

I checked my phone, noting I had five waiting texts but none from my sister. I was dialing her number before I knew I'd decided. "Was there anything about Phoenix on the radio?" I asked Stephen as the phone rang. "Or did you read anything on your phone?"

"Just that they had a storm warning like we did."

No answer from Bianca.

"I just talked to my wife," Ross volunteered. "She's keeping the kids inside, but she says it isn't too bad."

His words should have comforted me, but I was still worried about Bianca not answering her phone. Was a cell tower down in Phoenix? I scrolled through my contacts, looking for someone who might have heard from Bianca, and my eyes were drawn back to the message icon. Clicking on the notification, I saw the messages I hadn't yet read were all from Ruth Truman, one of our former foster sisters who still lived with Bianca in the apartment. Ruth had lived with Lily as long as we had, and we shared a similar darkness in our past, which made us closer than most. Her texts all said the same thing: *Is Bianca with you? Call me.*

Ruth answered on my first ring. "Please tell me Bianca is with you," she said without a greeting. "I'm going to kill her for making me worry."

Ruth was always playing mother, and at any other moment, I would have teased her about worrying. Now her words made me panic. "What do you mean? I'm in Valentine at the sanctuary. Bianca's in Phoenix, but she's not answering her phone."

"You're kidding, right?"

"Ruth! Where is she?" I became aware of everyone in the breakroom staring at me: Declan from the window, Stephen on the couch, and Ross at a table. I turned my back and pressed the phone tightly to my ear. "Where is she?" I repeated.

Ruth's words came spilling out. "She went to see you! Or to move in with you, I mean. She left like four or five hours ago. Before the storm. Oh, I can't believe this is happening! She wanted to surprise you, so she arranged to submit her final art projects early. Then we stuffed everything we could into her car this morning—not the pottery wheel or her pots, obviously, but practically everything else. I told her three times about the storm warning, but she said she'd be there long before it hit. Then she never called to say she got there. I've been calling and texting her for the past hour because of the flooding."

"What flooding?" Alarm filled me at the word. Declan said he'd seen the roads around here covered in water.

"On Route 93. But maybe she was past it by then. She's probably fine. She could have—"

"Ruth," I said, trying to stop the jumble of words, "did she say if she was going to my place in Kingman, or if she was heading to the sanctuary in Valentine?"

"I don't know." Ruth paused and I wished I could reach through the phone and shake her.

"Did she say anything that might give you a clue? Because otherwise, I won't know where to look for her."

"Well, she said something about seeing a raccoon. Do you have one at the sanctuary that's going to have a baby?"

I stifled a groan. I knew that meant my sister had been heading here, not to my house in Kingman. Bianca had driven to see me three times in the past month, and after the first time, she'd started using Hackberry Road instead of deviating to Kingman on the I-40 and then going up Route 66 to Valentine and the sanctuary. The unpaved Hackberry Road might be interesting to drive on a good day, but in a storm, it could be a death trap, especially in my sister's little Honda.

Ruth was still talking in my ear, but I couldn't internalize what she was saying. Something about Lily sending out her husband to look for Bianca on the road leading from Phoenix. "Call me if you hear from her," I said. "I'll let you know if I find out anything."

I hung up, standing for a moment rooted to the spot, unsure what I was going to do. In the end, though, there was no real choice. I was the only one who could get to Bianca, and it was up to me to find her. In two steps, I was grabbing my jacket and pulling it on. The left sleeve was slightly stiff with caked blood.

"What's wrong?" Stephen asked.

"My sister left to come here hours ago, and no one has heard from her." Now that I thought about it, she'd probably been on her way when I'd talked to her in the aviary. That seemed like a lifetime ago.

"You can't go out there," Ross said. "It's suicide."

I glared at him. "I guess that means you're not coming, huh? Why am I not surprised? You're such a jerk, you know?"

"Uh, Zoey, for once, I agree with him," Stephen said. "You'll have to wait for the storm to pass. Then we'll all go."

"*You* can't go anywhere. But I am going after my sister. Now." I grabbed a few water bottles from the fridge. We didn't have any more blankets in here, but we had some small animal print ones in the gift shop.

Please let her be okay. Maybe if I said it enough, she would be.

"Zoey, no!" Stephen tried to raise himself from the couch but sank back in pain.

I purposefully avoided his eyes—and Declan's, though I was aware of Declan going into the closet. Maybe he was checking on Betsy, but I was too panicked to care. He'd have to take care of both the raccoon and Stephen. Ross, of course, would take care of himself.

Without another word, I ran into the gift shop and stuffed a lap blanket, a sweatshirt, and a handful of candy bars into my backpack. Then I checked for the keys to my truck, pulled up my hood, and plunged into the darkness of the storm.

I hurried as fast as I could, stifling the fear that pummeled through me with the wind and rain. I was soaked before I'd gone ten feet, but at least the heavy deluge had cleared away much of the dust in the air so I could see my way to the muddy parking lot. The sky was still black and ugly, the wind battering. The raindrops felt like whips of ice.

Sprinting to my Toyota, I felt a sense of déjà vu. When Bianca and I had run away from our uncle's home all those years ago, it hadn't been storming, but the fear was exactly the same. Fear that if I failed, Bianca would pay the price. Fear that he'd find us and force us to go back. Grief for my mother—and anger at her for dying and leaving us with no protection from his abuse. I was fifteen when we left; she'd been dead three years. Then and now, Bianca only had me.

No, that wasn't fair to say, not since Lily Perez had found us in the park. We'd had Lily, her husband, and the foster sisters. An education. I wasn't really alone.

Except at this moment, I sure felt alone. Would Stephen had come with me if he wasn't injured? I really couldn't say.

I tried not to think about Declan, the man who would

face a raging tiger with the same aplomb he showed when he so tenderly felt Betsy's stomach. He must be disgusted with me after seeing the marks I could never hide. It was one thing to come to terms with what happened myself and an entirely different matter to expect others to understand.

His problem, I thought. *I don't care.*

It felt like a lie.

My hand shook as I tried to open the door to the Toyota. The truck was ancient, the green paint peeling, but it had new tires and the engine was reliable. Lily's husband had picked it out with me years ago when I turned eighteen, and now just touching the side made me feel less alone. The truck would make it over Hackberry Road in this storm, if anything could.

I'm coming, Bianca. Other words ran through my mind, chiding ones that would make certain she'd never risk herself again, but what if I never had the chance to say any of them?

My chest ached with the pain of it all. I shouldn't have left Phoenix. Finding my future meant nothing if something terrible happened to my sister.

Finally, the key twisted in the lock, but a clunk in the back of the truck startled me before I could yank open the door. I pushed my wet hair from my eyes and turned to see Declan, who had apparently thrown a tool box in the back of my truck. That was followed by a pickaxe and a shovel before he covered it all with a tarp and began tying it down.

"What do you think you're doing?" I yelled over the wind. I hated the relief I felt seeing him, but at the same time I wanted to grab onto him and weep with gratitude.

"Going with you," he yelled back, barely looking up from his task.

"Why?"

"Because you shouldn't go alone."

"What about Stephen?"

"I gave him a shotgun. In case the attorney acts up."

Despite myself, I sputtered a half laugh. "Good." Amazing how the situation looked so much more hopeful now.

Opening the door a crack, I threw in my backpack and climbed onto the bench seat. Seconds later, Declan tossed his canvas bag on the floor of the passenger seat and jumped in, his hair plastered against his face but still curling in a few places.

"Thanks for coming," I said.

He shrugged. "At least I got that bath we were talking about. Where're we heading? Kingman?"

The smirk died on my face. "Hackberry Road. You sure you want to go?"

Declan held out his hands as if weighing the options. "Hmm, let's see, facing almost certain death on a washed-out back road . . ." He let his left hand sink farther than the right. "Or putting up with that lying, pathetic excuse for an attorney." His right hand plunged to his knee.

I couldn't help laughing for real then. "Well, when you say it like that."

"No contest at all. Let's go."

"Anyway, my truck hasn't let me down yet," I mumbled as the engine caught, "so it's not certain death." As if to disagree, a jagged streak of lightning cut through the angry clouds. Way too close.

"I hear being in a vehicle prevents people from being hit by lightning. That's good."

"Yes, it is." I punched the gas and we shot forward.

The street from the sanctuary to Route 66 was paved, but in the few minutes it took to reach the highway, my arms ached from tightly clutching the wheel as I tried to keep us on the road. Rain fell in sheets so dense the wipers couldn't keep up, and once we reached Route 66, I had to slow to a crawl. The normally well-traveled historic highway was completely deserted.

By the time we reached Hackberry Road, my nerves felt stretched to the point of breaking. I steered onto the dirt, glad that here at the beginning of the road, the earth was rocky enough to give the truck a little traction. Regardless, I wouldn't give up. Bianca would know that I was coming.

I tossed Declan my cell phone. "Try to call her, would you? The unlock pattern is a backward C."

He dragged his finger over the face but shook his head. "Sorry, no bars. Not surprised in this storm. It was only a matter of time before the cell towers were affected."

"Try your phone."

He did. "Same here."

I wanted to scream and slam my hand against the steering wheel, but instead I breathed out a deep and steady sigh.

"You okay?"

"I will be." Breathing was one of the techniques I'd learned to ease tension, much safer than cutting or hurting myself. Actually, screaming was pretty good too, but that wasn't an option with Declan sitting here next to me. Running, swimming, and watching a good horror movie also helped.

"Oh, I meant to tell you," Declan said. "Betsy had one of her babies before we left."

"Really?" Hearing that was better than screaming any day. "Then she should be okay."

"I think so. She was taking a little break when I checked on her, but the others should come faster."

For no reason at all, I suddenly felt weepy, but at least I no longer felt like screaming or hitting the wheel. Maybe Declan had a soothing effect on me too.

We crept along the road. It was growing muddy now, but the truck was still moving. As long as I didn't stop, we shouldn't get stuck—I hoped. There seemed to be no letting up on the heavy downpour.

"Ever seen anything this bad?" I asked Declan

"No. I've heard old-timers talk about killer storms, but I've never been in one this bad myself."

"We're going to need a new quarantine, or fix that hole the tree made. I didn't mean to let the door blow away."

"I think that was one of the original structures that they modified when the sanctuary first opened. Believe me, a new one is long overdue."

"You've been here six years, right?" I risked a second-long glance to see him peering attentively through the windshield as if doing so helped me stay on the road. Thankfully, he hadn't come up with the stupid macho suggestion that he drive my truck. I knew my baby better than anyone.

"That's right."

"You think you'll ever do anything else?"

"Nope."

I didn't question him because I felt the same way. But with Stephen managing the place and the Careys owning it, there really wasn't any way for Declan to move up. I didn't know what he earned now, but my temporary wage here wasn't nearly as much as I'd been making at the research firm. I didn't care about getting rich—the sanctuary was a non-profit outfit—but even if they did have a permanent job open up, I'd need more if I was to make it a career. For the moment, I was content with the situation, but soon I'd have to make plans for the future. At least I knew now that I wanted to work with animals, and that was more than I'd learned during all my years in college.

We lapsed into a comfortable silence, the rain hammering out an irregular rhythm against the truck. Every now and then, the tires seemed to sink into the ruts, but a little punch on the gas kept us moving.

"Looks like trouble up ahead," Declan said after we'd been driving for over forty minutes but had only traversed about six miles of road. "I was worried about this spot."

I slowed but kept moving forward, trying to peer through the rain. Jerking the wheel to the left, I headed off the road, bypassing what looked like a mud slide. To his credit, Declan didn't look nervous as I gunned it over a couple of large rocks. I had to make sure the wheels hit just right so we wouldn't get high-centered.

"Nice," he said as I angled back to the road after clearing the water. "Reminds me of your first day."

"Ha. What do you remember about it? You barely talked to me." He'd been at the interview I'd had with Josh and Lena, but he hadn't said three words. Even as they took me around for a tour, Declan had only watched silently, unnerving me with his stare.

"My orders were to watch how you interacted with the

animals. Josh says I have a sense for it. But what I meant was the guts you showed when we introduced you to Cuddles. You didn't hesitate to go up and give her a nice scratch."

"Lena said she'd just been fed, and you were all petting her."

"Yeah, but she knows us." He held his hand out near the steering wheel. "She gave me this the first time I dared to go in her cage—and that was after I'd been there a month."

"Ouch." I couldn't see the nasty scar at the base of his thumb in the dark cab, and I wasn't about to take my attention from the road to try harder, but I'd seen it before and wondered at the cause.

"The moment you left, I told Josh to hire you, even though we wouldn't have the budget to keep you when Patty comes back from taking care of her mother."

"I knew it was only temporary when I signed on."

"No, it's not. We'll find a way to keep you." His voice sounded amused now, and I could imagine his lazy grin. "We're actually kind of hoping Patty doesn't want to come back." He laughed. "Even if she does, it'll work out."

A surge of energy bubbled up inside me. I had no idea they felt this way, and it made me hopeful, because if you peeled away all the worry about supporting myself and Bianca while she grew her pottery business, I belonged at the sanctuary. "Well, I hope Patty earns more than I do, or my sister will need to sell a ton of pottery to help pay a mechanic the next time my truck breaks down."

He chuckled. "Just as long as it doesn't break down tonight." After a few moments of silence, he added, "You know, you could always get more training in something we really need. Then they'll pay more."

"Guess you're all full up on biologists." Declan had a degree in wildlife biology, and Ewan had one in biology.

"Something like that. But Josh finds funding when he needs it. Six months ago, I hit him up for a hefty raise—and he gave it to me. He knows that with my experience, there are a dozen of other jobs I could take."

"Well, my double degrees in biology and chemistry don't seem to be in demand here."

"Actually, it's a good start, and one of the reasons I pushed for you."

I dared to take my eyes from the windshield for a second. "Why?"

"Because what we really need is someone who's studied animal medicine. If there is something we can't handle now, or one of our animals needs surgery, we have to call in a vet, sometimes clear from California, depending on the problem."

"A vet? That's a lot more schooling." Four years, in fact. "And expensive."

"Josh and I've discussed the possibility of sponsoring someone in exchange for a promise to work at the sanctuary for a certain amount of years. Might be worth looking into." His voice was a little too casual, which hinted that he cared about my response—maybe even a lot. Had he and Josh discussed approaching *me* with this idea? And where did Stephen fit into it all? He was the official manager for the sanctuary and should be able to weigh in with his opinion.

My emotions were all over the place just contemplating a new career. The physical sciences had been my favorite classes in college, but I'd never even thought about being a vet. I had heard it was hard to get in to veterinary school, though with the well-known sanctuary as my sponsor, my chances were infinitely higher.

"I might be interested." I was actually more than interested, especially if it meant staying at the sanctuary with the animals I loved.

"We hoped you might. Josh asked me to feel you out about it."

Interesting that Josh had asked Declan and not his nephew, Stephen, but I wasn't sure what that meant. "Well, you can tell him I'll think about it." As if to punctuate my words, the truck jolted as we rolled over a particularly deep rut.

"I think the rain is getting worse," Declan said.

I had to agree. I really couldn't see more than the occasional glimpse of the road through the driving rain. Another lurch and the truck rocked violently. Instinctively, I let off the gas and the truck stopped. Muttering under my breath, I punched the gas, but the wheels just spun.

I tried not to think about Bianca in her little car. Was she stuck somewhere as well? Was she even still on the road? There were several steep drop-offs along Hackberry Road, and if she'd driven off one, she could be hurt or killed.

Pushing back the panic, I shoved the transmission into reverse, somehow managing to back up and go forward again, steering away from the rut we'd been lodged in. We continued to creep along, rocking and lurching. The rain kept coming, worse now, as if God had opened up heaven and was dumping massive buckets of water directly on top of the truck.

I hit the brake. "I can't see anything."

What little I could see of Declan's face by the light of the instrument panel was grim. "It might pass in a bit. I'll take a look around." He hopped out of the truck.

I opened my door as well. My first foot sank calf-deep into the mud, my shoe disappearing altogether, and my second foot went even deeper. I could see several feet in front around me, and we were still on the road, but near the truck itself, most of the dirt had washed away.

I climbed back into the truck, shaking off as much mud as I could. Declan was already back in the cab. "Let's try to move the truck a bit off the road," he suggested. "In case someone comes along."

Maybe my sister. My heart lightened for the briefest moment at the idea, but just as fast I realized it wasn't going to happen. If my wheels were half-buried, those on her little car would be have been stuck a long time ago.

I wasn't going to think about the drop-offs.

Going forward wasn't successful, and going backward didn't work this time either.

I gave Declan a frustrated stare. "I'm afraid we aren't going anywhere."

6

Now what? I wanted to ask this aloud, but I was too afraid he'd say we had to give up, and I wasn't ready to do that just yet.

"We can use the shovel to dig out once the rain eases," he said.

That was a good idea, but in the meantime, I had another one. "Did you see any posts along that side of the road?"

Sections of Hackberry Road had posts marking the edge, normally when the road went close to an incline or to mark the location of a few cabins in the woods. In some spots they went for a mile or more.

"Yes."

"Then if we can't drive, I'm going to walk down as far as I can find the posts. That way I won't get lost and I can find my way back. My sister might not be too far. She started out before the rain."

Declan tilted his head and studied me. "You don't give up, do you?"

"She's all the family I have." I swallowed hard, honesty forcing me to add, "I mean, I have a lot of foster sisters, and we're pretty close, but that's different. Bianca . . . I've taken care of her since we were little. She's only a year younger than I am, and we've never lived apart until now. She's everything to me."

He nodded. "Let's go."

"You should stay here."

"Zoey, I'm coming." His voice was like a caress that sent shudders down my spine. I hadn't felt this way since . . . well, I couldn't remember when. I'd thought my past had made it impossible for me to ever feel this captivated by a man, no matter how much I'd dreamed about it happening.

"Thanks." My mouth was dry, as if stuffed with a wad of cotton.

Grabbing the shoulder straps of his canvass bag, Declan retrieved it from the floor, pulling out two small packets and tossing me one. I examined it in admiration. "You brought rain ponchos?"

"Hey, I'm an Eagle Scout."

"Good for me, I guess." I laughed as we put on our packs and then the ponchos. Now if I found my sister, the blanket and jacket I had for her should be mostly dry.

Declan debated on taking the shovel and the rope, but in the end he opted only for the rope because it fit into his pack. We started out, buffeted by the wind and the rain, the mud sucking at our feet. Walking just off the road in the rocks and vegetation made it slightly easier to navigate.

From post to post we pushed on. My bare hands turned numb with cold, but I didn't dare tuck them into my pocket for fear of losing my balance and ending up with my face planted in the sludge. We'd been walking about thirty minutes, covering maybe a half mile, when the posts gave out, angling up a sudden incline that had to lead to a cabin.

Declan stopped and looked at me. "If we go on, we'll probably veer off the road. We could get lost."

I surveyed the dark, muddy world around us. He was right. The only thing we had were those posts. "Guess we head back to the truck," I said.

He shook his head. "If there's a cabin up there, maybe someone's home. They might have a landline with phone service."

A particularly strong gust of wind sent me scrambling for a foothold. Declan reached out and steadied me through the plastic poncho. "Okay," I agreed. If we did find a phone, I could call Lily or Ruth to see if there was news about my sister.

I clung to that hope as we struggled up the hill. On a clear day, we would have been able to get my truck up the incline, but now it was a slick, muddy mess. I fell, one hand sinking into the mud a few inches before Declan dragged me back to my feet. Ten paces later, he went down on one knee, and I had to pull him up. Then we both sank into the same deep hole and had to shove and yank our way out together. Tears squeezed from my eyes. I was tempted to lie down in the mud and give up, but my past had taught me to survive. To move one foot at a time and to focus on surviving only the current minute.

Besides, there was Bianca to rescue. So I accepted Declan's help up yet one more time, and then five steps later steadied him before he fell.

The top of the hill leveled out and the posts stopped at a grouping of trees. We staggered a short way through them, grateful for the vegetation that made our footing more secure. Finally, we reached a small clearing where a cabin, overgrown with brush, stood like a forgotten memory. There were no lights, and from the appearance of the cabin, there hadn't been lights there—or anything else—for years.

That meant no landline. I wanted to start back down the hill to follow the posts some more, but I had to admit it would be useless. We could walk within five feet of Bianca in this downpour and not see her.

"Let's go inside," I shouted. "Rest for a bit."

We hurried to the porch, slipping and sliding on the patches of mud between the plants. The sagging porch threatened to collapse as we stepped onto it, and I had a sudden vision of the entire cabin crumpling with us inside.

Declan tried the door, but it was nailed shut. A board had also been nailed over the window, but when he pulled at it, the piece came loose and wind blew away into the trees. Declan used his elbow to punch out the remains of broken glass before climbing through. I handed him my flashlight, and he directed the beam around the place as I followed him inside.

An ancient couch was the only furniture in the modest room, and trash littered the ground, dancing now with the wind coming through the window. The holes in the couch and the droppings of several animals, mostly in the corners of the room, indicated that we weren't the first intruders.

Declan flashed the light over the roof. "Looks strong enough, I think," he said. "Not a single leak."

"We won't be here long. The rain has to stop soon." I don't know if I was trying to convince him or myself. I was relieved to be out of the deluge, but I needed to get back out there as soon as possible. My sister needed me.

"Let's look at the rest of the place." He started into a tiny hallway leading to a room that turned out to be a miniscule kitchen. It held a broken chair, several taped boxes, and an old wood-burning stove, which Declan eyed with interest. The kitchen roof did have a leak in one corner, but the rest looked sturdy enough.

Further exploration down a narrow hallway revealed a tiny bedroom. Declan ran the light over the room as I stepped inside. As the light touched the focal point of the room, an old bed with a shredded mattress, it came alive with movement. Tiny gray bodies erupted from the torn padding like a small volcano. Even over the storm, I heard indignant squeaks.

After spending years sleeping in my uncle's crowded junk room, and now working at the sanctuary, I wasn't bothered by mice, but that didn't mean I wanted to wade into the squeaking melee. Instinctively, I turned fast and banged right into Declan, propelling us both into the hallway.

We both froze as he reached out to steady me. His hands felt oddly warm even through my jacket, which had to be my imagination. It didn't matter. Every part of me was aware of him. My eyes raised slowly to his. I already knew he'd be looking at me, but I hadn't expected it to be with *that* expression. I recognized it because I felt the same desire.

My heart threatened to pound out an entire symphony. The rain crashed against the cabin and thunder boomed in accompaniment, but all of that could have been on another continent for the notice we gave it. Neither of us moved.

Panic grew inside me. I didn't know what to do. Rather, I knew what I wanted, yet something in me was terrified to make it happen.

It's just a kiss. I wanted to move closer, but my limbs refused the order.

Declan swallowed hard and took a step back. His eyes still pierced mine, but his voice was casual as he said, "The kitchen's probably better for us to wait it out."

"I guess the extended mouse family is a little much?" Just like that I could speak again.

Declan gave an exaggerated shudder. "I confess. Mice are the only animals I really don't like." He leaned past me and grabbed the door, pulling it shut. "We should try to put something over the window in that front room to block the wind."

My heartbeat was starting to return to normal, but there was a huge part of me that was disappointed. He'd felt it, hadn't he? Even if he had, being attracted to me didn't mean he wanted a relationship.

Back in the first room, we looked around for something to block the window, but nothing presented itself, so we ended up hefting the couch and standing it on end at an angle against the window. Two mice bolted from the couch and disappeared into the mounds of trash. The couch didn't keep out all the wind and rain, but it was better than before.

Declan waved my flashlight. "Let's see if we can start a fire. I think I saw some wood."

In the kitchen, he returned my light and dug in his pack for a larger flashlight that doubled as a lantern. He placed it on the floor near the stove. While he checked the flue and chose some wood from the scattered pile, uncovering several more mice, I cleared a place on the floor with the broken chair leg. Then I removed my poncho and scraped off as much mud as I could from my shoes and pants before taking out the lap blanket I'd brought from the store.

"I'm freezing," I said. "But it's not really all that cold in here, is it?" I hoped Bianca still had a blanket in her car.

"Cold enough." Declan withdrew a larger blanket from his pack. "Try this one instead."

I laid the surprisingly heavy blanket down on the wood floor, then settled on it, keeping my shoes and the bottom of my pants off the material. I was shaking now that I'd stopped moving. Declan pulled off his poncho and grabbed the smaller blanket from my backpack, settling it around my shoulders.

He dropped beside me. "Should get warm here in a minute."

"You brought matches."

"Actually, it was a lighter. Let me see your wrist. It might be getting infected. Maybe that's why you feel so cold."

"It's fine. Doesn't even hurt." That was mostly true, but I let him take my hand anyway.

He pushed up my sleeve a few inches. My hand burned with his touch, and something inside me ached. He started to push up my sleeve further, but I pulled it back down.

Instead of commenting on that, he said, "Does it hurt a lot when I squeeze it?" He pressed gently on the bandage.

"No." I couldn't feel anything except where a few of his fingers brushed my skin at the edge of the gauze.

"Good." He didn't let me go.

Wind rushed in my ears, wind that had nothing to do

with the storm raging outside the cabin. Panic slid around the edges of my mind, but I pushed it away. Being here with Declan, even in the midst of this ridiculous storm, was right in the way that breathing was right. All worry about my sister aside, everything in my life seemed to have led to this moment.

"Zoey," Declan said in a low, sexy whisper that played havoc with my pulse. His hand traced the soft inner flesh of my arm above the bandage, moving higher. I couldn't pull away. His fingers went still higher, snagging slightly on my raised scars. Was there any chance he'd think I'd run through a glass door?

No, of course not. No accidental scars could ever be so regular.

He looked down, his fingers continuing to glide over my skin. Why did it have to feel so good? "Something must have hurt you badly to make you do this."

I didn't look at him as I answered. "It was a long time ago."

Now would come more questions—and the disgust. He'd seen past the outer shell I showed to the world, and I felt naked, exposed. I started to pull away. He didn't resist, letting me slip from his hold.

"What happened?"

There it was. Question number one. I dragged my eyes

up to his, expecting distaste, but the only emotion I could detect was compassion and interest. That was surprising. But I didn't want him to like me for my brokenness.

"I mean, if you want to tell me." He waited, not pushing.

I couldn't seem to tell him that I didn't want to talk, or that it was none of his business. Because more than anything I wanted a chance with him, and if there was to be any sort of a romantic relationship between us, I had to tell him. Though I was healed, there were still ghosts in my past. There would always be, and they would color my future. They wouldn't control me or my choices, or decide my happiness, but sometimes the wounds of my past still hurt almost more than I could bear.

"My mother died when I was twelve. My sister and I went to live with my uncle." I looked away again, not wanting him to see my face. I stared at the black stove, felt the heat radiating from it, a heat that didn't reach my heart. My fingers plucked at the coarse blanket beneath us. "It took less than six months for him to begin touching me. I tried so hard to avoid him, but he . . ." I choked, unable to go on.

His hand reached for mine, interlacing our fingers. "I'm so sorry."

I let my eyes find his again—looking steadily at me without censure. There was no need to say more, not now. I didn't have to say how my uncle's friends had added to my abuse, and how isolated I'd felt with no one to turn to for help. "It took three years, but we got away. I could see my uncle was starting to look at Bianca *that* way. So I took her and left." I released his hand and pushed up my sleeve.

"This was the way I coped with the pain and stress. At the time, it was all I had. I didn't know there were better ways, or that I was making it worse."

He nodded as if he understood, but I didn't see how he could. Most people had no idea. "That was when you went to Lily's House?"

"Well, there was no Lily's House until seven or eight months later, but we did meet Lily then. She saved us. She's saved a lot of kids."

"Like you saved Bianca."

How easily he had pinpointed the one thing I was proud of in my life. "Yes."

His eyes wandered over my face as tenderly as any caress. "We'll find her, Zoey. We will."

My heart was doing that odd pounding thing it had done outside the tiny bedroom, and I was falling, falling down a hundred flights of stairs, no handrail in sight. His face moved closer. Slowly. Giving me the chance to flee. I didn't want to flee.

Yet a part of me was even more frightened now that I'd told him about my past. Declan wasn't like the guys I'd tried dating in college. He mattered.

As if seeing the hesitation in my eyes, he started to pull away.

No! Making an abrupt decision, I closed the last inch between us. Our lips touched, first gently and then with more passion. His arms went around my body, holding me tight. Heat seeped through me, clear to the ends of my fingers. Amazing.

His lips deviated from my mouth, trailing over my cheek to nibble on my ear and then tracing down my neck.

His warm breath made me shiver. Then his lips found mine once more, and time stopped. I had no idea how long we sat there kissing, but when we finally drew apart, I wasn't the slightest bit cold.

"Do you know how long I've wanted to do that?" he asked, his voice raw.

It seemed like a loaded question, so I shook my head.

"Since the moment you knelt down in front of Cuddles and started scratching her neck."

"Don't be silly. You didn't say two words, remember?"

"I've got eyes, Zoey Morgan. And you're one of the strong, bravest, beautiful people I know." He kissed me again, and I kissed him back. His touch sent passion racing through my veins. No panic. I trusted him. Maybe because I'd watched him with the animals, and that had given me a glimpse into his soul. All these weeks we'd worked together, and I thought he was unreachable, but he'd been as attracted to me as I was to him.

I came up for a little air. "Maybe you're just searching for a wounded soul like you search for wounded animals." I spoke only half in jest.

"We're all wounded." He leaned forward and kissed my nose. "Everyone. Just in different ways."

"Oh, yeah?" It sounded cliché.

"Take Kitcat. His wife has cancer."

I stifled a gasp. "What? I didn't know." Kitcat was a grizzled old man who had worked at the sanctuary longer than anyone except Stephen's family.

"It's not a secret, but he doesn't talk about it much. And Ewan's a recovering alcoholic."

I knew that much because when we'd all gone out for a

drink after the movie, everyone had ordered soft drinks to support him.

Declan leaned back on the blanket, propped up on his elbows. "And you've heard that Josh and Lena have a daughter they haven't seen in twenty years. Then there's Stephen . . . well, you've probably guessed his story."

Guessed? I had no idea what Declan was talking about. "I know his parents died in a car accident when he was a few years old, but he doesn't seem conflicted, if that's what you're hinting. He told me he doesn't remember them."

"Yeah, but he doesn't want to disappoint Josh and Lena. They've given him everything, and that's a pretty heavy obligation. He sees what their daughter put them through, and he feels a lot of pressure to be the son they never had."

Shock waved through me as I realized what Declan was saying. "He doesn't want to stay at the sanctuary, does he?" That made so much sense. I'd wondered why Stephen didn't know as much about the animals as the others and why he didn't seem to feel the need to work with them so closely. Instead, he buried himself in reports, fundraising, and ordering supplies.

"Right. He likes the animals well enough, but he doesn't love it like the rest of us—like I could tell you did that very first day."

"I can't believe I didn't see how he feels." I lay down on my side next to Declan, using the elbow of my good arm to prop up my head.

"I'm hoping Stephen will finally admit to his uncle that all those law classes he's been studying online for the past two years aren't just for fun."

"No wonder he didn't look all that upset when Ross appeared."

"You kidding? He eats up that stuff. It's his way of connecting with his real dream."

"We need to help him," I said

"He's already taking the first steps, even if he doesn't realize it yet, and when he does wake up, it's not like we can't run the place without him. Lena used to manage the office, we can hire a company for fundraising, and I can fill in for the rest. I do it all with the animals anyway. There's plenty of time for changes down the road."

"Does Josh know? He has to." He had to realize he'd been grooming Declan all these years to take over, not Stephen.

"Not in so many words, but his instincts are good. I think that's why he's held off on retiring so long, to see how things settle. He's not going to take Stephen's inheritance from him if there's any chance at all that he wants it."

"Stephen, an attorney." The thought made me laugh. "I can't wrap my head around it. He's a great guy, but my experience with lawyers so far hasn't been any good."

"I bet. Couldn't have been easy to get away from your uncle."

I shook my head. "I'm not talking about then. When I turned eighteen, I filed against him with the police, and we went to court. I didn't want to do it, but he'd remarried and had a step-daughter. She was only five. There was no way I was going to let him hurt her. Took two years, but he went to prison."

I tried to blink back tears, but in the next second it didn't matter as Declan reached for me, pulling me into his arms. We lay on the blanket, my head on his shoulder, his cheek against my forehead. I felt warm and safe, but my heart thundered at his closeness.

We lay quietly for several minutes, listening to the raging storm and the crackling of the fire. My thoughts returned to Bianca, the worry almost crushing, but there was nothing I could do about finding her until the rain let up. I had to believe she was all right. As if sensing my worry, Declan massaged my back, easing some of the tension away.

"What about you?" The words slipped out before I could stop them. I lifted myself partially up off Declan's shoulder to see his face.

His shrug somehow tucked me closer to him. "I'm not in any hurry. Even once Stephen's made his decision, I'll still be doing the same thing I'm doing now. Maybe just a little more of it."

"No, I mean . . . you said everyone's wounded. You're not wounded."

He stared at the ceiling for a moment, as if contemplating what to say. So there *was* something. Or maybe his life was so perfect that he was ashamed to admit it after what I'd told him. Silence stretched out between us until I felt I should be uncomfortable, but I wasn't. I wouldn't let myself be. He'd given me time, and I'd do the same for him.

As I watched, his expression changed. "Do you hear that?"

"What?"

"The rain. It's sounds different."

He was right. I jumped to my feet, scrambling for my things. "Maybe we can dig out the truck now."

He was up as fast as I was, scooping up the blanket and folding it into his pack. Maybe he was relieved that he wouldn't have to answer. I pushed the thought aside. He'd kissed me, and there was a real connection here. I'd hold onto that for now.

I checked my phone. Still no signal.

"We'll leave the fire going," Declan said. "With the stove door shut, it will burn out safely anyway."

I nodded. "We might need it again. There's no telling what's going to happen with this storm."

We hurried to the front room of the cabin and pulled the couch away from the window, letting it drop and bounce, dislodging a few more critters.

I stuck my head outside. "Still raining, but I can see a lot better."

"Let's go then."

I dropped my backpack and pulled on my poncho.

8

The rain might have eased, but it was still dark outside and windy. I slipped and skidded down the hill heading back to the road. My mind raced with plans: get back to the truck, dig out, continue driving for as long as we had visibility. If we couldn't dig out, we'd continue as far as the storm would allow us on foot. I *would* find my sister. It was already after eight, more than five hours since I'd last heard from her.

"Careful," Declan called. "You don't want to break an arm."

We were only halfway down the hill when Declan stopped walking. I turned around to see him shrugging out of his pack. "What are you doing?" Impatience filled my voice.

"I think I see something down the road. I have binoculars. Don't know how much good they'll do in the dark, but it's worth a shot."

I looked in the direction he'd indicated. From our vantage point, we could see what had to be Hackberry Road, but visibility wasn't very far, and I didn't see anything of interest. Wait. There was a glow some distance away, very faint, but different enough that it stood out in the dark, even in the rain. The wind ripped off my hood, but I ignored it, straining to see.

Declan had found the binoculars and was adjusting his pack to use them, but I hurried back to him and grabbed them from him. As I drew them to my face, my heart thudded slowly with both eagerness and dread. Even if it was a person, it could be anyone who might have been traveling on this road when the storm struck. Cabins dotted the area, however sporadically.

Where did the light go? I steadied my hands and moved slowly along the road. All dark. No, there it was, a glow that might be a car with a light on inside. But the shape was too dark to identify accurately, and I couldn't see any outline that might be a person.

I handed the binoculars back to Declan. "I think it's a car. It's not moving, but I can't tell if it's hers, or if there's someone inside."

Declan reached over and tugged up both the hood of my jacket and the poncho hood. Then he took a moment to peer through the binoculars. "Yeah, it's hard to tell, but something's there. So what do you want to do? Go back for the truck or continue on to the light?"

My truck was half a mile away, and I thought the light was closer than that. "Let's walk toward the light. We should be able to stay on the road now that the rain's let up. If we went back for the truck, it could take us an hour to dig out. Even if it's not Bianca, whoever it is might need help."

We finished our descent, and the light was obscured from view. As we walked, I tortured myself with images of my sister hurt and helpless. Shivering in the dark. What if the light wasn't actually coming from a car? What if I wanted it so much that I was imagining it?

The road was completely washed out in some places, and we had to deviate long distances to either side to get past the water. I was glad we hadn't returned for the truck because we probably wouldn't have made it through the deep grooves slicing over the road, now filled with mud and rainwater.

Mud soaked through my shoes to my feet, and I was cold again, but I couldn't stop. At last, we spied the glow ahead. "Can I see the binoculars again?" I held them to my eyes, my breath catching in my throat. "It *is* Bianca's car! No mistaking that silly daisy she painted on the hood. The light is shining right on it." I looked heavenward. "Thank you, God."

We tried to hurry, but the mud sucked at our feet and slowed our progress. "Is it just me?" Declan asked, "or is the light from her car getting dimmer?"

"It's probably been on for hours. She should know to preserve the battery if she's planning to wait out the storm and then drive home, but Bianca's always been afraid of the dark." Yet even with her fear, she *did* know better—so maybe she was hurt and hoped someone would see the light. My worry mounted with each step.

When we reached the car, we found it completely mired in one of the washed-out sections of the road. The tires were submerged and muddy water reached above the bottom of the doors. I angled my flashlight into the windows, fearing what I'd find, but there was nothing inside except boxes and piles of her belongings.

I scanned the area around us, first without and then with the binoculars. Nothing. No sign of my sister. "She could be anywhere."

"Where do you think she'd go?"

That's right—I knew Bianca better than anyone. I slowed my breathing and looked over the area again. To one side of the car the land was flat for a good two hundred feet before dropping steeply off. That way wasn't likely. The other side, where we were standing, slanted upward toward a small thicket of trees and brush. That was a possibility. But maybe she would have stayed on the road. She wouldn't have gone back the way she'd come because she was closer to the road's end on my side. "It's those trees or the road," I said, pointing the way we'd come.

"I'm not betting on the road, not with how bad the rain was. Would she have been able to see it? We couldn't, and there aren't any posts here."

He had a point. If Bianca had been worried about getting lost, she would have found someplace to hole up instead of taking the risk of wandering off the road.

"We have no idea when she left the car," I said. "Maybe it was when the rain eased." If so, she could be close to finding my truck by now.

Without warning, Declan stepped into the water around the car, sinking to his knees. Before I could ask what he was doing, he put his hand on the hood of the car. "Not even the slightest bit warm." Sliding his hand downward, he reached in past the tire. "Not warm here either. Even with the rain, the engine wouldn't have cooled too fast. I'd say it's been off at least an hour. Maybe two."

"Maybe she drove into this hole when it got too bad to

see." Just like I had. I glanced at the thicket of trees. "Let's look there and then head to the truck."

"The trees? Not the safest place when there's lightning."

"Maybe she hoped to find a cabin. She should have stayed with the car."

He shook his head. "Not with all this water. You get enough, it could be swept over that drop-off—and after that rain, I'm betting it's full of water down there."

I offered a hand as he climbed out of the dirty water. "She had an emergency pack in the car—not that the flares would do any good right now."

"The other stuff would make a difference."

We trudged toward the trees, the going easier with small rocks and vegetation under our feet instead of inches of mud. In the distance, thunder cracked. I hoped that wasn't a sign of more rain heading our way.

When we reached the trees, I started calling, "Bianca! Are you here? Bianca!"

Declan took up my cry. "Bianca! Bianca!"

It was darker in the trees, and colder. Despite the poncho, my jeans that had dried somewhat were completely soaked again as we waded through the bushes. I stopped and moved my flashlight over the area. Declan took out his larger one and used that too.

"Bianca!" I shouted again. Nothing.

We walked first to the right for fifteen minutes, calling and calling. Then we retraced our steps and went the other way, keeping in sight of one another but far enough apart to cover more ground. My voice felt hoarse from so much calling. What if I was too late?

I was beginning to feel despair when my light caught a

movement near some fallen trees. At the same time, a thin voice reached my ears. "Zoey?"

"Bianca!" I ran toward the sound of her voice, crashing through brush and jumping over rocks. As I neared, I saw her sitting up between two fallen trees, her figure drowning in the yellow rain poncho from the emergency kit. Spread over the two trees was the emergency blanket she'd apparently been using as a makeshift tent. A glow stick in her hand lit up her face.

She was okay! Tears leaked down my face, and for the first time that day I was glad for the rain that masked my emotion. All the scolding words I'd thought of saying to her vanished. Nothing mattered except that she was okay.

"You came!" Bianca's laugh sounded a little hysterical. "I knew you would."

"Of course I came."

She tried to climb to her feet but sank down almost immediately with a groan.

"What's wrong? Are you hurt?"

She nodded. "My ankle and my arm. I fell when I got out of the car. Rain was coming down so fast, I couldn't see. I was afraid the car would get carried away with me in it. My arm hurts the worse, but nothing's breaking through the skin or anything."

I almost laughed, thinking back to how I'd checked Stephen's leg for the same thing. Maybe Lily had taught us that—with dozens of girls at Lily's House, collectively we'd had numerous broken bones.

Avoiding her wounded right arm, I moved around to Bianca's other side to help her stand. She was covered in mud, as if she'd fallen numerous times, and my hand slipped on her back. Before I had her all the way to her feet, she collapsed on one of the fallen trees, panting with agony at the movement.

"I can't," she gasped. "My ankle. Left one."

"I can carry you." Declan angled around behind her.

Bianca looked over, noticing him for the first time. "So I did hear a man's voice. I thought I was hallucinating."

"That's Declan." I began gathering Bianca's belongings. "He works at the sanctuary with me."

"Nice to meet you," Bianca said.

"You too." Declan shrugged off his pack and handed it to me. "It's kind of heavy. Think you can carry it?"

"Absolutely."

He took something out first—a bottle of painkillers. He shook out two and handed them to Bianca while I gave her one of my water bottles. "Thanks," I told him.

"Yeah, I imagine Stephen's swearing at me about now for taking them."

I snorted. "Maybe that useless attorney can get some from the gift shop."

"I doubt it. But the others will make it back to him soon."

I shoved Bianca's blanket and glow stick back inside her emergency bag, next to her purse that was already inside. When I was ready, Declan picked Bianca up, one arm under her back and the other under her knees, carefully balancing her hurt arm on the outside as it draped over her stomach.

"I'd bring the truck closer, but the road's impassable right now," I said for Bianca's benefit.

"She hardly weighs anything," Declan answered.

Unlike me, Bianca had never gone through a fat stage,

and I'd often worried about how thin she was. She'd work for hours on her pottery without remembering to eat. But she always protested if anyone called her too thin, and the fact that she didn't contradict Declan worried me.

Bianca gave a little sob as Declan stepped over a large rock. "Sorry," he muttered.

We trudged on, reaching the road and starting up it. Declan's pack and Bianca's emergency bag felt heavier with every step. I had no idea how long it would take us to get back to my truck, and the rain felt heavier now. Our progress was slow—too slow. Bianca wasn't sobbing anymore, but whenever I caught a glimpse of her in my light, her teeth were clenched and pain etched lines over her face.

The rain picked up. "I don't think we're going to make it to the truck." Declan leaned over slightly to speak close to my ear.

"The cabin then."

He nodded. By the time we reach the hill to the cabin, the rain was heavy, though not nearly as bad as it had been when we'd stopped the truck. "It'll pass again," Declan said. "We'll make it to the truck soon enough. Meanwhile, we'll take a break and get warm."

Passing Bianca through the window was a bit of a challenge, but soon we had her lying on Declan's thick blanket, spread once again on the kitchen floor. Declan put the rest of the wood inside the stove, leaving the door open to emit more warmth, and we began discussing using the broken chair for fuel. "We can also use the mattress in the bedroom," I said, "if you've got a knife, Boy Scout. Or parts of the couch."

Declan pulled out a knife much larger than any approved

for Boy Scout use. "Sounds like fun." He went to work, while I tucked the blanket I'd taken from the gift shop around my sister, topping it with the sweatshirt. I'd managed to remove her wet jacket, but we wouldn't worry about putting on the sweatshirt until it was time to leave. I was sure her arm was broken. Maybe her ankle as well.

I took off my wet jacket, snuggling up to her back and lending her my body heat, my hand splayed over her side just below her arm. She reached for my hand with her good one. "I love you, Zoey."

"I love you too."

"I was coming to surprise you. I know it's been hard on you being so far away, and I thought you'd want . . ." She trailed off.

"Of course I want you to stay with me for as long as you can. Just promise me you'll never drive in a storm again."

"I promise." She was silent a moment before adding, "I'm grateful for that emergency kit you got me. That stupid glow stick—who knew it would give me so much comfort?"

I laughed. "Try to rest, okay? As soon as the rain lets up, I'll get you to the hospital."

Obediently, Bianca closed her eyes. Too obediently. I moved my hand to check her forehead. She was burning. I sat up and stared at her face. By the dim light from the wood stove, Bianca looked flushed.

Declan came in at that moment, carrying a load of mattress pieces. "Those mice . . . ugh." Seeing my face, he dropped the pieces quickly near the stove and came to me. "What's wrong?"

"Fever. She's burning up."

He frowned. "She might be hurt worse than we thought."

"What should we do?" It felt odd asking. For so many years I'd made all my decisions by myself. Or with a little distracted guidance from Lily.

"*We're* not doing anything. *I'm* going to get your truck." He held out his hand. "Can I have the keys?"

"No. It's too dangerous."

"The rain isn't as bad as it was when we had to stop. I've dug out cars before."

"I can help."

He motioned to Bianca, who appeared to be sleeping. "You need to stay with her. You'll have to trust me."

Trust him? Before today, the only man I'd ever trusted was Lily's husband. But Declan was right that I couldn't leave Bianca. I handed him my keys.

He took them and went down on one knee, kissing me with a delicious slowness that sent tingles up my spine and warmth throughout my stomach. "I'll be back as soon as I can."

I watched him go, remembering that he still hadn't told me what his wounds were. I couldn't help but wonder.

Declan was gone a long time. Bianca awoke, and I made her eat a candy bar and drink more water. It was all I had.

"Thank you," she murmured.

"How do you feel?"

"Like your truck hit me." She turned her head, looking around. "Where did your friend go?"

"To see if he could bring the truck closer."

"He's really cute. All those blond curls. Like a younger version of that guy who used to play on all those *Mentalist* reruns Lily loves to watch. Only longer hair."

I spluttered a laugh. "Simon Baker? Yeah, Declan looks even better when he's not soaked."

"You like him."

"Yeah. A lot."

She roused herself enough for a little squeal. "I'm so excited for you!" She moved as if to hug me and gasped. "Ouch."

"Just hold still. We'll talk about this later."

She drifted off again, and I threw a couple mattress

pieces into the stove. They smelled odd as they burned, and I hope the mattress had been here long enough that any dangerous chemicals had already leaked out. At least the room was warm.

Leaving the lantern for Bianca, I went to the front room in the dark, peeking past the couch I'd pulled back into place over the broken window. No sign of Declan yet. Had he managed to get the truck unstuck? Had he fallen into a worse rut? I itched to go help him. I didn't like depending on anyone else.

Time dragged on. I tried to doze next to my sister, but sleep eluded me. Bianca's forehead felt hotter despite the pain killer I'd given her, and I wondered if I should make her take another one. I checked my phone again for service, but like the other dozen times I'd looked, there were no bars. *I'll have to go find him,* I thought. Maybe he needed help. But how could I leave Bianca?

A loud bang had me jumping to my feet. In the front room, Declan had pushed aside the couch and was climbing inside. I ran to him, and he held me tightly, his lips finding mine. His jeans and poncho were covered in mud, but I didn't care. Fire spread through me.

"How'd it go?" I managed to ask.

"Couldn't get it up the hill, but it's close. Let's get her to the hospital."

I kissed him again, hard. "Thank you."

"You keep that up, and we won't get far," he joked.

Laughing, I started for the kitchen, but Declan's hand grabbed my arm. "Zoey," he said, slightly hoarse. With the flashlight angled down, his face was mostly in shadow. "After we get Bianca safe, I want to tell you something . . .

about myself. My past. I know you wondered . . . I just don't want you to think I'm hiding anything, because I'm not."

For a fleeting moment I was torn between wanting to help Bianca and hearing his story right now. Obviously, he'd had to work up to telling me this much. But my sister needed immediate help, and she had to come first. "Okay, but I'm holding you to it."

"I know. That's why I told you." His hand released mine, going up to my face, trailing fire across my skin. "I think I'm falling for you, Zoey Morgan."

I kissed him again, and for a tiny moment, I forgot about the storm and even about Bianca. He tasted of rain and warmth, and breath-taking promises. "Good, because I think I'm falling for you too."

Getting Bianca down to the truck turned out to be the easy part of our journey to the hospital in Kingman. The hard part was creeping down the road and digging out the three more times we became stuck. But we finally made it to the paved road, where we could increase our speed. Even then, it took ninety minutes to traverse the Route 66 to Kingman, a journey that usually took me only thirty minutes.

We drove straight to the emergency room and carried Bianca inside. They found her a bed right away and started X-rays, but there were so many people needing attention that an hour passed before an older doctor came to explain her injuries.

"Your sister has two breaks in her right arm that we're calling in a specialist to pin," he said, his face grave. "Her left ankle is also severely sprained, so I'm guessing she'll be in a boot for six weeks, but the orthopedic surgeon will talk to you about those injuries. The most pressing thing is the internal bleeding in her abdomen, and I think she might be showing signs of infection related to that. She needs surgery to repair the damage."

"Is she going to be all right?" Anxiety made my voice sharp.

The doctor cracked a confident smile. "Oh, yes. Definitely. Barring any unforeseen complication, of course. This is extremely minor surgery compared to my usual fare, plus she's young and healthy. Meanwhile, we've put her on an antibiotic. I think her lethargy is due more to the combination of injuries and exposure rather than the bleeding and infection. But it's a good thing you got her here so quickly. Another day and the infection could have made this a very different story."

"Thank you." I was speaking to the doctor, but I really meant the words for Declan, who reached for my hand and squeezed it gently, telling me he understood.

"You can stay with her until the surgery," the doctor said. "But first, why don't you clean up a bit in the bathroom? I'll have a nurse get you some scrubs. The authorities are still warning people to stay put, so you probably don't want to leave." He winked as he added, "We certainly don't want you back here with any injuries."

By the time we were cleaned up and Bianca was in surgery, it was after two and the rain had stopped. We settled in the ER waiting room, where the receptionist had promised to give us Bianca's room number once it was assigned.

I took Declan's hand, stifling a yawn. "So, back at the cabin. You wanted to tell me something. What happened?" I said it casually, the way he'd asked me about my past.

He grimaced, and under the fluorescent lighting, his eyes looked more gray than blue. "It's just . . . my father was killed by a drunk driver. I was eleven."

Tears stung my eyes. "It's hard to lose a parent." My father had never been in my life, but I still longed for my mother.

"Everything I missed with him, I blamed on that man. My mother told me it'd eat me up inside, but I didn't care. For a long time, I couldn't get past it."

From his haunted tone, I could tell there was more, so I waited.

Declan pulled my hand into his lap, sandwiching it between both of his. "The man who hit him came to me five years later, asking for forgiveness. I was sixteen at the time and told him exactly where he could go—it wasn't a pretty scene." He paused, releasing a heavy sigh. "Less than a month later, he committed suicide, leaving behind a wife and three little kids. The oldest was eight."

"Oh, no!"

"It was a wakeup call for me. I felt that maybe if I'd just forgiven him, he'd be alive and those kids wouldn't be missing their dad the way I missed mine."

I tried not to rush too fast to excuse him, because it didn't matter if I thought he wasn't responsible—he felt he was, and he still hurt over what had happened. "I'm so sorry. That's really sad. Of course there had to be other factors that contributed. You know that, right?"

He nodded. "Yeah, but I'll never know if my words

would have made the difference." His hand clung to mine. "It took me another three years before I was able to face his family. I expected anger from them, but the guy's wife took me in her arms and said it wasn't my fault. She forgave me and made sure her kids did too. She didn't want the cycle to continue."

"Did she ever remarry? What happened to the kids? Do you know?"

A glad laugh escaped him, and his voice was lighter. "She eventually remarried a great guy, but for three or four years I did all the activities with those kids that their father would have done. It didn't make up for not having a dad—I can never change that—but it made a difference for them. And for me. The oldest just graduated from high school. I still see them all occasionally."

"You did a good thing."

"I just did what anyone should have done. Once I realized it was up to me."

I understood too well. "Like I did with Bianca and my little step-cousin."

His face angled toward mine, and my pulse raced in anticipation of another kiss. But the ER doors chose that moment to open, and Stephen came inside, half hopping and half carried by his uncle. There was an awkward moment as Stephen's eyes fell on my hand tucked inside Declan's.

Declan released me and jumped up, hurrying to help Josh carry Stephen to the chair Declan had just vacated. "Good to see you guys are okay," Josh said. "We were worried."

"I'm just glad to see Stephen survived his time with that attorney," Declan quipped.

Josh ran a hand through his white hair, firmly plastered to his head with water. "Yeah, he's still back at the sanctuary driving my wife mad. He's too afraid to leave until the rain stops completely, so she might kill him before we get back." He nodded at Stephen. "Keep an eye on him while I go check in." He hurried to the desk.

"You take up medicine?" Stephen asked me.

"What?" I said. "Oh, you mean the scrubs. Yeah, we were pretty much covered in mud, and they didn't want us tracking it through the hospital. Look, they even gave us these sock booties because our shoes were soaked." I lifted my feet to show him. "Anyway, we found my sister. She's in surgery, but the doctor says she's going to be fine. We found her in time." I would still worry until she was home with me again, but I'd asked enough questions in the past hour to know that Bianca's doctor was highly skilled.

"That's good," Stephen said. "I bet you have a story to tell."

"We sure do." Declan sat on my other side and reached for my hand again. I felt grateful for both his steadying touch and his message to Stephen. Hopefully, there would be no more awkwardness. I valued my friendship with Stephen, but after what happened tonight, I was pretty sure that what I felt for Declan was the real thing.

Stephen leaned back and tented his hands on his stomach. "So that's how it is, huh? For what it's worth, I'm happy for you both. Really." He paused, catching my eye, tapping the tips of his fingers together. "Who knows? Maybe if I'm lucky, Zoey will introduce me to her sister."

"We'll see." I spared a glance at his uncle, who was still talking to the receptionist. "It depends if you're finally ready to go after what you want." My sister already knew what she wanted, and I didn't want to set her up with someone who lacked the courage to grab hold of his destiny.

Stephen's hands stilled. "I don't know what you're talking about."

Declan snorted. "Yeah, you do—those law classes you've been taking? You know that's your real future. But we can argue about it later. I think that nurse with the wheelchair is coming for you. Don't hold your breath on getting to see a doctor any time soon, though."

Stephen didn't respond as Declan and the nurse put him into the chair, but his eyes held the same interested gleam I'd noticed when he'd gone off to debate with that useless attorney at the sanctuary.

As the nurse rolled Stephen away, Declan put his arm around me and pulled me close. "Now where were we before he arrived?"

I moved closer until our lips were almost touching. "Just about here."

RUTH'S CHOICE

Ruth

I stared at the music store as I had done so many times before. Huge signs proclaimed discounts as deep as ninety percent off. Good deals, to be sure, but it wasn't the sales that interested me. I was here for the building.

The store was located in a strip mall that sat far enough off the main street to have decent parking, and yet was close enough not to inhibit customers from making the trip. The surrounding shops looked trendy and successful. The perfect retail location. I believed the demise of the music store had more to do with two nearby competing businesses than the location. In fact, this street had been on my wish list long before the discount signs appeared in the windows.

I'd talked to the owner last week about leasing the property and learned the rental for the fifteen hundred square feet was sixteen hundred dollars a month. Not cheap by any standards, but far less expensive than the more upscale rental properties of the same size. The required first and last month's rent was a challenge I was up for, but I'd also have to buy a new stove and refrigerator for the existing kitchen, which was currently storing guitars. I'd need to put in tables and glass cases to display desserts like in a European café, which was my model even though I'd never been to Europe.

When I'd shared my plans for opening the café, the owner of the building had been encouraging and offered me an allowance for paint. We both agreed that the tiled floor would work fine. But the first three bids I'd received for the renovations and the equipment were each over twenty thousand dollars. Too far out of reach with my current job as a junior dietician at the hospital during the day and my second job as a waitress-slash-cook at a small family Mexican restaurant across town.

Which was why I was all dressed up on this beautiful Thursday afternoon in May and staring morosely at the store. I'd been applying for loans all over Phoenix, but no one seemed interested in loaning money to a too-tall, half African-American woman, with limited time on the job and a miniscule credit history. My five-month-old college degree in food science and two years waitressing didn't impress anyone.

I heaved a sigh and started to take off my D-backs cap to fan myself before I remembered I wasn't wearing it. Or my favorite jeans and T-shirt. Instead, I wore a borrowed purple dress that was supposed to be retro trendy but was a tad too short and fit far too snugly for my comfort. The black heels that had seemed reasonable this morning now made every step torture.

In fact, there was no way I was going to make it to my car wearing them. Gingerly, I slipped first one and then the other off my feet.

A movement in my peripheral vision caught my attention. But it was just a man with a camera, a baseball cap pulled low over his brow, brown hair curling out beneath it in wide ringlets. His camera, a serious-looking affair with a huge lens attached, was aimed upward at a small brown bird perched on the scraggly tree several yards from the bench where I sat.

I couldn't see what interested him in the shot, but he'd have to be a genius to make it appeal to the masses. Or at least to the people here in downtown Phoenix, Arizona, who were passing by without so much as a second glance at the little creature. But the man's intentness and the steadiness of his hand hinted at experience, so maybe he could see something everyone else missed.

Refocusing on the store, I considered how many weeks it might be until the doors closed for the last time. The contract gave the lessees until the end of this month, with the possibility of extension, and since it was only the first of May and their sales were winding down, it was doubtful they'd extend. But how much time after that would the owner need to get it ready for a new tenant? At my current jobs, it would be at least a year, and probably three, before I scrimped and scraped up twenty thousand dollars and an extra month of padding. By then, this building would be rented to another lucky business owner.

I hated the idea of defeat and losing this location. There had to be something I could do, but my mind was drawing a complete and utter blank. I hadn't felt so alone and frustrated since leaving my biological mother's home for good when I was thirteen.

Wait. I pulled myself erect on the bench. I wasn't alone, and there was nothing to compare to that terrible night when I'd run away. Now I had my foster parents, Lily and

Mario Perez, and all the girls who'd ever been through Lily's House to help me. I couldn't ask them for money because cash was always tight, but if they would help me do the work, and if I stripped down my original plan to the very basics, and bought everything secondhand, maybe it was still possible. I could give up my apartment and stay with Lily to save rent. I could offer to work more at my current jobs.

I folded my arms in determination, reminding myself of all the meals I would make in my café, and all the people who'd come in and chat, taking a moment from their busy lives to eat one of my pastries. It was a beautiful dream, and I'd make it happen somehow. There was still time.

Of course, I wasn't going anywhere just staring at the music store. I needed to get working on my new plan. I bent over to grab my shoes, glancing around to see who might notice—only to realize the man with the camera was no longer aiming it at the tree but at me. For an instant, I froze, worry and upset zipping through me and making my heart pound against my ribcage.

Shoving my poor abused feet into my heels, I bounced up and faced him, hands clenched at my sides. "What are you doing?"

He slowly lowered the camera, revealing laughing brown eyes that were opened wide, giving him a somewhat startled expression. His skin was several shades lighter than mine, but he still had plenty of African American blood running through his veins. His smile was wide and friendly, and I found myself wanting to return it.

With effort, I resisted. "Well?"

"Uh, taking pictures?" He raised the camera slightly for

emphasis. The words were matter-of-fact, with no mockery implied, but it had been a rotten day, and I wanted to take offense.

"I can see that," I retorted. "What I don't understand is why that *thing* is pointed in my direction."

His smile widened. "It might have something to do with the fact that you are the most beautiful woman I've ever seen."

The rest of my protest died on my lips. Even through my irritation, I could see he was one fine man. Intelligent eyes, lean body, and tall enough even for me. Not that I was looking for any man.

"Well, uh . . ." I said, finding my voice. "Thank you. But I'd rather you not take my picture." His stare made me uncomfortable.

Again the slow smile that was like a key turning something inside me. "Why?"

I shrugged. Being told I was beautiful was nice, but I was experienced enough to know it usually didn't end there. Years of counseling had helped me deal with my past, but I'd only had one real boyfriend to practice a relationship with, and we'd broken up when he'd taken a job in New York. Jamal was a good friend, comfortable like a warm blanket, but I didn't love him enough to move that far away from my adopted family. I still shared an apartment with two of the girls who'd gone through Lily's House at the same time I'd been there, and they were my sisters and my support, far more support than Jamal had ever been. I also enjoyed being able to go home to see Lily and the others whenever I wanted. Jamal hadn't loved me enough to stay, either, but we remained good friends.

"There's no law against taking pictures," the man continued. "At least in a public place because no one has any expectation of privacy. I could even sell them. Of course, you can't actually publish photos without a model release because . . . Never mind. You want to see them?"

Before I could stop myself, I stepped toward him. "I guess."

He slipped around to my side, bringing with him the faint aroma of cologne. "Just a moment," he murmured. "I have to enable the screen. I don't normally use it when I shoot."

"Oh, you mean you use the little square that messes up your makeup. At least that's what my sisters call it."

He laughed. "It's called a view finder. Ah, here we go."

Images appeared on the two-inch screen. In the first picture, I was turning toward him. The second, slightly earlier in time, showed me staring in determination, and the third caught me with my lips parted, my expression thoughtful. The shot was fantastic.

"Wow, you're good." I looked amazing, beautiful—like someone I didn't know.

"I had a great model." He thumbed through a few more. Not all of them made me look as amazing as that third picture, but none were blurred or embarrassing.

"I'm not sure what's so fascinating about that store," he said. "But they're already advertising ninety percent off, so whatever you're waiting for, it's probably as good as it's going to get."

"Yeah, I know." I knew it too well, and someone was going to scoop the building right out from under me if I didn't figure something out soon. But I wasn't going to tell this stranger about my dream.

Finally, after about twenty shots of me, the little bird appeared, looking wide-eyed and intent. Nothing at all like the bird I'd seen. This guy had made the waif-like creature as cute and appealing as he'd made me look beautiful.

"You're not going to make me delete these, are you?" he asked.

I lifted my eyes to his and tried not to drown in their depths. The rapid beating of my heart was ridiculous. He was just a man and those were just eyes. "I thought you said it wasn't against the law and that I had no say."

"Well, not in the eyes of the law, but I don't like to take pictures of people if they don't want me to. The problem is, once you tell them you're shooting pictures, it's harder to get great natural poses unless they're trained models, and even then, it's not as appealing, at least to me. I prefer candid shots." He tilted his head and gave me another smile. "Please?"

"Fine. You don't have to delete them. But no selling them."

"Couldn't get much for them without a model release anyway. Want me to email copies to you? I won't charge you for them."

I really wanted that third picture, and I'd even pay for it, but it was silly because it didn't really look like me, and I almost never dressed this way. Besides, then he'd have my email address. My eyes ran over his brown curls and sincere face. Maybe that wasn't so bad.

Yes, it was. Especially if he went around telling all the

girls he met that they were the most beautiful woman he'd ever seen. *What a line.* I knew his type, and I didn't want or need the distraction right now.

"I don't think so. But thanks."

He sighed, his smile wavering slightly. "Look, these are great pictures. I do freelancing for a couple of magazines. If you're interested, I could shop them around, but I'd need a model release."

Shopping the photos around was something I definitely didn't want. Next, he'd be asking me to strip down to a bikini to pose, and all the counseling in the world hadn't prepared me for that. No way was I going on display. Consciously, I opened my hands that were beginning to ache for clenching them so long. "That's really nice of you, but I'm not interested in being a model."

"What do you like to do?"

"Cook." So much for not giving him any personal information.

"Cook?"

"Yes, and bake and experiment with any kind of food." I glanced to the side at the music store, wishing he could see it as I did . . . and wondering why it mattered if he did.

"Food's good," he said. "I like eating."

Now I was grinning. "So do I."

"We're both creative people, you and I." He reached into his pocket and took out a business card. "Look, here's my contact information in case you change your mind and want to see if I can find a home for the pictures. Or if you decide you want me to email them to you after all." He paused, eyes roaming my face as if putting it to memory, which was a silly idea since he already had the pictures.

"Or if you ever need a taster. I'm good at tasting. I have a cousin who works on this food show, and he's always bringing me stuff to try out before they choose the final menu."

I wanted to ask which food show, but I didn't need to add more of them to my watch list. And I didn't want to encourage him if he was working up to asking me out. Was he interested? It was possible, but most likely it was because he wanted me to sign that model release.

To mask my thoughts, I concentrated on his card. His name was Zane Thomas, apparently, and he had a website. He shot weddings, anniversaries, graduations, baptisms, and bar mitzvahs.

"It's my cell number," he said, ducking his head a bit so he could look into my eyes.

"Thanks." I wasn't going to change my mind, but with all my foster sisters, a photographer might come in handy, so I'd keep the card. "Are you expensive?"

"A bit." There was no apology or offer of a discount, which made me like him more and feel less like he was trying to sell me something.

I glanced down at the card again. "Well, it was nice meeting you, Zane. Good luck with your photography. Thanks for the card. And I guess if I suddenly show up in a magazine, I'll know who to send my attorney after." I could have kicked myself as the words left my mouth, but he just laughed.

"It was nice to meet you, Beautiful-woman-in-the-purple-dress."

"Shouldn't that be lavender dress? Or lilac? I thought you said artists were creative."

"Well, I'm still a man." He emphasized the words with a little wave of his body that hinted he might be a good dancer.

"*That's* your excuse? Really?"

"Okay, Beautiful-woman-in-the-amethyst-dress, it was nice talking to you." He extended his hand, and I put mine into it. His touch was warm and slightly electric, and my breath caught in my throat.

"Ruth," I said. "My name's Ruth." Ruth Truman, but I wasn't going to tell him all of it.

He grinned. "Hi, Ruth. I hope you call me."

I pulled my hand from his, turned, and walked to the car, scarcely noticing the pain of my high heels.

Zane

I watched the most beautiful woman I'd ever seen walk away. It wasn't as if I could stop her, though I wanted to—and I hadn't known until that moment how much I wanted to. Why hadn't I asked her out for a drink? Well, at least she hadn't told me to delete the pictures.

Would I have done it if she asked? Deleted them all? I was glad it wasn't a choice I had to make.

Usually people were flattered when I wanted to photograph them, and even those who were annoyed became happy to accept twenty bucks in exchange for a model release. In the five years I'd been photographing full time, not one person had threatened to break my camera. I'd learned to be unobtrusive as I recorded the world through my unique lens.

I had thousands of photos now up on stock photo sites. A couple of best sellers and a few hundred pictures that sold regularly paid the bills, and the magazine gigs on the side allowed for any luxuries. I was doing what I loved. Living the life. I had no desire to visit war-torn countries and risk life and limb. I wanted to depict normal life, to find the beauty—and the sadness in it. Real life.

At the moment, I regretted that I wasn't more aggressive, that I hadn't somehow obtained Ruth's contact information or convinced her to pose for more photographs. There was something about her, compelling and familiar, but there she was walking away, limping slightly. High heels were ludicrous things, but I had to admit they did wonders for a woman's walk. I had a picture of Ruth's shoes and her feet next to them—a picture I'd taken before going back to the bird, so it hadn't been grouped with the others and she hadn't seen it. I suspected she'd have wanted me to delete the photo, even though it told more than all the other photographs combined.

Scratching an itch on the back of my neck, I sat down on the bench and studied the music store. What had she been staring at? She'd been here a long time, so that store meant something. Now I would never know the story behind her presence.

I wouldn't have put her pictures up on the stock sites, not before checking my magazine contacts. She was a cut above most people I photographed, and I was almost sure I could sell them for a big payoff, but the magazines wouldn't buy a photo without a release.

Besides the photos of the bird, who didn't need to sign a model release, it had been an unsuccessful day. I'd still had no luck finding the woman in the baseball cap, whose picture I'd taken here a month ago after the big storm. She'd been sitting on this very bench wearing slightly baggy pants, a loose T-shirt, and a D-backs baseball cap, talking and laughing with a couple other girls. I'd taken the pictures on a whim, loving the natural way she tilted her head as she leaned in to talk. She was dressed so plainly compared to the others, yet she shone like a rare diamond. She was the kind of girl I'd like to take with me camping on landscape photo shoots. The kind who would jump into a lake without fear of getting mud in her hair. My kind of compelling.

Unfortunately, the girls had received a phone call that made them rush away before I could approach them, so I'd chalked the photos up to ones I'd print and show in my portfolio but never use commercially. Then last week a resort manager saw her picture when I bid on his project, and when he offered me the job, he expressed an interest in using the woman in the D-backs cap as one of the models. He'd been so enthusiastic that finding her and getting her to agree seemed important.

To be honest, I wanted to find her, and his interest only gave me an excuse. I wanted to discover if she was anything like my idea of her. I wanted to make her laugh, and see her jump into a lake. Maybe she wasn't anything like I imagined . . . but maybe she was. So I'd taken to photographing everything I could up and down this street for the past week, hoping to run into her, with no luck.

Funny that I'd found two women at this very place that drew my eye. Not everyone transferred so well to film.

The thought brought me to my feet, gripping my camera tightly and staring in the direction the woman in the purple dress had disappeared. No, they couldn't be the same woman. The coloring and build was the same, and they both had wide-set brown eyes, but the woman today was sophisticated and a bit standoffish, and her hair was long and smooth. The woman in the D-backs cap was warm and friendly and loved to laugh, and her hair hung in tight, sexy ringlets to her shoulders, poking out from the cap a little crazily. Like my sister's hair before her latest hair-straightening phase.

I hadn't seen the older photos up close in the past few weeks, but the sinking feeling inside told me I'd made a big mistake today. I'd been thrown off by the dress and straight hair and high heels. Why had I assumed my mystery woman would always wear a baseball cap?

I unshouldered my camera bag and sat again on the bench, rifling through the pockets to find my extra memory cards. Had I deleted the pictures after transferring them to one of my external drives? Usually I did, unless the card wasn't that full. Finding the card and placing it in my camera, I brought up the pictures of the girl in the cap, enlarging the details.

Definitely the same woman. And she was incredibly beautiful by any standards.

I put a hand over my mouth, closing my eyes in thought. Now that I'd actually found—and lost her again—what were my choices? Maybe if I haunted this bench for two more weeks, I could find and convince her to go out with me, even if she said no to the photo shoot. People were creatures of habit, and she seemed to have some fascination with the music store, so she'd probably be back here at some point.

No. My hand fell to my lap. Sure, I'd dropped the ball in recognizing her, but I had offered to take her pictures to my contact, and she'd refused. I'd also offered to email her and had given her my contact card. Any more than that might be misconstrued as stalking.

I straightened my shoulders and removed the memory card from my camera. I still had a half hour of good light. A stroll down the sidewalk might reveal more treasures I could uncover, like the little sparrow, who would likely bring me enough money on the stock photo sites to pay my phone bill.

I started off, then stopped, glancing again at the bench. Maybe it wouldn't hurt to pass by here in a day or two. I could shoot photos anywhere, and there was a skate park not too far from here where I'd been meaning to grab a few photos. If I happened to see her, I'd smile and invite her out to coffee, keeping my camera in the bag.

The worst she could do would be to say no.

Ruth

I drove up to the sprawling house at the end of the street that had recently been painted a light shade of blue. A sign over the front gate read *Lily's House*. Early May had always been my favorite time at the house. The grass was a verdant green, not yet parched by the long Arizona summer. Lily's garden would be planted and some of the tomatoes ripe. In a few weeks the early peaches would be ready, and I loved peaches.

I'd started living with Lily when I was thirteen, before she and her husband bought this house and became certified foster parents with the state, but this place had been a constant throughout my teens and would always represent home to me.

Making my way under the arch and down the front walk, I stepped over a few toys. Lily's foster girls—currently ten of them—were all in their teens, but she had three biological children ranging from five months to six years old. The youngest was Cherie, Lily's first daughter, and while I loved Lily's two boys, I adored Cherie.

I went through the unlocked front door, calling to Lily

as I walked through the living room. "I'm home, Lily. Here to visit Bianca." The house smelled wonderful. I'd definitely come at the right time.

Lily appeared in the doorway leading to the kitchen, her hair in its customary ponytail. Cherie sat on Lily's hip. "You only want to see Bianca?"

I laughed. "You know what I mean. Of course I want to see you and everyone else." There were only eight years between us, and we were more sisters now than foster mother and daughter, but she was still the woman I most looked up to. In large part, she had inspired my love of feeding people and taking care of them.

She handed me the baby before I could ask to hold her. Cherie bounced up and down with happiness to see me, her hand immediately tugging on my straightened hair. "How'd the meetings at the banks go?"

I grimaced. "Not that great. But I may have a way to go forward. I'd like to run it past you and Mario." I hesitated, knowing I had to be careful how I went about asking for support because Lily would sell the shirt off her back to help me if it didn't endanger her children, foster and biological. But running a foster home, one that was more like a real home than any I'd had with my birth mother, cost more money than Lily usually had access to, even with the trust fund from her grandfather. Lily's love and care never stopped at eighteen when the state checks did, and I knew she was paying to help keep two of her former foster girls in college.

"I'd love to hear about it and help in any way I can. That location is perfect."

My eyes tickled a bit with unshed tears, not because I

was worried about losing the store, but because even with all the girls she had to keep track of, she loved me like a "real" mother or sister.

"Thanks. I'll stay until Mario gets home from work." I bounced Cherie to make her laugh. "But where is everyone?"

Lily grinned. "Out picking peas. We're watching a movie tonight, and I like to have something besides popcorn and chocolate for them to munch on. Plus, they were all getting up in each other's faces like they do sometimes, and a little work always helps their attitudes."

"Good for you." I couldn't help laughing because I'd been at the other end of those kinds of chores too many times to count. "What are you going to watch?"

"*Annie Get Your Gun.* The last time we saw it, Lois and Andy did an amazing rendition of 'Anything You Can Do' right in the middle of the musical. Using their own words. Stuff about how many boys' numbers they could get, how many children they could have, and how many days they could ditch school until the principal suspended them. None of it made any sense, but we didn't stop laughing for a week."

"If it happens again, you should film it."

"I already have the camera charged and ready."

I glanced to the left where stairs led up to the second floor. "Is Bianca in her room?" At Lily's nod, I added, "How is she?"

"Better today, I think. She's been able to use the cane instead of the crutches and her boot should be off in a few weeks. Her side still hurts sometimes, but that's to be expected. She is having a little trouble sleeping, though. She might be taking a nap."

I patted the big canvas bag that I'd stuffed with my jeans and some new pastries I'd made early this morning. "I brought her nightlight. She left it when she moved out of our apartment. I should have found it before now."

"Maybe it will help. You know how she is about the dark. Take the baby up with you—she'll distract Bianca." Lily started toward the kitchen but stopped to ask, "You staying for dinner?"

"If you have enough."

"We always have enough."

I'd expected as much. Lily's food wasn't something anyone bragged about, but she never scrimped on the quantity, and she did make some mouthwatering rolls. The only things given out in more abundance than food at Lily's House were love and chores.

"Then I'll stay. Thank you."

"Oh, and before I forget to ask," her gaze dropped to my feet, "is there a reason you're barefoot?"

"I got a blister, so I left my shoes in the car. I don't know how women walk in those torture devices."

"Moderation in all things," Lily murmured.

Chuckling at that, I bounced up the stairs as wildly as possible to entertain the baby, who was giggling when we entered the bedroom at the end of the hall. Inside the room, Bianca was teetering on a chair, balanced on her good foot and reaching for a book on the top shelf of a built-in bookcase.

"Bianca Mendez," I said, "what on earth are you doing?" I set Cherie and my bag down on the floor and ran to help her. "You should have asked for help."

Bianca turned her head, her tiny figure nearly falling

from the chair. I reached out to steady her, grasping her arm and half helping, half carrying her down and back into the unmade bed she'd apparently just left. She only weighed maybe a hundred pounds, and she'd lost weight she couldn't afford to lose since her fall during the storm last month. She'd ended up with a severely sprained ankle, an arm broken in two places, and internal bleeding—all of which required surgery.

Afterward, she'd come back here to recuperate instead of moving in right away with Zoey, her biological sister, in Kingman, which was where she'd been headed the day of the storm. I'd tried to visit Bianca as much as I could since the accident. Both of us, and Zoey, were part of the originals—the six runaway girls Lily had with her before officially starting Lily's House. Bianca and her sister were fourteen and fifteen when I'd first seen them in a park a month after I'd been taken in by Lily. Bianca had been crying. When I told Lily, she found them and brought them to our little apartment. We'd been family from that moment on.

Bianca wrinkled her nose. "I just need that book up there on the top shelf. I must have left it here when I moved out."

"Yep, you did." I was a year younger than she was, and we'd shared the room for a year after Zoey had left for college. Then, since I graduated from high school early, we'd both joined Zoey at the apartment where I still lived. "I thought you did it on purpose. You should have asked for help. What if you'd fallen?"

"I didn't."

Standing on tiptoe, I retrieved the book and handed it to her, but not before glimpsing the title: *Pottery through the Ages.* I should have known. Pottery was Bianca's passion and life's calling.

"I'm thinking it's time to get back to work," she said. "Or at least in a couple weeks. And this will give me some ideas for new projects. My arm's probably not strong enough to throw pots, but there are handles and other stuff I can make. Can't let my suppliers down."

"Anyone can throw pots," I teased. "Even Cherie." I mimicked tossing a basketball before picking up the baby, who had crawled over to the bed. With so many hands to carry her around, you'd think Cherie wouldn't have any incentive to move on her own, but in the past week she'd gone from rolling everywhere to full-on crawling, even up the stairs. Unfortunately, she hadn't yet figured out how to go down.

I set Cherie on the bed, and Bianca zoned out for a full minute, immersed in baby talk to Cherie that had me laughing. Finally, Bianca tucked the baby in beside her and patted the bed for me to sit. "You're giving my neck a crick. So, tell me about it. Did you find anything?"

I slumped to the bed with a sigh.

"Oh, that doesn't sound good." She scooted closer, awkward with the walking boot that nearly reached to her knee. "What happened?" Her dark eyes willed me to spill my secrets.

"What happened is no one wants to lend me money. I'm a big risk. I'd need a co-signer, and you know how Lily and Mario feel about risking what they've worked so hard for. I wouldn't dream of asking them anyway. But"—I straightened, holding up one finger—"I'm not giving up. I have a plan."

"Yes! Let's hear it then." She reached under her pillow and pulled out a baby toy to give Cherie. "Don't ask," Bianca said. "She's been up here a lot. So, tell me the plan."

"Well, you know I have enough to pay the first and last month's rent, and maybe enough for a month of food supplies. Plus, I get paid tomorrow, and I can ask for more hours at my current jobs until the end of the month when I'll need to quit. It obviously won't be enough to cover the equipment and renovations I wanted, but maybe I can cut it all down. Make do with what I can afford. There's that counter along the back wall that I can use to put toasters and drink stuff on. I mean, it's that ugly orange, but it's functional. And what if I bought one of those cheap folding tables to put in front of that for the register. I can also use another folding table for food prep in the back and nail some crates above them as temporary cupboards. No one would see it after all, right? It's out front I have to worry about."

Bianca was listening thoughtfully, so I rushed on. "Instead of that big glass floor case I wanted for pastries and other desserts, I could buy a few of those clear plastic serving containers like they have in breakfast nooks at hotels. They could just sit by the register for now. Even used floor cases cost several thousand dollars, so that's a huge savings right there. I'd have to be careful about anything that needs refrigeration, but . . ." I trailed off because Bianca was shaking her head.

"No, you need at least a couple curved glass countertop cases—not those cheap plastic ones. Remember you're shooting for chic, not bargain basement. The small ones can't be more than a few hundred used, and I'll bet we can get at least one of them with refrigeration for your custards."

"That would work. Maybe I can sell my contract at the apartment and move in here. I know there aren't any extra beds at the moment, but I can sleep on the floor." I couldn't remember which foster girl was sleeping in here with Bianca, but I knew she wouldn't mind.

"What if you used my old pottery table to hold the register? I know it's as ugly as sin, but it's really sturdy and not too deep so it won't take up a lot of room. Mario can help us put it on a platform to raise it somehow, and Lily can make a curtain to go around the base to cover the legs. I can cover the top with ceramic tiles. I have boxes of them in Lily's shed out back, and I can make more if we need to. We could even put handprints in them and color them any way you want. It'll be new and original."

I knew if Bianca designed them it would be amazing. "It'll look custom."

Her eyes sparkled. "That's the idea. You can also have some of my pottery pieces, and you can hang any of those paintings I did in college. They're up in the attic. They aren't professional, but they're bright and cheerful, and they'll fill the space until you get something better."

"Are you kidding? You know I love your work. Thank you!"

She laughed as I hugged her. "It beats sitting here feeling sorry for myself. I know the others will pitch in too. Washing walls, painting—whatever you need. It'll be fun. Just like when we moved in here, remember?"

"Boy, do I. What an utter mess. Remember that horrible

carpet?" I shuddered. "I plan to talk with Lily and Mario about the café, so Mario can help me crunch numbers to see if it'll work. I need to make sure it's even possible before I take the jump. Oh, that reminds me—I'll need a new refrigerator."

"We'll find a great used one. Hey, when you get back to your apartment, ask Halla to write up a news release for the local papers about your business. And she can post it on her blog. She's good at that stuff. Speaking of which, we should take pictures of you right now for the article. Do you know how hot you look in that dress? I was doubtful when Halla lent it to you, but you are one sexy babe."

I popped up and gave her a little bow. "Why, thank you." Without wanting to, I thought of the picture Zane had taken of me. Maybe I should call him and ask for the picture? No, that was silly and it wasn't that important. I didn't need his picture, even if it was the best one I'd ever had taken. Any picture would do.

"Ruth?" Bianca was staring at me.

"Huh?"

"You zoned out. Where were you?" She reached over and pulled baby Cherie away from the edge of the bed.

I thought of telling Bianca I was daydreaming about the café, but my blush gave me away. If only Zane's smile didn't make my heart pound like a girl with her first crush.

"Ruth! It's a guy, isn't it?"

I sank back down on the bed. Both Bianca and Cherie were staring at me, the baby with her hand shoved into her mouth. "Maybe."

"Tell me! Who is it?"

"Just a guy who was taking pictures of a bird outside the strip mall. I was sitting there thinking what I'd absolutely need to get the café up and running, and what I could do without, when I look over and see he's taking pictures of me."

"No!" Bianca's jaw dropped.

"Yeah. So I ask him what he's doing, and he starts talking about how it's not against the law to take pictures of people in public."

"Seriously? What a jerk."

"It wasn't like that. He was nice and funny about it. In fact, he said he'd erase them if I wanted, but they were really good. Actually, better than good. And he was so cute and polite and . . ." I felt warm all over just talking about him. This was definitely a case of absence making the heart grow fonder.

"What did he look like?"

"Tall and lean. Wears a baseball cap." I went on to tell her about his eyes, the loose brown curls, and his coppery skin.

"Woah, you certainly checked him out. I don't think I've ever heard you describe any guy like that before."

"He was rather hot," I admitted.

"Well, did he ask you out?"

I frowned, pulling up my legs and folding them against my chest, tucking the ends of the dress in the bend of my knees so it wouldn't slide down to my thighs. "I think he might have been trying to, but I'm sure his main goal was to get me to sign a release for the pictures so he could plaster them all across those stock photo sites Halla uses for her blog. He talked about a magazine and said it might mean money for me, but it was all iffy. Nothing concrete. He's probably one of those smooth-talking guys, who tell all the ladies what they want to hear." At least that was the way I felt now. I was no model, however good his picture had turned out.

"That's too bad. But I always said you could be a model if you wanted."

I made a face and tightened my arms around my knees. Attention on my face and body was the last thing I wanted from a bunch of strangers. My privacy was more important. My looks and figure had caused me enough pain, and while I was over that, and happy with the way I was now, I didn't want to invite attention to myself. "It's this dress. He wouldn't have noticed me at all if I'd been wearing my regular clothes."

"You mean everything two sizes too big?" Bianca's lips pursed. "Look, you know you can't dress in jeans for your café. Not if you want it to be upscale. You'll need to have some kind of uniform."

"I could call it a diner. You can wear anything in a diner. From what I've seen, you can at least wear jeans."

"Diners usually have more food choices and waitresses. I think you'd better stick to the basics and your yummy desserts. Black pants, white top, and an apron with your logo on it will be easy enough. Your employees can wear their own clothes, and you provide the aprons."

"Employees?" A well of panic bubbled inside me.

Bianca chewed on her lip a moment before saying, "Well, I think you'll need at least two other people, even in the beginning. I'm sure the girls here can help. It'll be fun for them to do something different, and it'll keep them out of trouble. Lily will be all over that. Remember when she had us walking those dogs?"

"Hey, back then we needed the money. But my café won't be very busy at first."

"You never know." Bianca paused, her mouth curving in a sly grin. "So about this guy, did you give him your number?"

"So he could hound me into signing a release? No way. It's not as if he believed in them enough to offer me real money. I should have made him delete them."

"I thought you said he was nice."

"Because he wanted something."

She sighed. "Well, did you get *his* number? If he's a real photographer, maybe he has connections and the offer to pay was real. Even a couple hundred dollars could help you set up the café. At the very least, we could get a picture from him if they were that good."

I thought of telling her about the card, but if I did, she'd have it out of my bag inside thirty seconds and be punching in his number. "Forget it. He was just trying to get me to sign a release."

"Oh, fine. I'll do the picture. Stand there while I take a few with my phone. The camera on it is surprisingly good, and I did take that photography class. Comes in handy when I photograph my pots. Open the curtains, will you? And turn on the light. It's starting to get dark in here. Too bad we don't have any of your pastries for you to hold or something."

"I have plenty of food pictures," I said, popping up from the bed to do her bidding. "Halla and I've been taking them for months for the menu, and she's got them all laid out for printing and laminating. But, you're in luck, because I brought you my new pastries."

"Oooh." Bianca turned to Cherie. "You hear that sweetie? We're going to spoil our dinner."

"Why not? Eating a pastry when you're hungry is much better than eating it when you're too stuffed to really enjoy it." I retrieved my bag from the bed and dug inside. Seeing her nightlight, I tossed it onto her bed.

"Thanks, I wondered where that got to."

I hesitated. "Lily said you're not sleeping well."

Bianca's gaze dropped to Cherie, and she ran her fingers through the baby's dark hair. "I dream about being stuck out in that storm sometimes . . . and it reminds me of when Zoey and I lived with my uncle. She used to cry at night, and I felt so helpless, like I did in the storm after I left the car because I was afraid it would wash down the ravine. But the feeling will pass."

"I'm sure it will. Maybe you should talk to Tessa." Tessa was Lily's sister and the psychologist for all the foster girls. She and her husband lived next door, and they had horses they let the girls ride and take care of as part of therapy.

"It's really not that bad. I just need to get back to work." She raised her hand. "Don't go all mother hen on me. I'll talk with Tessa if I need to."

"Good." I pulled out my jeans and T-shirt to uncover the container of pastries. My mouth was already watering from the smell of Lily's dinner, and now my stomach started growling anxiously.

"Mmmm," Bianca said. "First the pictures, then we dig in."

Probably a good idea since I was anxious to get out of my borrowed dress. She snapped a half dozen pictures, including a couple of me holding a pastry. Then she unzipped my dress, and I changed while she looked at the pictures critically.

"Well, a couple turned out okay, but depending on what Halla can do to lighten them, we may have to take them again on another day. Outside with more light, I mean."

"No way. I'm not flattening this hair again for at least a month. Maybe three. Too much work. Those will have to do."

I sat cross-legged on the bed and set the pastries between us. Cherie crawled into my lap, eager for the small piece I broke off for her.

"These are called mil folhas," I said. "Puffed pastry, egg-based filling, and frosting glaze on the top with chocolate designs. A Portuguese lady from the hospital gave me the recipe." I offered Bianca the container. "Give it a try. This is my sixteenth batch, and I think I finally have it right. At least my friend says so."

Bianca was already reaching for a rectangular pastry. As she bit into it, her eyes shut slowly as if experiencing a kiss. "Ooh, perfect. It's like the French thousand leaves pastry, only the filling is much better."

"My friend also gave me another recipe for custard egg tarts, which are tastier than they sound. I could eat them all day and be happy getting fat."

"Well, you'll need to gain weight to have your own restaurant. They say you can't trust a skinny cook."

I laughed. "I plan to."

Bianca licked her fingers. "This is heaven," she said.

"If these are any indication, you are going to be a raging success."

I hoped so. But I still needed Lily and Mario to weigh in on my plan. Until then I could only cross my fingers that I wasn't overlooking something important.

"I wonder," Bianca said, swallowing her last bite, "if photograph guy hangs out taking pictures often on that street. You could track him down."

"No way. And just for that, you get no more pastries." I shut the container, but left it on the bed for her to eat later. I liked seeing her happy. Plus, she might need them after what else I was about to say, though they'd be small consolation for the thing I'd been dreading bringing up from the moment I walked in. But I knew I had to tell her. In fact, that was most of the reason I'd gotten up early this morning to make the pastries.

"There's one more thing," I told Bianca. "Last night when I was combing the city looking for other possible locations for my café—cheaper ones—I went into one of the shops that sell your ceramics. They were having a sale, so I went in to see how your stuff was doing. They had a whole shelf dedicated to your work and were even setting out more. At first I was really excited and couldn't wait to tell you, but then I remembered you haven't been working this past month, so how could they have a new shipment? And the quality . . . well, see for yourself."

I reached for my discarded bag and pulled out a small pink-marbled candy dish, handing it to her.

Bianca ran a finger over the dish. "Wow, this is bad. Jagged edges. Uneven glaze. Is this my competition? Six bucks? No wonder it's so cheap. I mean the form is all right but the—"

"Turn it over."

She did, gasping when she saw her own logo. "I didn't make this."

"I know."

Color drained from her face, and she looked ready to cry. "What am I going to do?"

I'd been thinking about it every minute that I hadn't concentrated on my café. "Research. Track down who's behind it. In a couple weeks when you get that boot off, you'll know better what your options are and what to do. Try not to stress too much. Anyone with eyes can tell the logo's a copycat—the whole piece in fact."

"Okay. You're right. I'll take it slowly." Bianca's voice was slightly more upbeat, but her color didn't return. "Can you hand me that water bottle over there and the pills?" she asked, pointing to the items on a lower shelf of the bookcase. "I've been trying not to take them because they make me a little loopy, but my arm ached all night and the medication might be wearing off again."

Climbing up on the chair to get her book and then taking all those photos of me probably hadn't helped. I watched her swallow the pill, mentally kicking myself. "It's going to be okay. You know that, right?"

"I know. For both of us. Let's go downstairs and talk to the others about your café. But please don't tell them about the candy dish yet. I'll talk to Lily tomorrow, but I want more information before we tell anyone else."

"Sure. Let me know if you need any leg work for the

research. I can visit all the pottery shops. Make phone calls. Whatever you need."

"Thanks. I'll let you know."

I carried Cherie to the main floor, hesitating at the bottom of the steps to watch Bianca swing her boot down as she gripped the railing. For some reason, she reminded me of the little bird in the scraggly tree—and the man with the camera.

A thought skittered across my mind: maybe if I rented the store, I'd see him again.

Ruth

The next evening, I drove back to Lily's House after my Friday night shift at the Mexican restaurant. It had been a good night for tips, and I was excited to add to my funds for the café. But now as I pulled up in front of the house, my stomach tied in knots. I'd told Lily and Mario about my plan and left them my notebook of expenses and projected income, and I trusted them to tell me if I should take the plunge or if I should wait a few more years. The very thought of waiting made my heart wilt, but I'd rather succeed than go too fast.

Mario had a degree in accounting, but he worked at a place called Teen Remake in downtown Phoenix. His day was spent mostly with troubled teens, but he also did their books. Having so many foster children at Lily's House made the job a perfect fit, and more than one of the girls from Lily's House had ended up in the program. But my trust of Mario and Lily went beyond simple accounting. They knew me and believed in me. Any doubts they had were something I'd need to address because they would never stop me from going after my dream without good reason.

I found the whole crew out on the back lawn, roasting marshmallows and making s'mores. Always something going on at Lily's House. Lily's two sons were on the swings, and Cherie was being passed from girl to girl around the gas fire pit. All ten current foster children were present, plus Bianca. Halla and Elsie, two of my current roommates, both part of the original six foster girls, and also Saffron, the oldest of the original six, sat near Lily.

"Don't you have a date?" I teased Saffron. She lived across town, and I didn't see her as much as the others, but she always came for the monthly Sunday dinners with a new guy in tow. She had more ex-boyfriends than the rest of us combined.

She flipped her blond hair over her shoulder. "Yeah, but I think we're breaking up anyway. Besides, you're more important."

"Wow, I didn't know it was going to turn into a party."

"Are you kidding?" Bianca said. "Just wait until—" A look from Lily hushed her.

My stomach flip-flopped. "So," I said, sitting on the side of a log next to Halla, who had scooted over to make room, "what's the verdict?" The question was directed to Mario, who had my notebook in one hand, his other holding Lily's. His black hair and dark eyes, a result of his Spanish heritage, were a complete opposite of Lily's pale features. They'd come from two very different worlds, but the look in Mario's eyes whenever he was with Lily and the way he treated her—and all of us—made me believe in true love and that there were good men left in the world, men worth knowing and loving.

Someone passed me the sack of marshmallows, but the lump in my throat made it impossible to eat anything now. I set them on the grass, my eyes not wavering from Mario. He grinned, and suddenly I knew everything was a go. I should have known from the moment I arrived, because if it wasn't, there was no way they would have had everyone over.

"After looking over your financials," Mario said, "I believe you could be ready to do this at the end of the month."

"Really?" I reached out to grab Halla's hand, and she squeezed it encouragingly.

"You'll need to work hard this month to make sure you have enough padding," Mario continued, "and it's going to be hard to get the place ready by then—especially because you'll need to schedule a visit from the health department—but I think you've thought everything through. You will have to give up your apartment and eat here, though, because the first couple of months, you'll probably barely break even." He paused. "I would feel better if you had a little more padding, but . . ."

"But we've solved that!" Bianca put in from across the fire pit. "Because all the girls here have volunteered to work for free until you can pay, even if it's for a year."

"As long as we don't have to do chores here that day," someone mumbled. Laughter rippled around the fire.

"And Mario says he can make my old table into a counter for the register, with sides and everything," Bianca continued. "And we'll all paint. Well, not me because I'll be doing the tiles for the counter. And Halla said she'd make flyers for everyone to hand out. I'm so excited for you!" To show how excited, she threw a marshmallow at me.

I popped it into my mouth and chewed, glad that she seemed to have recovered from the shock I'd given her yesterday. "You know that's a health violation, unless you just washed your hands."

"Hey, that's your worry, not mine," she retorted through the ensuing snickers.

"It'll be everyone's worry who works there," Lily said. "All the girls who don't already have them will need food permits. Mario and I will donate the cost of the licenses. It'll be a good investment for the girls and the café."

"Plus, we have this." Bianca reached behind her for a black top hat and passed it to the girl next to her, who passed it to the next person. Everyone was quiet, and when the hat got to me, I was shaking too badly to take it. Halla reached across me and grabbed the hat.

"Four hundred dollars," she said, jiggling the hat for emphasis. "We think it'll buy an awesome used latte machine, and maybe even some industrial pans for your pastries."

"Thank you so much!" I blinked back tears. This was really going to happen.

This was never going to happen—and just when everything had been going so well. Over the weekend, I'd found a used oven large enough for my pastry pans and a stove top which was more costly than I'd wanted but that I knew would save me money in the long run. I also bought cute, mismatched café-type tables and dozens of equally mismatched plates and glasses, which Halla assured me would add character to my café. I'd picked out the paint color for the walls and decided which of Bianca's artwork to use. I gave notice at the hospital and at the Mexican restaurant, and both places wished me well.

Then the problems began. Another party had offered to rent the store, and I'd had to agree to pay a hundred dollars more per month to match their offer. Plus, the store was now going to be vacant in mid-May instead of at the end of the month. Which meant a half month's extra rent to come up with to beat out the other interested party. That was when Lily's sister, Tessa, stepped in and promised to buy the industrial-sized used refrigerator I'd found, which was the exact price of the extra rent. I swore I'd pay her back when I could.

Crisis averted, or so I thought, I tried to dwell on the bright side—two weeks of extra time to make the store nice, instead of trying to crowd the renovations into a week so I could meet the opening we'd tentatively scheduled for the seventh of June. So on Tuesday, I paid the first and last month's rent and applied for a business license. An inspector agreed to come out to do a pre-assessment of the location, but I wasn't worried because the place had been a restaurant ten years earlier.

Now, barely a week since roasting marshmallows, I stared at the health inspector, listening to his report, my heart falling and never seeming to reach bottom. Beyond the man, I could see the signs in the music store window, proclaiming *One Day Left!* I might as well leave the signs in the window because it looked like it was over for me before it really began.

No, I *had* to find a way. "But this place was used as a restaurant before," I said. "You know that, right?"

He checked his papers. "True, but that was years ago. We have new policies in place to make eating safer for the public, and that ceiling must be fixed. It's simply too old to be sanitary. You saw all the gray powder in the kitchen. That's definitely dust from the ceiling tiles, and it'd end up in the food. Also, the crates you want to use as cupboards." He shook his head. "Not going to happen. The surface would have to be smoothed and stained so they can be easily cleaned. Otherwise, dust will collect, and that could be a danger for the food. I'm sorry."

"How much do you think it would cost to fix the ceiling? Any idea?"

"Well, I wouldn't recommend putting in those kind of ceiling tiles again. They're dust magnets, and the space only invites rodents. I'd put up drywall and texture over it before painting. Something that size will cost at least a few thousand dollars. Could be four thousand depending on the contractor. Unless you can do it yourself, or have friends help, and then the cost would probably go down by more than half. But ceilings are hard if you don't have the right equipment."

"Right. Okay." I wiped my hand on the black skirt I'd worn to impress him. At least I'd been smart this time and hadn't worn heels.

He handed me a card. "Please call me to schedule

another visit when you have the café set up—with the new ceiling. If you decide to go through with it."

"Thank you." I felt numb watching him walk away.

My first thought after the disappointment was that maybe I could continue working at my old jobs through June instead of until the end of May. If I put in enough time at the Mexican restaurant, I could pay for the ceiling, and then I could use my paycheck from the hospital for rent. I would probably have enough, as long as I found someone to buy my apartment contract, and if I lived with Lily. That would also leave me more time to market the opening of the restaurant.

Except I was already training my replacement at the hospital, and the owners of the Mexican restaurant had promised my job to their niece's daughter. I was betting no one else would hire me for only a month.

Maybe the owner of the store would agree to redo the ceiling. Our contract said the maintenance was limited to major things like busted pipes, structural damage, or broken windows, things her insurance covered. I was responsible for getting licenses and upgrading the interior according to my specific needs, but maybe she'd feel this was important enough to invest in. It wouldn't hurt to ask.

I still had a few minutes left of the early lunch I'd taken before I had to be back at the hospital. I wandered to the bench I'd sat on before when Zane had captured my photo. Instinctively, I looked around, but he was nowhere to be seen. *Of course,* I thought.

I dialed the phone number. "Hello, Mrs. Gunderson? Ruth Truman here. I'm the one who's going to rent your—"

"Hi, Ruth. Of course I know who you are. I'm glad you called. I've talked to the renters, and they're planning to be out by Wednesday morning next week. I really don't know how clean they're going to leave the place, but I'll inspect it that day, and I'll keep their deposit if it's not all cleared out. If it is ready to go, I want you to know that you can get in whenever you want after that. I know our contract doesn't start until the 15th, but if you want to get in sooner, feel free to do so. It would be nice to have your café open and get a buzz going before summer gets into full swing."

"It would. I don't see that it's going to take a lot of time to paint and arrange the dining room. And the menu is all ready. I'm keeping it simple with pastries and a few main dish staples. The kitchen is the biggest issue right now, and about that . . ." I paused, taking a breath before rushing on. "Remember when I asked it if was okay to have a health inspector come out just to make sure there were no surprises?"

"Of course. It was a good idea. Better to know up front how many coats of paint or whatever."

"Yeah, well what he found came as a surprise to me. He said the ceiling tiles are too old and need to be replaced because they're a health hazard around food." I went on to explain his recommendation about putting in drywall.

"Oh." Several long seconds of silence and then, "Look, you know I think your café is a great idea, and I accepted you over the second party who was interested even though you are a lot younger because you impressed me with your seriousness, but it's not feasible for me to put in a new ceiling. However, if you want, I can call the other people, and see if they're still interested. If they are, I can let you out of the contract with no penalties." Mrs. Gunderson gave a soft chuckle that was more kind than amused. "They're planning on opening a basket store, so I don't think the ceiling will matter to them."

My words clogged in my throat, and when I finally spoke, they tasted like failure. "If you will ask them, I would appreciate it. Meanwhile, I'll see what I can come up with."

"All right. I'll let you know."

"Thanks." I hung up, my mind reeling with disappointment.

I leaned over, elbows on my knees, head in my hands. What could I do? What had I been thinking starting a business with only a bit of reserve? I should have been more patient. And now I'd not only risked my entire savings, but so many others had donated or put in work because they'd trusted in me. I was letting everyone down.

There has to be a way.

The thought calmed my mind enough that I could stop the swell of panic threatening to choke me. I would find a way to get the money—at least to buy the materials. Did Mario know how to lay drywall? He could work wonders with wood, and he did most of the repairs around Lily's House, but there might be an end to his abilities. Plus, he worked full time as it was. We'd have to find more people to volunteer, or hire someone, which meant more money.

Around and around my mind went in circles. It had to be possible. There was no way it was possible. I couldn't give up. I had to give up.

If Mrs. Gunderson found another renter, I could store

my café equipment in Lily's shed until I was ready for a new place, and on a worse-case scenario, I'd lose all my money while waiting for another renter to take over the contract. It would take me years to save that money again.

No, even if I had to bake and sell pastries door to door, I'd find a way. If only I had more hours in the day. Some way to earn enough money for the ceiling. I glanced around the street, hoping for inspiration. If I'd learned one thing growing up in Lily's House, it was to never give up. If one door closes, or the ceiling leaks dust, you find another way.

My eyes landed on the tree where the little brown bird had perched the last time I was here. Now there were two birds and a small nest. They'd certainly been busy. It would make a nice picture.

Picture.

I dug in my purse, searching for the card. Where had it gone? It had been in this black leather purse—the only dressy purse I owned. There it was.

I lifted the card and read it. He probably hadn't been serious about his magazine connection. Maybe he'd sold my photos anyway and forged a model release. I didn't know anything about this guy, except that he was hot and I'd dreamed about him twice in the past week.

"You are pathetic." I shoved the card into my purse and jumped to my feet. I'd just have to go back to my friends and family and ask for more help. Help I knew none of them could afford.

I'd gone only five steps when I took out the card again. It wouldn't hurt just to call, would it? I was pretty good at telling when people were insincere, and he had seemed so nice.

Well, I'd think about it as I walked to the car. If it still sounded like a good idea by the time I got there, then I'd call. Maybe.

I passed the birds, who stared down at me, their heads tilting jerkily. One of them began singing.

Zane

"Thanks for dropping by," Mason said as I chewed a mouthful of chicken taquito. "Well, how does it taste?"

"Not bad, except for the slight burned flavor." I was hungry enough to take another bite.

"I knew it!" Mason paced away from me and back again in the studio kitchen, running a hand through his spiked blond hair. "Sylvia says it's perfect, but she's doing something wrong. Oh, this is a disaster."

"No one's going to care," I told him. "They'll just think they did something wrong when they followed her recipe."

"Maybe. But too many failed recipes, and they'll go watch another show." Mason tugged his hair again, a habit that might be why his hair seemed thinner than it had last year. "I knew I should have gone into sitcoms. I don't even like cooking."

I stifled a laugh. "Yeah, but you sure like to eat."

Mason's head jerked in my direction. "You think I'm gaining weight?" He ran a hand down his lean chest. "I've been in the gym every night."

I wasn't even going to answer that. Mason was my favorite white cousin, which wasn't saying much because he was the only cousin on my mother's side, but he was easily distressed for someone who had chosen to become a TV producer. His show, *Turn Up the Heat,* was popular on the West Coast, and was slowly gaining ground in the East.

"It's fine." Although now that I'd stopped eating, the burned flavor remained in my mouth.

He pointed at me. "See? Now you're feeling it. We'll have to go with the other recipe."

The other dish was the braised pork belly sandwiches, which tasted much better than they sounded, even though I wasn't a huge pork fan. Especially when they called it "belly." It didn't sound like something people should eat, but the rest of the world didn't seem to share my view.

"Go with it," I said.

He gave a sharp nod of decision. "I will. You can never go wrong with something that is essentially bacon."

"Right." The pork belly tasted nothing like bacon to me. Bacon-flavored butter was a better description, but either way it should be a hit.

"Thanks for coming down, man. I needed an outside opinion—a truthful one. Everyone here"—he waved his hand around the studio, though there were only two cameramen in sight—"is so afraid Sylvia's going to quit that they'll praise anything she makes. But the last thing we need is an audience taster to make a nasty face on live television. I mean, usually we can grab one of the set people to taste it, or I'll come out and do it, but this could be a disaster."

"Live?"

"Didn't I tell you? Sylvia is insisting on at least one live show a month. It's driving us all crazy. She wants to meet her audience. As if two hundred thousand Twitter followers isn't enough. Not to mention two book deals." Mason's nostrils flared. "I swear, if she threatens to quit one more time, I'm going to pack up and move to the Australian outback to produce a wildlife show."

Mason had been threatening to do that as long as I could remember. "I'd visit you," I said. "I could take some sweet photos there."

He rolled his eyes. "Which reminds me. You think you could take a few more publicity shots next week? Sylvia has an internet article coming up, and we have to supply the pictures. She doesn't want to use the older ones. She likes each article to be exclusive."

"Sure," I said. Mason was the cheapest of all my clients because of the family discount, but he occasionally sent real jobs my way, so it worked out in the end. Besides, he was family.

"Thanks, Zane." He patted me on the shoulder awkwardly. "Gotta run. I owe you one, cuz. Go ahead and take one of the sandwiches—or all of them."

"I will." I waited until he was gone before rifling through the set refrigerator. Ah, there was the pomegranate jelly. The jelly would make me overlook the fact that the pork in my sandwich was mostly fat. In fact, I'd eat anything with pomegranate jelly, especially homemade. Sylvia Blakely might be a prima donna, but she knew how to make an awesome pomegranate jelly.

I'd eaten half a sandwich when a sound alerted me that someone had arrived in the studio, and I looked up to see Sylvia. She always reminded me of a younger, thinner, slightly flatter-chested Dolly Parton, and we'd always been friendly until the last six months. Now she seemed upset and angry all the time—a manner that vanished the minute the cameras started rolling. I chalked it up to pressure and a growing ego. Either way, she wouldn't be pleased to see me adulterating her pork belly sandwich with jelly. I slid a napkin over the sandwich and wrapped it up tightly before starting toward her.

"Well," she asked, "did you like it?"

"Absolutely."

She smiled at me like she wanted to pat my head. In the old days she would have hugged me. "I knew it. I'd better make sure I have enough chicken."

That was my cue to leave. I'd let Mason break the news that it was the sandwiches she'd be making for the next show and not the taquitos. Dropping bombs was not in my volunteer taster job description.

My phone rang on the way out. "Hello?" No answer. I checked the number to see if I recognized it. The service was sometimes sketchy in the studio, and I'd hate to miss an important call. The number wasn't familiar, but I passed out cards every day, so that wasn't unusual. If it was someone wanting to employ me, hopefully they'd call back.

The phone rang again, and this time I saw it was Landon Bass, my contact from the resort, whose sales booklet was my next big project. "Hey, Landon," I said. "Good to hear from you. What's up?"

"Hey, Zane. Just calling to see if you can push back our meeting for another half hour. I've had to resolve some issues here, and I have to meet with an electrician before I can leave."

"Sure, no problem."

"So, were you able to work out a deal with that model? The one from your portfolio?"

The moment I'd have to break it to him had arrived. "No, sorry. She isn't going to be available, but I have more photos to show you. I think you're really going to love them. I've made sure to have the whole ethnic gamut like you requested."

"Okay, sure. Too bad. That girl was perfect, but I'm sure you've found others just as good."

Relief rolled through me. Had I mentally exaggerated his attachment to Ruth's pictures? Maybe I'd been looking for her more for myself than I wanted to admit. At any rate, if everything went all right at the resort, I'd finally be able to upgrade my printer. My current one worked reasonably well, but the newer ones had more ink choices and a larger paper width, which meant I wouldn't have to go to a printing shop to print bigger photos.

"I think you'll find these new models every bit as appealing. For the shoot, I recommend using at least three. You can have your pick."

"How about moving our meeting back to one o'clock this afternoon? And I've blocked off four to eight Monday evening for the photo shoot as you requested. It works out well, since that'll be our least busy time for the week."

"Perfect. We'll do the inside shots first while we wait for the right angle of the sun outside."

"Sounds good. See you in a few."

I breathed a sigh of relief as I disconnected. I'd photographed every model I knew, as well as two dozen strangers on the street this past week, and I was sure he'd find a least three to use. I'd already advised the most promising women of the Monday shoot, so it was only a matter of calling to set it up.

I reached my Toyota Tacoma that still had the pop-up camper on the back from the last time I went camping on my hunt for the perfect landscape shots. The camper was small, but it beat setting up a tent.

I had just taken a bite of sandwich when the phone rang again. What did Landon want now? I chewed enough to be able to answer. "Hello?"

"Uh, hi, um." Long pause and then, "This is Ruth."

I sat up, dropping the sandwich on my lap, and nearly dropping the phone as well. After eight days, I'd given up hope that she'd call. I tilted the phone away from my mouth as I hurriedly chewed.

When I didn't respond, she rushed on, "I'm the woman you saw on the bench outside that strip mall about a week ago when you were taking pictures of a bird. You know, purple dress?"

I swallowed quickly and a bit painfully. "Hi. Of course I remember you, Beautiful-woman-in-the-amethyst-dress. Good to hear from you. What's cooking . . . uh, get it?" Man, that was so lame, I could have kicked myself. I picked up my sandwich and set it on the decidedly dusty dashboard.

She laughed. "Oh, quite a lot actually. Pastries, mostly."

"Sounds tasty." I was full of corniness today—not exactly the way to impress a woman.

There were two seconds of awkward silence, which she finally broke. "Look, I know this is really unusual, but I was thinking about what you said . . . about the pictures.

Something's come up, and well, I need to earn some money, and I wanted to ask you if you were serious about possibly selling my pictures and how much it might pay." Another pause before a hurried addition, "I understand if that was just conversation, or if you already found someone . . . or if it's not much. I'm only calling to ask what you meant, but maybe that was a bad idea."

Time to jump in before she talked herself right out of it. "Are you kidding? It's a great idea. In fact, I just got off the phone with a guy at a resort here in town. They attract a lot of older people, but they're trying to appeal to a younger generation to widen their market, and they've hired me to shoot and design a new sales booklet. The photo shoot is Monday, and I think you'd be perfect for it, if you don't mind posing for a few pictures on location. You know, just pretend to be a guest enjoying the place."

I heard a swift intake of breath and then a quiet, "Okay, I appreciate that. What time?"

"Four in the afternoon. Is that good for you? It'll run at least three hours. Possibly more."

"Yes, I can work that out. Is there anything I need to know . . . or wear? And how much does it pay?"

I typically paid twenty-five bucks an hour to models the first time I worked with them—as long as I wasn't forced to go through an agency, which often charged me six to ten times more. But for women I'd worked with before, I paid fifty dollars. It wasn't a lot of money when compared to how often models were able to get gigs, but at least they kept it all and ended up making about the same as they would with many agencies. I wasn't crazy to work with like some photographers, and the models liked the free copies of the pictures I provided for their portfolios, so usually even the more experienced models agreed to pose for me.

"I can pay fifty an hour," I said. "As for what to wear, this is a resort, so there's no clothes to model. I do have access to some outfits, but on this level, I usually ask the women to bring any clothes they think might work for them."

"Oh, I see. That makes sense."

Clothes were one of the reasons I normally hated doing photo shoots that weren't for clothing companies, unless they were hiring and dressing the models themselves. I much preferred shooting nature or candid shots that didn't require clothing changes. But this opportunity had been too good to pass up, and I had to pay the bills, just like anyone else. Most of the inexperienced models were excited to bring everything in their wardrobe, and the more experienced often had expensive clothing given to them from past photo shoots. It was all a matter of making it work.

"The clothes themselves aren't really important," I said. "It's more a matter of having them fit and looking nice in the photos. You'll want a variety of what you'd normally take to a resort."

"How fancy is this resort?"

"Not too fancy. In fact, we'll want some shots in jeans and shorts. They have a mini golf course, tennis courts, and a pool, so if you have anything along those lines, that would be great. Something an average person your age might wear. And maybe something dressier as well. They have a nice restaurant on the premises. Like I said, I do have some clothes to choose from, so don't be too concerned." Most of what I had were purchased for one-time use for past shoots when the client requested something specific. I always added it to their bill.

"Where is the resort?"

"If this is a mobile phone, I can text you the address."

"It is." The words came hesitantly, as if she was already having second thoughts about letting me have her number. "One more thing," she asked. "Is there anything in particular you'd like me to do with my hair? I mean, I'm assuming I should come with it fixed, but when you saw me my hair was straight, and it's usually curly . . . very curly. What's better for the shoot? I could send you a picture if you'd like."

"Curly," I said. "The other girls will have straight or slightly wavy, so it'll balance out."

"Oh, great." She chuckled. "Guess I get to sleep in an extra hour on Monday morning."

"That's always good."

"Thank you. I'll see you Monday."

"I'll see you then."

I hung up, pumping my fist into the air. Things were absolutely working out my way. Well, except for the sandwich. I got out of the truck to toss it into the garbage near the building just as Mason hurried out the door. He looked harassed but determined.

"You still here?" he asked, slowing when he saw me.

"Had some calls to make. What's the rush?"

"I'm just getting out of here before Sylvia threatens to quit again, and I tell her to go ahead and do it. She'll cool off, and so will I."

"Good luck," I said.

"You, too, cuz. You too."

I didn't need luck because on Monday I was going to photograph the most beautiful girl in the world.

Ruth

Fifty bucks an hour. If it panned out and wasn't too degrading, maybe I could see if he had any more work. The hundred and fifty might buy enough materials to get us started on the ceiling, and maybe there was something else I could do to add to the funds. Halla might know of something. She had a zillion contacts on social media compared to my measly forty Facebook friends. If it wasn't for her, I might not have even uploaded a picture.

Modeling was the last thing I ever thought I'd do, and even the idea made me nervous. However, despite my unease, I couldn't help the sliver of excitement that worked its way into my thoughts. If this was a real job, then maybe everything else Zane had said wasn't a line.

At that thought, more butterflies than Halla had social media contacts swarmed in my stomach. I clutched the steering wheel and replayed the conversation in my mind. He had been professional and encouraging, not personal, and I needed to be careful not to romanticize him in my head. I was doing this only for my café. That was all.

Still, I couldn't wait to get home and tell my roommates I was going to be a model. If they didn't fall down on the ground laughing, they might be the tiniest bit impressed.

My gaze snagged on the car's dashboard clock. Oh, no, even if I hurried, I was going to be late getting back to the hospital, and I hadn't eaten my lunch. I'd have to work late and go directly to the Mexican restaurant afterwards, and on Fridays I could never leave there before nine even though I was normally scheduled only until eight.

I started the car before digging into my bag for the sandwich I put inside that morning with a little ice pack.

It was going to be a long day.

The next morning Halla stared at me, her ultrashort, blond hair on end and her cheek still printed with a strange pattern made by her pillow during the night. "You're kidding."

"No, the whole ceiling needs to be replaced."

"Not that!" She jumped out of bed and settled next to me, pushing me over toward the wall. "You're going to model? Like dressing up in fancy clothes and strutting around in front of the camera?"

"I guess so. You make it sound awful."

"It will be for you. You *hate* stuff like that."

I pulled my knees up to my chest. "Mrs. Gunderson texted me that the other people who wanted to rent the building already signed another contract. That means one way or the other, I've got to pay for the restaurant for the next two months or more if she doesn't find anyone by then. I have to make this work."

"If you go into the café unprepared, you'll fail," Halla retorted. "Maybe it's better to wait."

My heart plunged, but I lifted my chin and said, "If I fail, I fail. At least I know I gave it my all."

Halla laid her head on my shoulder. "Okay, you're right. If anyone can do it, you can. I just hate to see you so stressed. Have you told Bianca and the others about the ceiling?"

I tilted my head to touch hers. We were as different as milk and chocolate, as we'd been called in our teens, but I considered her my best friend, even better than Bianca and Lily. We'd met on the streets and had been roaming Phoenix together for some time—I couldn't remember how long now—before Lily had found us at a church where she was serving Thanksgiving dinner to the homeless.

"There's really nothing any of the girls can do," I said, "except paint the place when it's done. I'll go talk to Mario and Lily today, see if they know anyone who can help. If I can get the money, that is."

"Well, you have to," Halla said. "In fact, you'll have to do that first, before you even buy food basics. We still have three weeks before the opening to get the rest."

"Three weeks? I'm opening mid-June. That's five weeks."

She lifted her head. "About that. I think we should move it up to the first of June, take advantage of the fact that we're getting in early. We can still do marketing all of June and beyond, but you won't have your current jobs after the end of this month, and you might as well be at the café making some money, even if it's only a bit."

She had a point. "If we get the ceiling done in time," I reminded her. "I'm still working two jobs until the end of the month, so I only have some of the weekend and two nights off a week."

"I know, but we'll get it done. The minute they let us in, we'll all start working, even if you aren't there. Let's shoot for raising two thousand dollars. And with the hundred and fifty for this modeling thing—if it's legit and not just this guy trying to take advantage of you—that puts us a bit closer." She rubbed the smattering of freckles on her narrow nose. "But I think I'd better tag along on Monday."

"What?"

"Yeah. Just in case he isn't all that he seems. You don't know this guy."

A sensation of fear crawled over my left shoulder and up the back of my neck. I closed my eyes, willing the sensation to go away. "Okay." I sighed. "But I wonder—when do we get to meet guys and not be afraid?"

"Not afraid. Cautious." She smiled, and her blue eyes sparkled with her usual humor. "In a way, we're lucky we learned that lesson early in life because now maybe it will keep us from making the bigger mistakes—like marrying a jerk. We know what to look for."

"I hope so." Halla's past was different from my own, but still as emotional—like all the girls that went through Lily's House. She was back in contact with her timid mother, but she hadn't spoken to her abusive father since she'd run away all those years ago.

"Oh, that reminds me." Halla jumped up from the bed. "I printed a proof of the menu yesterday for you to approve. I sent it to three friends online, and I'm sure there are no typos, but I wanted you to have a final look. I ended up doing it folded only once because it made more sense for the organization, and I really hate trifold menus. Wait right here."

She ran from the room and returned shortly with the menu. I took it, running my hand over the images. "I don't know how you made it all look so appetizing."

"You did that, not me. It's your food. I just lightened and sharpened the photos we took. I'll wait to print and laminate a few days before you open so we can use that money instead for the ceiling. In fact, they'll be on me."

"You can't afford that," I protested. Halla was two years older than I was and should have finished college a year ago, but while I graduated from high school early and crammed four years of college into three and a half, graduating last December, she had taken a year off to explore her inner muse. Now she had just finished up her junior year in college, as an English major, and her part time job at the college print shop barely covered her expenses. "You've already spent hours on this."

"You've taken care of me all these years," she retorted. "And it's my contribution. Besides, since it's not a sit down and take your order type of place but rather an order and sit down with your food deal, they're really just at the tables to advertise to those already eating what else you have available. I won't make too many because you're bound to want to shake things up in a few months. Now, come on, if you need to take clothes to this modeling thing, we'd better start picking them out."

"First I need to price drywall."

"That can wait. Monday will be here before you know it."

She went to the closet and opened one side. "You can borrow anything of mine that you want. I'm sure Elsie will let you too."

"You're both so much shorter than I am."

She laughed. "That means our clothes will just make your long legs that much more visible. Anyway, it doesn't matter. You have to borrow things. Practically all you own is jeans."

Halla stared into the closet and began ticking things off on her fingers. "Let's see. We'll need a few dresses, hats, shorts, shirts, jewelry. I wonder if Audrey next door would lend us a few pairs of shoes. She's your size, right? Didn't you lend her some shoes once?"

"I think she still has them."

Halla snorted. "Probably. We'll also need a swimsuit or two. Do you have any that fit?"

"Swimsuit? Really?" My stomach churned. What had I gotten myself into? "It's a resort booklet, not an ad for sunscreen. He didn't mention taking shots at their pool." Or had he? I couldn't remember now.

"He said to bring stuff you'd actually take if you were staying there."

"I know but . . . you know what we really need? Blueberry muffins." I popped out of bed. "Since I have to go talk to Mario and Lily about the ceiling, I'll take Bianca some. She loves them. I'll go make them now."

"You're not getting out of this," Halla called after me. "But go ahead and stuff your face while I start working on the wardrobe. And by the way, if this guy is rich, you take him some of your muffins. Maybe he'll buy enough of them to pay for the ceiling."

I grinned at Halla's comment because I knew she was joking. But mostly because the burden I'd felt since learning about the ceiling yesterday had been lifted by sharing it with her. I was either going to do this thing or go down burning in flames. At least I'd go down with style.

I was also smiling because one of the Portuguese pastries from my last batch was still in the fridge, and I could eat it while I made the muffins. Pastries solved a world of problems.

When I arrived at Lily's with my muffins, Bianca was in bed, talking to her sister, Zoey Morgan, who'd come to visit from Kingston. Zoey had her dark hair pulled up into a ponytail, and her naturally bronze skin had been darkened by the sun. She was wearing shorts sleeves for the first time that I could remember, seemingly uncaring of the old cut marks on her arms. She looked healthy and happy.

By contrast, Bianca's hair splayed around her in tangles, and she had huge circles under her eyes that told me she'd had trouble sleeping. But she smiled and waved as I came in.

Zoey bounced up for a hug, which I returned enthusiastically, knocking off my D-backs cap. Of all the original Lily's House girls, our pasts had the most in common, and we'd been in group therapy together to learn to deal with the sexual abuse we'd endured. She knew things about me that I had never even shared with Halla. She'd once told me how grateful she was that we had each other, not only because I understood her, but because of my support, she'd never had to burden Bianca with any horrifying details.

"I hear you're going for the café," she said.

"And I hear *you* have a new boyfriend."

She laughed. "It's true, I do, and he's amazing. Do you know he's buying that little cabin where we hung out during the storm? He was looking for a place, and while it's off the beaten track, it's closer to work than where he lives now."

"Oh, so romantic," I said. "He bought the place where you first kissed."

"That rat hole," Bianca added.

"Mice," Zoey corrected. "And they're gone. Every last one of them. As soon as you're better, I'll take you there. He's ripped out most of the kitchen. It's going to be really nice. Still small, but it *is* a cabin, after all."

"Can't wait," Bianca mumbled unconvincingly.

"These are for you." I opened the container of muffins and held them out to Bianca.

"Thanks." Bianca scooped one out and nibbled at it. "Really good."

Zoey sighed and grabbed one for herself, taking a huge mouthful. "Oh, I've missed your cooking. Once your café is open, I'm definitely coming to town as often as I can to eat there."

"I'll give you the family discount."

"Stop that." Bianca slapped at my wrist. "Full price for everyone until you can pay your bills."

Zoey sat on the end of the bed. "That's right, and I've been wracking my brain for what I can do to pitch in. They don't pay me enough at the sanctuary yet to be much help with funding, and I live too far away to come paint, except maybe on a weekend. However, I think I've finally hit on something better. I can't bring any of the animals from the sanctuary—the whole point of the place is so animals don't have to be hauled around and made uncomfortable or afraid—but I talked to the owner, and he'll let you have one hundred tickets to the sanctuary to use to publicize your café launch."

"One hundred tickets?" I gaped. "That's huge. How can he afford that?"

"Well, let's be honest, it's a basic ticket, so we'll still make money on safari upgrades and gift shop sales. Plus, it's publicity for them as well."

"Still, it's a lot."

Zoey grinned. "He offered twenty at first, but I'm a good negotiator. Besides, I'm dating the new manager, and that helps." She pulled her legs onto the bed and sat cross-legged. "Instead of using them for the first one hundred guests, I think you should hold a drawing. Every time someone buys something, they get an entry. More purchases, more chances to win. And you could draw ten tickets a day for the first ten days to keep up the excitement."

"You'll have to get their names and email addresses so you can contact them," Bianca said. "Then every now and then you can send them coupons and notices about new specials."

They'd really thought this through. "I love it!"

"I figure it's unusual enough to get attention from the newspapers—and once they taste your food, you'll win them all over."

I was overwhelmed with the generosity. I knew Halla would have fun writing up blurbs about the tickets for her blog and the newspapers, and for the flyers the girls had agreed to hand out.

We discussed the possibilities as we ate our muffins, but I noticed Bianca only consumed half and then set it back in the container.

"Are you okay?" I asked.

"Just a little nauseated. I walked around a lot yesterday and I think I overdid it. I had to take one of the stronger pain pills this morning."

Zoey's smiled vanished. "I was telling her when she arrived that she should wait until the boot is off next week before going all over Phoenix tracking down that jerk who's using her logo. It's too heavy to drag along. Besides, she needs more time to recover."

"I agree." I sank to the floor, suddenly feeling a little weary myself. "But did you find out anything?"

"Well, I think I have an address for the guy. It's a shop for pottery supplies." Bianca pulled one of the many pillows from behind her and lay back on the bed. "But I am going to wait until I'm a little stronger to, uh . . . what's the word? I hate how these drugs make me feel stupid. Oh, confront him. And I'll either ask Mario to go with me or do it on the phone."

"Good idea. I'll go with you too." I hit my right fist into my left hand and deepened my voice. "This guy is going down."

Bianca smiled, if a bit weakly. "I just want him to quit."

"He will," Zoey said. "But before I forget, I want to give you this." She reached in her back pocket for a white card and handed it to Bianca. "My friend Stephen just started working at a law firm here in town. He's not an attorney yet, but he assists one and he's really knowledgeable about this sort of thing. In fact, you know that case I told you about involving the sanctuary? Well, for the past year, he's been our liaison with the attorney he's now working for."

Bianca stared at the card somewhat blankly. "I know I should remember at least some of that, but I don't right now. Do you think you can put the card in my purse over there on my dresser? Put it with the other cards inside the zip pocket. I'll look at it when I'm off these drugs." She yawned widely. "I know it's not even lunch time, but I think I need to take a nap. Do you two mind? I'm missing half of what you're saying."

"Of course we don't mind," Zoey said. "I'll go visit with Lily while you sleep. When you wake up, I'll make us lunch and we'll watch something on Netflix until I have to drive back. How does that sound? Nothing strenuous for the rest of the day."

"Sounds good," Bianca mumbled, her eyes closing. "Thank for the mu . . . mu . . . little thing I was just eating."

Zoey and I laughed. "She's funny on drugs," I said as we tiptoed to the door.

"I know. Can't wait to tease her about it when she's better."

Zane

W as she going to show? That was always the worry with an inexperienced model, but the fifty bucks an hour should have been all the convincing Ruth needed.

The other two models were already here. Under my guidance, Landon had chosen a beautiful Latina and a woman with hair so long and blond, I'd have to be careful to get decent photos of her face. Needless to say, Landon was happy Ruth had agreed to come to the shoot after all, but if she wasn't here by the time I finished setting up my equipment, I'd have to call a backup.

I hoped something hadn't happened to her. Maybe she'd decided my motives were questionable, and that bothered me more than I wanted to admit. Mostly because where Ruth was concerned I really didn't know what my motives were.

The clothes I'd hauled here in my camper were already inside a room Landon set off for us. I'd decided to start dressy for the inside shooting, and then work toward more casual outside. My sister had come along as she usually did to touch up the models' faces between takes. She did this for me in exchange for fifty bucks and a night of me babysitting her two children, which I secretly enjoyed more than they did.

"Kassidy," I called to my sister. "I'm going outside for—" I broke off because through the partial glass wall in the lobby that overlooked the parking lot, I saw a car driving up. I took a few steps forward to see if it was Ruth.

Sure enough, Ruth gracefully unfolded her tall form from the car and walked toward the resort. Or rather, swayed. She wore a flowing sleeveless print dress in yellow tones that contrasted beautifully with the deep bronze of her skin. Her hair spiraled in tiny ringlets to her shoulders, obviously tamed with some kind of product. A decorative clip on one side gave her an air of exuberance. With her smooth skin, wide-set brown eyes, and the many tiny ringlets, she looked as if she'd come prepared for a high-end photo shoot, not just this low-end job.

Ruth entered the building through the double doors, smiling in my direction, and I realized I was staring. Why did I feel as if I were melting and that the earth had stopped rotating?

"Good, you're here," I managed to say.

She wasn't alone, I finally noticed. With her was a blonde with large blue eyes and short hair, wearing a camouflage tank top and khaki pants, and also a younger girl in a blue T-shirt and jeans whose curly dark hair hung nearly to her waist. I recognized them from the very first pictures I'd taken of Ruth in her baseball cap. Both their arms were full of clothes.

"These are my roommates, Halla and Elsie," Ruth said. "I hope it's okay they came with me. I needed their help carrying things. We brought more in the car, but this is the stuff we like the best."

"They're welcome." I nodded at them both. Neither was dressed up, so I didn't think they were trying to push their way into the photo shoot. They were both attractive, but had nowhere near Ruth's appeal, at least not for me. "We're all set up. I think we'll start here at the front desk, and then move to their restaurant. What you have on looks great."

A soft touch on my arm told me Kassidy had heard my call from earlier and was standing behind me. "Oh, this is Kassidy," I said, bringing her forward. "She'll be doing any makeup touch up that might be necessary between takes. Mostly for shine. I can do a lot with Photoshop, but the more I can get right in the original picture, the better it is."

"Nice to meet you." Kassidy reached out and shook Ruth's hand. "Love your hair. Mine doesn't look nearly that nice when I wear it curly—so I mostly straighten it."

"You're more patient than I am." Ruth indicated her friends. "These two hiding under these mounds of clothes are my roommates." She made the introductions to Kassidy, while I tried to remember what I'd been planning.

Oh, right. The pictures here in the lobby and then in the restaurant.

"Could you get the yellow scarf for Ruth to wear?" I asked Kassidy. "And tell the others we're ready."

"Will do," Kassidy said. To Halla and Elsie, she added, "Come with me and I'll show you where to put the clothes." My sister winked at me with a huge grin on her face as she left, which made me wonder what she thought was so funny.

"I'm glad you came," I said to Ruth.

"Me too." She met my gaze with an unwavering one of her own.

Heat rushed through me, and I turned from her to hide it. "Why don't you walk on up to the desk and chat with the receptionist there? Just like you're a regular customer. Ask her about anything." Landon had chosen a pretty young woman to clerk the desk, and I hoped she wouldn't freeze when I started taking pictures. If she did, I'd have to dress one of the other girls up in a uniform, which would leave me with only two models to act as guests.

Ruth nodded. "Just talk to her. That I can do."

"Pretend I'm not here. Well, that's not exactly right. You should always try to smile. Naturally, of course. Think of something funny."

"Got it." She turned and sauntered up to the counter as I began to snap pictures. I thought I'd have to coach her more, but she chatted with the clerk like they were old friends. Was Ruth asking her about recipes? Oh, they must be talking about the fresh chocolate chip cookies at the desk. I'd already had three myself. Ruth bit into one, and I snapped pictures as fast as I could. I'd never seen a model eat a chocolate chip cookie before, and it might go well in the booklet.

"Go join her," I told the other girls as they came out of their makeshift dressing room. "Go ahead and introduce yourself. Take a cookie." Miranda, the blonde model, shot me a dirty look.

When I finished shooting in the lobby, I posed them going to the elevator, sitting in the restaurant, and in one of the rooms. Then I had them change and we took more pictures in the room and then in the breakfast nook, where

Landon had provided a partial breakfast for the shoot. So far so good.

"Are we about done?" asked Ruth's short-haired friend.

Halla, I remembered. "No, we still need to go outside. The sun's almost right."

She frowned. "I don't know that this is a good idea."

The younger roommate nodded. "Ruth's miserable. But you know she'll do anything to save the café."

I abandoned the shot I was going to take. "What makes you say she's miserable? She looks great."

"Her back," Halla said. "She's stiff like that when she's uncomfortable, and see the way her foot is twisting as she leans forward? She does that when she's worried."

The two things were making the photographs better, because the twisting foot made her look more natural, and her posture was elegant. "She's a natural," I said.

Halla rewarded me with an unyielding stare. "Maybe, but she's hating every minute."

I didn't know what to say to that, but I decided I had enough footage inside. "Let's take a break, everyone."

Ruth rose from the breakfast table and went to her friends, who drew her away, talking at high speed. Ruth shook her head at them, and once she glanced over at me and smiled.

See, she's fine, I thought.

Kassidy and I picked out the clothes for the mini golf and the tennis courts. We didn't have uniforms, but most guest wouldn't, so shorts and blouses would do.

"What's with all the banter?" Kassidy asked. Her voice lowered to mimic me, "Look natural, like you're going for a stroll. Talk to each other. Ask what the others had for breakfast." Her voice returned to normal. "And you can't take your eyes off her."

"Who?" I said.

"Ruth. Who else?"

"Of course I'm looking at her," I hissed. "Would you prefer that I take pictures with my eyes closed? Now keep your voice down."

Kassidy gave me a sassy look. "Well, you're trying too hard. Tone it down. You're making me nervous." She leaned forward and whispered. "For what it's worth, I like her."

Kassidy was my only sister, but at that moment I'd trade her for a brother. Men didn't draw such silly conclusions.

"Let's just get this done," I growled. "And grab that D-backs hat. I want Ruth to wear it."

My sister smirked at me like she had as a child. "And just for that," I told her, "next time I watch your kids, I am loading them up on ice cream. They'll be on a sugar high for days."

She rolled her eyes. "What else is new?" With a flip of her straightened hair, she hurried off to see if the girls had finished changing.

I gathered my equipment—and tried to do the same with my thoughts.

"Need any help?" It was Halla.

"Sure, can you grab that bag? It's got my extra lenses."

"I'll be careful."

We started for the tennis courts, and I asked. "So, what café is Ruth trying to save?"

Halla turned to look at me. "She didn't tell you?"

"No," I said with what I thought was extreme patience since I wouldn't be asking if I already knew.

"She's opening a café in three weeks. She's been planning this for years, and it's finally coming together, but the health inspector told her last week that she needs to put in a new ceiling. It's setting us back quite a bit."

That explained why she'd changed her mind about the photographs, and I shouldn't be surprised that she'd been telling the truth about needing money. Even so, an unreasonable disappointment lodged in my chest, which didn't make sense unless I'd hoped perhaps she'd just wanted to see me again.

"Thanks for telling me."

Halla nodded, turning away as the others caught up to us.

The pictures on the tennis courts went well, but we'd picked up a few observers and now that Ruth's friends had pointed it out, I could see the tenseness of Ruth's shoulders. How her smile was becoming more forced with each addition to the crowd of observers. The other models played to the crowd, sometimes waving or blowing kisses, or striking sensual poses that garnered good-natured catcalls. Ruth remained quiet, and I suspected she'd rather be pulling off her fingernails with pliers than posing in front of this crowd.

The pictures were still coming out good. More than good. Despite Ruth's tenseness, the camera loved her.

"Okay," I said. "Let's hit the pool." I'd saved it for last in case I wanted the women to get wet. Hair would be a mess after that.

Back in the dressing room, Kassidy had already chosen their swimsuits. "Change and we'll meet you out there," she said as she handed the bikinis to the models.

Ruth's suit was a bright yellow, perfect for her skin tone,

but her face lost color as she accepted the bits of cloth. Her tongue ran across her bottom lip. "Are all those people going to be out there watching?"

"Some of them," I said. "Do you want me to tell them to leave?" I wasn't sure how I could do that, seeing as they were guests at the hotel, but I was willing to do anything to wipe that stricken look from her face.

Ruth didn't reply, but now her gaze went to Halla, who was by the door. Halla hurried over. "You don't have to do this," she said to Ruth in a low voice.

"What's wrong?" I said. Maybe Ruth had scars she didn't want anyone to see.

Neither of them replied, but Ruth looked ready to cry. Watching her struggle awakened something inside me, an urge to protect her, though I wasn't quite sure what I needed to save her from.

I had to shoot at the pool, though. One way or the other. But I was an artist, so as much as the man inside me wanted to see Ruth in that suit, I would improvise.

Ruth

I f anything, Zane was better-looking without his hat than he had been with it, and I loved men in baseball caps. His hair was curly, but not anything like mine. More like Elsie's, except shorter, just past his ears. He stared at me now with concern in his eyes—concern when I'd expected anger at my hesitation.

Even if there had been anger, I wasn't sorry for my feelings. They might have root in my past abuse, but they were part of who I was now. I was never going to be the kind of girl who loved posing in front of the camera. I didn't want to see my face—and especially my body—plastered on the pages of a magazine or spread over the Internet. Nearly every moment of these past hours had been torture. Why had I even agreed to this?

The café. Yes, I had to remember that.

Yet try as I might, I couldn't even think about changing into the yellow bikini. I couldn't go out there with all those people staring. I felt too vulnerable, too exposed. Zane probably thought I was crazy. What would he do if I walked out and ruined the rest of his photo shoot?

He took three rapid steps toward me, and my stomach tightened, but I didn't cringe or shrink away. I had a right to my feelings, even if they weren't something he would ever understand. He reached past me for something from the mound of clothing on the bed near where I stood and tossed me a white cover up.

"On second thought, this will make a greater contrast with your skin. And keep those shorts on too. A lot of people wear shorts to hotel pools, especially when they're outside."

My heartbeat began to slow. "Okay." Maybe I could finish this after all.

"I thought you wanted some shots of them in the pool," Kassidy said. For a second, I hated her, though that was probably more to do with how familiar she seemed to be with Zane than for the casual statement. Was she his girlfriend?

Zane shook his head. "New plan. Ruth'll be on the deck with some playing cards. We'll get the others in the pool. It'll be a more natural shot with the three of them talking if someone stays on the deck. Come on, let's get this done. You girls change while I clear the pool area. I don't want anyone else in the shots, and it'll be easier if no one is there."

The other women were already pulling off their tops before he was completely out of the room. I went into the connecting bathroom to change, and Halla followed me.

"Are you okay?" she asked.

I slumped against the sink. "This is awful. How do women do it? Did you see them strutting around, and waving at everyone? Do girls really wear such tight shirts in real life? Oh, I just want to go home."

"I know, and we can, if that's really what you want. He can take pictures of the other two in the pool."

But now that wearing the bikini in front of the crowd was off the table, maybe I could stay. "He might not pay me if I don't finish. I think there was something about that in the release I emailed him. And that means everything I've done today will be for nothing."

"So what are you going to do?"

I pulled off my blouse and put on the yellow bikini top, followed by the cover up. The cover up was large and comfortable and I could barely see the suit. "That was Zoey's," Halla said. "She left it at Lily's when she lost all that weight. It's a little big."

I pulled it up on my shoulder. "It's perfect."

We walked out to where the other girls were waiting. "Sorry you have to wear that awful cover up," said the blonde, whose name I hadn't been able to fix in my mind. "Maybe you should think about getting a boob job." She stuck out her well-developed chest as she headed for the door. "It really helps in the modeling business. We just have to stay too thin to maintain good breasts." The brunette nodded her agreement and flounced out of the room after her.

I looked at Halla and Elsie, who was seated on the bed waiting for us. "You think he wants me to wear this to hide the fact that I'm not as endowed as the others?"

"Of course not," Halla said in her practical, no-nonsense voice. "It's because you looked like you were going to run away. Which kind of makes him a nice guy. But who cares what he thinks? Let's just get this finished."

"You go with her," Elsie said to Halla. "I'll start putting the clothes in the car."

"Good idea." Halla tossed her the keys.

When we reached the outside pool area, there was no one in sight but Zane, the other models, and Kassidy, who dabbed powder on my face before I sat on the warm cement bordering the pool. She handed me a deck of cards.

"Fan them out," Zane called. The other girls tried to approach me, but he waved them off. "Dangle your feet in the pool. Move them up and down. Good. Okay, now you others get in the water. Ruth, hand them some cards when they reach you."

More pictures, but Zane was having us do funny things, like smelling the cement or trying to balance cards on our heads and noses. I completely forgot to be self-conscious. Then my foot accidentally splashed water on the other girls, and they splashed back. We all ended up wet and laughing.

"And that's a wrap!" Zane called. "Thanks, everyone. You go ahead and get changed. Kassidy will have your checks ready by the time you change."

There was a clock by the pool that told me we'd been here nearly three hours. It felt more like ten. My face was stiff from so much fake smiling.

Zane reached out a hand and pulled me to my feet. "You did a great job."

"It's harder than I thought," I admitted. He was still holding my hand, and my heart was doing all kinds of odd flips. Over his shoulder, I saw Halla give me a thumbs up as she went out of the gate.

"You're a natural," Zane said, releasing me.

"Thank you, but it doesn't really feel natural."

"Well, you could go far, if it was something you wanted."

I couldn't seem to look away. "I don't think so."

"That's right. You're opening a café."

"How did you know?"

"Your roommates. I guess you really do like to cook."

"I do."

I should be walking back to the changing room, and he should be storing his equipment, but neither of us moved. I thought about Kassidy. If he was staring at me like that, she couldn't be his girlfriend, could she?

"You're wet," he said. "You should get changed."

I looked down at the cover up, which wasn't nearly as wet as my hair. "I guess." I slipped my feet into the flip flops Halla had thought to bring, and together we turned toward the pool gate.

"Zane," I said, "about those pictures you took on the park bench. Would you still be okay with emailing me one of them? I need a publicity shot for the café news release. One of my sisters took a picture, but she's kind of on drugs right now, and when she sent them to me they weren't as good as I'd hoped."

He opened the gate. "I'm sorry about your sister. That's terrible."

"Oh, no." I chuckled as I preceded him to the walkway outside of the pool area. "Not that kind of drugs. She was in an accident and it's a prescription. She only takes them when she's in pain."

"Good. And, yes, you can have any of the photos. But I already downloaded them to an external drive, so I don't have them here. Why don't we meet and you can go through them to decide which you want?" He smiled and stopped walking. "I mean, I could put the best ones on Dropbox or Google Drive, but it would be more fun to meet. Don't you think?"

He wanted to see me again, no photo shoot involved! I felt like running back to the pool and screaming as I cannonballed into the water. Should I ask him about his relationship with Kassidy before I agreed? No. He wasn't asking me to marry him, just to meet for the photos. "It would be more fun."

His grin widened. "Okay, then, it's a date."

"A date?"

"A date." His gaze brushed my lips before coming back to my eyes.

Oh, man, I thought. I hadn't kissed anyone since Jamal left a year ago. I hadn't even had time to think about anything but my plans for the café.

I was thinking about something else now.

"How about tomorrow night?"

I had to work at the Mexican restaurant, so Wednesday would be better, but that was the day I might be able to get into the shop, and nothing was stopping me from that. But I did want to see him.

"I have to work my second job tomorrow night, but I get off at nine, possibly eight if they aren't busy."

"That works." He adjusted the camera bag over his shoulder. "Should we go out for dinner?"

"It's probably better that we don't. I work days at the hospital, and I have to be there at six in the morning. I know . . . why don't you come over and we'll make dessert together?"

"You sound busy. I could just bring some."

"Not as good as mine, you can't."

He laughed. "Okay, then. Text me when you're leaving and I'll meet you at your place."

"Just a warning—my sisters will probably be there."

"Sisters? I thought you lived with your two roommates."

"Oh, I do. I meant them."

He blinked. "Halla and Elsie? They're your sisters? Really?"

Now it was my turn to laugh. "I didn't want to go into it earlier, but we all spent a lot of years together in the same foster home."

"Sounds like a good story."

"It is—one with a happy ending."

We started walking again, entering the resort where the others waited for us. Halla was smirking, one hand resting on her hip, and Elsie winked.

Zane leaned over and whispered. "Is it okay if I admit that Halla scares me a little?"

He was so funny. "Halla, she's like a little kitten."

"Yeah, with razor-sharp claws."

"Maybe sometimes."

I left him to continue on to the others, while I ducked into the changing room. When I emerged, Kassidy handed me an envelope. "I hope to see you again."

"You too." *Except not as a model,* I added silently. "Thanks." She seemed happy and not at all put out about the time I'd spent alone with Zane, which meant I'd read too much into their closeness. *Good.*

I was almost to the door when Zane called out, "Don't forget to text me."

"I won't," I told him. He'd probably be all I could think about. "See you tomorrow."

Halla and Elsie grinned knowingly, and I knew the moment we were out the door, they'd be full of questions.

Zane

I was getting ready for my date with Ruth when someone banged on my apartment door. I opened it to see Mason, who pushed his way inside my apartment, throwing his hands in the air.

"I'm finished. Everything's a mess. What am I going to do?" He stomped through my living room into the kitchen and pulled open my refrigerator. "Where's the beer? I need a drink."

I followed him into the kitchen. "Sorry, I haven't had time to shop. What's up?" I almost didn't dare ask because Mason made a big deal out of little things. Like the time his mother, my aunt, started using cottage cheese as a salad dressing when he preferred Thousand Island. "Now's not the best time; I'm going on a date."

Mason grabbed a half-gallon of orange juice and began chugging it straight from the bottle. For a seemingly fastidious guy who worked out in a gym and wore all the right clothes, he had some annoying habits, especially when he was stressed. "Well, I'm sorry to interrupt you, but you always have a date so it's not all that important. That camera is like a babe magnet. Maybe I ought to take up photography." He gulped more juice.

I took the bottle from him and set it on the counter. "This girl is different."

"Yeah, yeah." He waved his hand in dismissal. "But I'm your cousin. That's more important, and I'm in a crisis."

I glanced at my phone. It was almost eight, and Ruth could text any minute. "The studio took away your assigned parking space? No, that's not it. Maybe they stopped offering bagels at the shop you go to for breakfast?"

"Oh, right. Now he's a funny guy." Mason glowered at me.

"Well, then, tell me already. I'm in a hurry." Maybe I should wear jeans instead of these black slacks. I'd be more comfortable, and it was just a casual thing at her apartment. I didn't want to overdress.

Mason lowered himself to a bar stool at the mini center island that doubled as my dining table. "It's Sylvia. She quit."

That *was* news. Mason had produced several shows over the ten years he'd been in the business, but *Turn Up the Heat* was decidedly his most successful venture yet.

"I guess you're moving to Australia then?"

Ignoring me, he jumped up and started pacing. "It wasn't even because one of the cameramen refused to eat her sushi. That just put her in a bad enough mood so when the word came down that the station denied the time change she's been pushing for the past year, she just quit."

"Are you sure?" I sat down on a stool with an internal sigh. This was obviously not something I could solve in a few minutes.

"Well, the fact that she said 'I quit' was a big clue. And she cleaned out her dressing room." He plopped down again on the stool next to me, letting his head fall into his hands.

"She'll probably change her mind. She's threatened to quit before."

"She's never cleaned out her dressing room."

"What does her contract say?"

He lifted his head. "Right. Her contract . . . It's not up until the end of the year, so unless she's ill . . ." The glowering look was back. "I wouldn't put it past her to fake something."

"She'd be ruining her career, you know. Who's going to hire a prima donna who up and quits?" I pushed the orange juice back in front of him.

"She had two million viewers last Friday, and this Friday was supposed to be her first live show. Otherwise, I'd play one of the two backup shows we filmed last year. You know, give her time to calm down. But we can't do that with a live audience."

"No way is she going to miss that. Wasn't she the one pushing for it?"

"Yeah, she was." He lifted the jar of juice to his lips. "Man, this is good stuff. Where do you get it?"

"At any market. Look for 'fresh-squeezed' on the label. Maybe if Sylvia doesn't show up by Friday, you should just cancel the live show and play the recording."

He dragged his eyes from the bottle. "What about the viewers? We've passed out tickets."

"Did you charge for them?"

"No, no. It doesn't work like that." He thought a moment. "But we could turn them away. Say the show was delayed. People expect that in show business. In fact, the tickets say right on them that the day could be changed." He brightened. "You know, I'm going to send out notice right now that the date is changed to a week later. I think we can juggle the studio schedule. That way even if Sylvia does come back, she'll have to wait for the live audience."

"You'll teach her, huh?"

Mason sighed. "Gotta pretend somehow that I'm still in charge. But if she's really walked out for good . . ."

On the counter, my phone buzzed, and I reached for it, hoping I could get rid of Mason soon. "You'll just find a replacement. You know, a substitute chef."

He laughed. "Yeah, that'd really get her."

I checked the text. *Leaving now,* it said. *I should be there in fifteen. See you soon.*

"So, are we done here?" I asked Mason. "This text is my signal to leave."

"Yeah we're done." Mason stood. "Thanks. You're the best."

"I'm always here for you." I lifted a hand and he slapped it, but he didn't move toward the door.

"So who's the girl? Another model?"

"No, but she should be."

Mason's brow furrowed. "That's new. And good. Some of those women you've been dating—they make Sylvia look like a lamb. Modeling's a cutthroat business."

"Which is why I'm doing more and more landscape photos. Look, I have to go now."

"Well, if your date works out, bring her around to the studio on Thursday. We're filming the pilot of that new show I told you about, *Food for Tots.* I got a bunch of the cutest kids you've ever seen to taste the food. I think it's going to be a hit."

"Maybe next time. She works days." I started walking to the door, hoping he'd follow.

He grabbed the bottle of juice. "Mind if I take this? I think it has healing properties. I feel much better."

"Knock yourself out."

"I owe you one, buddy. Have fun on your date."

"Thanks."

After the door closed behind him, I hurried to change into my jeans. If we were baking, it would be a better choice, and I wanted this to be right.

I checked her text again. No cute emojis or excessive exclamation marks that were used by some of the women I dated. Just the simple message. Was she having second thoughts? But it was silly trying to read anything into a text message. I grabbed my car keys, my camera bag, and the flowers I had bought earlier and hurried out the door.

Driving to her place took a full fifteen minutes, and by the time I arrived, I felt as nervous as I'd felt on my first real date back in high school. Her apartment was just a couple blocks away from where we'd first met, and it was one apartment in a group of four-plexes. Maybe a little more upscale than where I lived in my small two-bedroom apartment. If I hadn't needed the extra room for my photography business, I might have chosen a better place, but in the beginning it had been all I could afford without a roommate. The lease was up in a couple months. Maybe it was time to upgrade.

After I bought my new printer.

Ruth opened the door, wearing jeans and a loose V-neck tee that somehow seemed to hug all the right places. Her hair was in those tiny ringlets, but no D-backs cap. "Hi," she said.

My heart banged against my chest all out of proportion to the simple word. "Hi."

Her eyes fell to the camera bag, a little furrow appearing between her eyes. "You planning on taking pictures?"

"Not really. I always bring this, just in case. Sort of comes with the job. But I can take some if you want, especially if this dessert is any good." I hoped she could tell I was teasing.

"You won't be disappointed."

"So where are your roommates? Uh, sisters."

"I'm sure they'll be back. They made a big show of leaving us alone, but they can always smell when I'm cooking, even if they're across town. They have a second sense about these things."

I laughed. "That good huh?"

"I hope so anyway. If not, my café is doomed. Come on, let's get right to the pastries."

I set my camera bag on the coffee table next to a dark green linen couch that looked more practical than comfortable and followed her into the kitchen. Supplies were already laid out on the counter and table.

"I made the puffed pastry last night and this morning," she said. "It's not hard but takes a long time since you use a boatload of butter, and you have to keep refrigerating it for thirty minutes between foldings. So now we'll cook that and get to making the cream filling." She tossed me an apron, which had sunflowers on it.

I tied the silly thing on. "And what are we making?"

"It's a Portuguese pastry called *mil folhas*. It's my latest favorite. I've adjusted the recipe slightly from the original that I was given, and even the woman who gave it to me likes mine better. No one else in town sells this kind, so I'm hoping it catches on."

"Is the recipe secret now?"

She laughed. "Definitely. So no telling."

She put on a pink frilly apron. "Don't laugh, or I'll make you switch with me. Elsie made this in high school when she went through a weird pink stage. She's still kind of proud of it. She's actually making more for the café, only I asked her to make them blue and with fewer ruffles."

I laughed anyway. "You kind of look like a piece of taffy, is all." Our eyes met, and for a moment that seemed like the most sensual thing I could have said to her. I wanted to lean forward and kiss her, to taste the living taffy, but instead, I cleared my throat and reached for a spatula. "All ready. Put me to work."

"Nope. Wash your hands first."

"Oh, right." I headed to the sink.

Next, we rolled out the pastry dough, dividing it into two large baking sheets. "We have to be careful not to burn it. There's a French pastry shop I know that slightly burns them like it's supposed to be some kind of delicacy. Totally ruined the pastry for me. Here, make little holes all over. Like this." She jabbed her fork into the dough at regular intervals. We slid them inside the oven and set the timer.

The cream filling consisted mostly of egg yolks, water, and sugar. "The trick with creating authentic Portuguese mil folhas is not using cream," Ruth said. "And in getting the egg yolks thick enough. Otherwise, it becomes too much like the French or Italian versions."

"And that's bad because . . ."

"I like these better." She grabbed the pan from the stove with the boiling water and melted sugar. "Pour this into the egg yolks slowly while I stir."

I did as she requested, and then the whole thing went back onto the stove for more stirring and thickening. I wiped a bit of the warm mixture from the edge of the pan with my finger and licked it. "Mmm, that *is* good." Weird for simple eggs and sugar to taste that good.

We spread the cream onto the baked pastry dough that was cooling on the table. She'd cut each panful into three equal pieces, and layer by layer we created two large rectangles of pastry. For the topping, she made superfine sugar in her blender from regular granulated sugar.

"I had no idea superfine sugar was a thing," I admitted.

"You're not alone," she said as she poured the sugar into the bowl with butter and milk.

After spreading a thin layer of icing, she mixed the remainder with melted chocolate, drew thin lines on the top, and created an interesting design with a toothpick.

My mouth was already watering. "How long do we have to wait?"

"We don't. They're best fresh. Or at least within eight hours. Although, I freeze some to take for lunches—mostly when I have too many—and they're still yummy."

She was cutting smaller rectangles as she spoke, her movements fluid and sure. There was no hesitancy or self-consciousness, but rather an intrinsic beauty in her connection with her creation. I couldn't tear my gaze away. I'd been wrong about her looking at home in front of the camera; this was home to her. Now I could see why her friends had thought she looked uncomfortable. I wanted to hug her, to tell her I was sorry about the photo shoot. To tell her I understood.

She handed me a plate and fork. "Go ahead."

I dug in. It was like tasting a piece of heaven. "This is amazing."

She smiled. "Good. Have a seat and finish it. Take another, too, if you want. They're kind of sweet."

"Wait, first let me take a picture of them. Is that okay?"

"Sure. Whatever."

By the time I returned with my camera, she'd set some of the pastries on a fancy plate. I snapped those first and then the ones still on the wax paper, followed by a few shots of the dirty dishes and a couple of Ruth in that pink apron. She didn't seem the least bit self-conscious now.

She laughed and stole the camera from me. "Show me how to take a picture of you. Never mind. I see how." She snapped multiple shots, while I made serious and funny poses.

Finally, we sat laughing at the table and dug into the still-warm pastries accompanied by iced tea.

"I'd offer you something stronger," she said, "but we don't keep anything like that in the house."

"You mean like beer? You don't like it?"

"Oh, I like it a little too much." She gave me a smile that didn't quite reach her eyes. "I told you I lived in a foster home. Well, there were reasons, and for a while before I left home I drank to get away from them. Turns out, I have a predisposition for alcoholism, so I . . ." She shrugged. "I just don't. But it doesn't bother me when others drink. I don't go all glarey-eyed and upset.

I mean, we could go out for a drink, and I'd just have something else."

I absorbed the information. Apparently, my guess about scars hadn't been all that far off—except they were scars that couldn't be seen. And maybe these other scars had something to do with why she'd been so uncomfortable at the shoot yesterday. Was her baggage something I even wanted to get involved in? My life was good right now. I was working. I was starting to make a name for myself. I had more chances of dates with beautiful women than I could ever want, and I liked beer. Did I want to complicate things?

I didn't have to think long to find an answer. Yes— wholeheartedly. She made me laugh, she was honest and refreshing, and the mysteries of her life had made her who she was. And right now if I didn't kiss her, I might go crazy without the help of anything alcoholic.

"Does that bother you?" she asked.

"No, it doesn't bother me. I got over the drink-myself- blind stage way back in college. It doesn't bother me at all." I scooted my chair closer. "But you do have a bit of pastry on your face." I reached out and touched her chin, turning her face one way and then another. "Yep, it's right on your lip."

Her hand started up, but I captured it with my other one. "Let me." I leaned in slowly, watched her eyes widen. Her mouth was slightly open, and I could see the tip of her tongue and smell the sweet pastry on her breath. Then our lips met. I tried to keep it casual, but it quickly ran deeper. My hand slipped from her face to the back of her head. My other hand tightened on hers.

Whatever demons she had in her past, she was one

incredible kisser. I wasn't sure where we'd go from here, but I knew I wanted more of her. Much more.

The door slammed, and she eased away, her eyes opening slowly. That act alone sent a raging heat through me, and it took all my willpower not to lean in for another kiss. "I think my sisters are home," she said. "I told you they would be. Now before they eat them all, let's get a few of the pastries into a container for you to take home."

I caught her hand. "Okay, but when can I see you again?"

"I'm not sure. I think I'll be able to get into the café tomorrow evening, and I'll be spending a lot of time trying to get it ready. Only three weeks left, and we have a ceiling to put in."

At last something I could do. "I have a hammer and a paintbrush. Need any help?"

Her eyebrows raised. "You know how to work a hammer?"

I wasn't exactly Handyman Joe, but I could figure it out. Maybe. "Sure. What's to know?"

Ruth

The soon-to-be café was empty of everything except the built-in counter along the back wall and one long shelf in the kitchen. The first thing Mario did was to put up the sign he'd made in his garage that proclaimed, *Eats and Treats*, which was Halla's brainchild after I'd discarded the idea of calling it Ruth's Café.

We had ordered a neon sign, but Mario felt it important to start the advertising as soon as possible. Later the wood sign would hang inside the café itself.

"Everyone ready for demolition?" Mario shouted.

The girls all cheered, especially Bianca who was still in her boot and would begin cementing her ceramic tiles to Mario's table. Lily was also there to help, having left her children with her sister. Mario and Lily's brother-in-law, Gage Braxton, went straight up the ladders to the ceiling and started pulling down the tiles. As the inspector predicted, they found rodent nests and droppings.

"Ew and ew and ew," Elsie mumbled. "I am so glad that ceiling is going. I hate thinking about what it would have meant to have mice in your café."

As I hauled tiles out to toss into the bed of the truck with the other girls, I kept an eye out for Zane. Besides the café, he was the only thing I could think of all day. Where was he? Maybe he'd changed his mind about coming tonight. Maybe he'd had another photo shoot with glamorous models.

I felt guilty the second I had the thought. I'd learned a lot about Zane the past two days, and one of those things was his love of shooting landscapes and candid shots of people. While the magazine gigs paid well, they weren't what he loved.

I hefted another armful of ceiling tiles into the truck and turned, bumping into someone who had come up behind me. "Oh, sorr—" The words died on my lips as I stared up into Zane's eyes. "Hey, you came."

He lifted his hammer. "I sure did." He'd worn his baseball cap and was dressed in old jeans and a T-shirt, which on him looked far too sexy for my heartbeat.

"Well, I think they're more using pliers or something at this point, but come on in."

His eyes ran down my body, and belatedly I saw that I was already covered in dust. "You have some in your hair too," he said helpfully, brushing it below my D-backs cap.

"Thanks, I've a feeling it's going to get worse."

"Probably." He glanced behind him at the store before giving me a quick kiss. "You look beautiful," he whispered.

I *felt* beautiful when he looked at me like that.

Straightening, he touched the ever-present camera bag slung over his shoulder. "You want me to take a few photos for history's sake? You know, this is how the Eats and Treats began. That sort of thing."

"I think someone's trying to get out of work."

His grin didn't waver. "I promise, it won't take long. Someday you'll be glad."

"Fine. Shoot away."

Inside, I made the introductions, though apparently Halla and Elsie had been talking about him because no one was surprised to see Zane there. Lily asked all kinds of questions as he took photos, and I knew before long she'd have him out to the house taking free portraits of the girls or maybe giving lessons on photography. Lily was an expert at utilizing everyone's abilities to benefit her girls.

True to his word, Zane was soon up on a ladder pulling down ceiling tiles near Halla, who smirked as she showed him how. The tiles had been glued together at the edges, and removing them sometimes was a matter of brute force, so before long, it was Zane who smirked as he helped Halla. Several times we were laughing so hard, it almost didn't seem like work.

I liked this man. A lot.

By the time ten o'clock rolled around, we'd only torn out half the ceiling, but the truck was completely full and we had a mound on the floor waiting to be hauled away to the dump. "Let's call it a night," I announced. "We all have to get up early tomorrow. Thank you so much."

"It's going great." Mario shook dust from his hair and patted it from his clothes. "We should get this finished tomorrow."

I made a face. "I have to work at the restaurant, but I'll be by as soon as I can get off."

"Don't worry. We'll be fine until you get here. And my dad's coming Friday night and Saturday to help with the drywall. With him helping, we should be able to get at least the kitchen done. The taping and sanding will take longer, and probably be our biggest challenge, but the texturing should go fairly fast with a special roller. I just wish I didn't have those camping trips at Teen Remake coming up." Mario shrugged. "But we'll finish it on the weekday evenings."

Somehow. I heard the word he didn't say aloud. "Just finishing the kitchen will be huge," I said. "It'll be the biggest setup for me." I hugged him and then Lily. "Thank you both for everything. I couldn't do this without you."

Lily grinned. "I think you'd find a way. But we're glad to help."

Everyone filtered out, the younger foster girls grabbing more of the fresh custard tarts I'd brought in a huge plastic container. "I'll wait for you in the car," Halla said to me.

Zane paused in his last-minute picture-taking of the disaster that was now my café. "I could give you a lift."

Halla smirked. "Fine. Have her home by eleven. She has to get up at five."

"Yes, Mom." Zane laughed and winked as Halla and Elsie left. "So," he said, looking around the café, "this is a big project."

"A lot bigger than we expected. But I'd already signed the contract, and I love this place."

"It's a great location, and I can totally see you here."

"I'm hoping I can swing it. I just need to find a little more money."

"How much?"

"Since we're doing the work ourselves, probably another eight hundred."

He thought about that for a moment. "I don't have anything in the works right now, but I can let you know if a modeling gig comes up."

Flashes of the shoot and the ogling crowd ran through my head. My stomach started to churn. "Zane," I began, leaning against the wall by the door, "I appreciate the offer but I . . . I'd rather try to find some other way. I'm not comfortable with . . ."

"With having your picture taken?" He stepped close, his eyes searching mine. "Last night and today—did that bother you? Because I'd hate to be making you uncomfortable."

"Oh, heavens no. This is all in fun. It's the dressing up, I think . . . modeling . . . the clothes, people staring . . . it's just not for me."

"Because of what happened when you were young?" He took my hand, and his touch felt warm and secure . . . and more than a little exciting.

I hadn't meant to talk about this for months—if we lasted that long—but maybe it was better now, before I fell in love with him. Because I already felt halfway there. "Partly, yes. I was. . ." I paused, not wanting to say more but forcing the words out just the same. "I was sexually abused by my mother's boyfriend when I was barely into my teens, and it was exactly because of my looks that he targeted me." I shook my head, trying to make Zane understand. "I don't have any hang ups on a normal basis, but I don't want to be a model. I don't want men thinking about sleeping with me because of how I look in a picture. I don't want who I am to be defined only by the way I look."

His jaw clenched, his hand tightening on mine. For a long moment, he didn't speak, and then, finally, with a deep breath, he seemed to find words. "I can understand that. Makes sense. And I'm very sorry about what happened to you." Silence fell between us once more, but it was less awkward than I'd expected. He didn't grill me for details I didn't want to relive. He didn't rant and rave or ask if they'd thrown the guy in jail.

After a while, he said, "My sister's ex-husband . . . he was . . ." Again the jaw clenching. "Well, let's just say, he was abusive. It's not the same thing, but she felt helpless. I might understand a little."

That was unexpected. "Your sister," I repeated, trying to remember what else he'd told me about her. I knew he'd mentioned she had two children.

"Yeah, Kassidy. You met her at the photo shoot."

I tried not to gape, but I couldn't help noticing the relief I felt that Kassidy wasn't competition. Somewhere in the back of my mind, I'd kept wondering. "She's your sister? I didn't realize. You seem close."

"We are. Anyway, I'm glad ordinary photos aren't a problem." His smile held a touch of wistfulness. "Taking photos for me . . . I think it's like cooking is for you."

If that was true, could it ever work between us? Would he be satisfied with not displaying photos of me, even if he thought they were his best work? If I had to make certain pastries only for him and not serve them in my café, I suspected I wouldn't be satisfied.

It's not the same thing, my mind whispered. I thought Zane would agree. While that didn't mean he'd always be okay with my desire to stay out of the limelight, it didn't mean he absolutely wouldn't be okay with it either.

For a full minute, we stared at each other. Then he leaned

over and kissed me slowly and gently. My hands went up around his neck. It felt new and delicious and wonderful.

"Let's both keep our eyes open," he said. "Something will turn up. But I want you to know that if you need the money, I'll give it to you. I was planning on buying this insanely expensive printer that I need, and you could use that money. I'd like to say the loan comes with no strings, but it probably wouldn't be true. I want you to keep going out with me. I like you, Ruth. I like you a lot."

I wouldn't burden our promising relationship with a loan, but it meant a lot that he'd offered to rescue me. I kissed him. "I like you too. And I don't want your money, but I'll still go out with you."

Zane

On Saturday morning, I placed the final picture in the resort booklet, pushed print, and breathed a sigh of relief. I'd been up practically all night typesetting it in InDesign after working on it all week. I was supposed to have finished it yesterday so I could print a proof for the resort, but I'd told them I'd bring it by this morning instead because the past three evenings I'd spent at Ruth's café helping her foster father and two other men tear out the rest of the ceiling and begin putting in the new one.

Unfortunately, even after working until midnight Friday evening after our day jobs, we were far from finished. The ceiling was so uneven with exposed water pipes and heating ducts in the kitchen that we'd been forced to construct a frame first before laying the drywall. Only Mario's dad had any experience, and he was growing older and couldn't really climb a ladder anymore. So we'd ended up being his eyes and hands.

But it felt good, the physical labor, much like camping in the mountains and shooting the landscape after a good climb. The only bad thing about it besides missing my original deadline was that we still hadn't finished the kitchen ceiling—or started on the dining room. And though I'd been to the café each day, Ruth had worked her second job every night, so the moments I'd spent with her weren't enough.

In the few hours we had spent alone, she hadn't brought up her past again, and every time I thought about it, I had to push the thoughts away before anger boiled up inside me at what she'd endured. My instincts were to hunt down all those responsible and make them pay, but I knew from experience with my sister's abusive ex-husband that I wouldn't be doing Ruth any favors. She'd worked through her demons, and my anger would only hurt her and bring it all up again. Unless she wanted to talk, I had no business doing anything but leaving it in the past. Maybe in time, she'd trust me enough to talk if she needed to. Maybe in time, I would lose the urge to punish someone for her pain.

I did want to see more of her than I was. Yesterday before going to the café, I'd even stopped by the Mexican restaurant where she worked and asked to be seated in her area to get a glimpse of her.

"Hey," she'd said as she approached my table, pen and paper in hand, smiling in that way of hers that lit up my insides. "What are you doing here?"

"I just felt a hankering for tacos."

She chuckled. "Did you now."

"Actually, I just came to see you in that lime green apron. I have a thing for women in aprons. Especially frilly pink ones."

Her chuckle became a full-blown laugh. I loved the wide smile and the brightness of her eyes. "Good," she said.

I lifted my camera. "Smile. This is for posterity's sake. Where you began and all that." She didn't object when I took the picture.

I'd ended up buying tacos to go for all the men working at the café that evening. Ruth had come by later after work and impressed me with her willingness to climb a ladder and pound in nails. Even at midnight, I hadn't wanted to leave her.

A loud banging on the door brought me back to the present. "Who on earth?" But I already knew. Unless the building was on fire, it had to be Mason.

"Ever heard of ringing the bell?" I grouched as I let him in.

"I just heard from Sylvia," he said without preamble. "She came to my house an hour ago. Who goes to someone's house at eight on a Saturday? It's insane." His hair was slicked back, still wet from his shower, and he wore a silk shirt and a pair of dress slacks. Pretty snazzy for any time on a Saturday in my book. But his face was pinched, and the way he squinted told me he had a hangover. He might also have a smear of red lipstick on his cheek—or had Sylvia hit him?

He walked past me, beelining for the kitchen and the pot of fresh coffee on the counter, where he poured himself a mega dose in one of my soup-bowl mugs.

"So, she's back?"

"No, she was just mad that I used the old recording for Friday's show. Says her hair was different and that viewers would notice. I have no idea what she's talking about. Her hair has always been the same." He looked in my fridge and took out the container that still had three of Ruth's pastries from Tuesday. I'd been eating at least one a day, and I didn't know how good they'd be after this long, but Mason deserved what he got at this point.

Mason sniffed the pastries and set the container on the counter next to his coffee. "I'm not sure what to do. Her contract does say that she's allowed sick leave, and she had her doctor fax me an excuse. It says she might be out for months. I'm going to have to cancel another live show, but if I do that, they'll probably pull it from us altogether."

"Did you tell Sylvia that?"

"This morning. She claims she doesn't care."

"That's totally unlike her."

"I know, right?" He scooped up one of the pastries and bit into it. "Ooh, nice. What's this anyway? Looks like a Napoleon."

"It's similar. Anyway, Sylvia will come around, and if she doesn't, there must be a ton of people willing to step in for a guest show."

Mason gulped his coffee. "Ah, that hits the spot. Guests are one thing, but someone big enough to please our following is going to cost an arm and a leg, especially on such short notice. So far, one woman agreed to come for two hundred and twenty-five thousand for one show. There's a guy I know who might come for eighty, but that's still too much."

"Use someone without a name, then. It's just one time."

"No way the other producers would go for a no-name.

Or the network. They don't want to lose their viewers to another cooking show." With a sigh, he took another bite of pastry. "This is really good."

"You should have tasted them fresh. Those are from Tuesday."

He made a face but started into the second, holding his hand protectively on the container, as if also claiming the third.

An idea began percolating in my mind, much tastier than even Ruth's pastries. She hadn't let me give her the money for the café, but maybe there was another way I could help her. "I think you might be wrong about the other producers wanting a name," I told Mason. "They have to worry about the bottom line just as much as you do. You've had no-name guests before."

"Yeah, but they were on with Sylvia. Even if I did find someone they'd agree on, there is no telling how the substitute would be on a live show."

"Unless you paid the big bucks."

"Right."

"But you have to do something."

He swallowed and licked his lips. "You know what? It's just too bad we can't have the person who made these pastries because they are really something. I know every pastry shop in town—where did you get these?"

He couldn't have walked into it better if I'd written his script. I leaned on the counter, my face close to his. "I can get you the woman who made these. And I saw her make them, so it's doable in forty minutes with some preparation beforehand."

"You know the chef who made this?" Mason laughed.

"Well, she's probably old and looks like a trucker. I was kidding about putting her on. You know this is TV. Whoever it is has to not only be a fabulous cook, they have to be attractive and translate well to film." He sighed. "Like Sylvia."

I ran to the spare bedroom and grabbed the mockup of the resort booklet. Mason was biting into the third pastry as I shoved the pages in front of him. "This is what the chef looks like. Careful, I have to take this mockup to my client today."

Mason's jaw dropped. "Wow. Seriously? She's stunning."

He was impressed enough that I got my laptop and showed him more. Ruth wearing the frilly apron, waitressing at the Mexican restaurant, and hammering nails.

"She's opening a café here in town," I said, hoping Ruth wouldn't hate me for what I was about to do. "This is what I propose. Let's do a test shoot, and see how she does on film. If it works out, you show it to Sylvia and tell her Ruth's either her replacement or her guest on the first live show next Friday. Her choice."

Mason's eyes gleamed. "It might work, but only if this girl"—he gestured to the photo—"is good in the kitchen. And comfortable behind a camera."

It was this last part that worried me. Ruth hated being in front of a camera or a gawking crowd, but would doing something she loved and wearing whatever she wanted make a difference?

Mason frowned. "What if Sylvia still doesn't come around?"

"Then you air the test run with no live audience, or you pay eighty thousand dollars for a replacement. Your choice.

Look, you know Sylvia best. Do you think she's serious about quitting?"

Mason shook his head. "Uh . . ." he began. "I might have left out a few details."

I folded my arms across my chest. "What?"

"Um, you see, uh . . ."

"Spit it out."

"Sylvia and I've sort of been dating."

You could have picked me up off the floor after that statement. "Wait, isn't she like ten years older than you?"

"Five. And she's still hotter than I'll ever be."

I took a napkin from the holder on the counter and wiped his cheek. Lipstick. "Let me guess. Sylvia's problems have more to do with you than with the show."

"Maybe a little. She wants a commitment."

"I see. Well, five thousand dollars for Ruth to do the show," I said, not feeling the slightest bit bad for taking advantage of his predicament. "And you mention her café opening. If it's successful, you have her back as a guest again in two weeks so we can help her launch the café."

"One thousand and no second show. Sylvia already has menus planned."

"Sylvia can adjust her menu. Three thousand, and a second free guest spot, even if it's only for five minutes. Come on, you're always saying you owe me. Now's the time to pay the piper."

"Two thousand."

I shook my head. "No. You'd better start calling that guy for eighty—or go make up with Sylvia."

"Fine. It's a deal," he growled. "But only if the higher ups sign off on it after they see her test run."

I shook his hand. "Good. Now come with me, so you can ask her yourself."

"It's not like she'd say no," he said, rolling his eyes. "Everybody wants to be on TV."

"Not this woman. She said no to modeling for me, and you saw the pictures. She could have been big. And I've seen her cook. She's a natural."

Mason gulped more coffee and stood. "Okay, let's do it. Get her to agree before she can back out." That was just like Mason. He dragged his feet and then suddenly pounced like a predator.

"Hey, it's her choice." I felt a little guilty about setting the wheels into motion. For any other person, it would be an incredible opportunity, but would Ruth see it that way? Or would she think I was trying to force her into doing something she didn't want to do just because she needed the money?

I was beginning to wish I'd kept my mouth shut.

"Did you say these pastries were from Tuesday?" Mason asked. "Wasn't that the night you had that date?"

"Yeah."

Mason slapped me on the back. "Go, Zane. I approve."

Ruth

We should have started on the dining room by now, but the kitchen framing was still underway. Even if we finished today, Mario could only help three nights each of the next two weeks. How could we possibly finish in time? I could use the café food money for the rest of the ceiling supplies and to pay men to put it in, but that would mean having nothing to serve customers. No. Somehow I had to find more money. But everyone had already done so much to help me. How could I ask for more?

I should have waited. I realized that now. Instead, I'd let my excitement get the best of me. I'd let my desire infect everyone, making them believe I could follow through, and they had all fallen in behind me. I bet Lily was home even now, going through her expenses and deciding what to cut to buy my dream. Not the decision I wanted to force on her.

I caught a glimpse of Zane through the café window, and despite my anxiety, my heart lifted. He'd been here every day, though I knew he had work to do and pictures to take. He'd offered me the money, but if I took it from him, there would be an obligation that would shadow our relationship. And it was so beautiful and perfect right now—could I risk it?

Maybe I should go see my mother and ask if she could pitch in.

Nausea churned in my stomach and rose in my throat. I had only seen her a couple times since a social worker had convinced her to relinquish custody, but the possibility of having to go back to her was a constant paralyzing fear that had stayed with me until my eighteenth birthday.

No way would I go there now. Not even if I was sleeping on a park bench—I *had* slept on a park bench to get away from her. I would rather give up the café entirely than make myself vulnerable to her ever again.

Zane came through the door, his smile turning to concern. "What's wrong?"

"Nothing." I forced a smile. "I'm just taking a break." I thumbed toward the kitchen where occasional silences punctuated the steady pounding noises of the hammers. "They don't need me right now."

He came closer and took me in his arms. "You look like you need a hug."

Boy, did I. I clung to him as a single tear slipped from my left eye. "I should have waited to open the café," I whispered. "I'm being a burden on those I love most—I hate that. And with Mario out of town the next two weekends, I don't think we'll be able to finish by the end of the month. We'll have to push back the opening. And then I'm not sure I'll have enough funds to launch. What I need is a miracle."

He pulled back and looked at me. Tenderly, he wiped the tear from my face. "Miracle. You hold on to that thought because I ordered one up for you today."

I blinked, unsure if he was trying to make me laugh. Next, he was probably going to offer the money as a partner buy-in. Or to rent a permanent table. I might be desperate enough to accept. Maybe I was ready for him to swoop in on his white horse to save me.

"Really," he said. "Now hear me out before you say anything. I have this cousin who needs someone to fill in as a cook for a show he produces. You can wear whatever you want—well, you know, within reason—and they'll mention the café opening." He swallowed a bit noisily the way I noticed he did when he was nervous. "All you have to do is talk about whatever it is you're cooking. And they'll pay you three thousand dollars."

"What?" I gasped. Three thousand meant I could pay for someone to finish the ceiling. I might not even have to move back in with Lily or sleep on a cot here at the café. "Why would they do that?"

"Because they really need someone, and my cousin ate the rest of your pastries from Tuesday night and loves them."

I didn't know what to say, but it seemed too good to be true. "This isn't some way of you trying to get me to model again, is it?" I felt bad the second the words were out, but he just laughed.

"Come on. I'll show you. I told Mason to wait outside. He'll tell you himself."

"I take it Mason's the blond man peeking through the window." I frowned. "Which is really dirty, by the way."

"We'll clean it after the construction. Come on." He took my hand and pulled me toward the door. Zane's cousin saw me looking at him through the window and jerked himself upright, turning away. He seemed familiar.

"What cooking show?" I asked, resisting Zane's pull. "I know them all."

"*Turn Up the Heat.*" He spoke with the same tone and expression as if he'd said, "Nice weather we're having, isn't it?"

"With Sylvia Blakely?"

He stopped tugging me. "That's the one. Look, you don't have to do it. There will be a lot of people watching during the filming—I know how you feel about that. But the opportunity presented itself, and I suggested you. It's still your decision. And you'd have to pass a test run to make sure you can cook and teach how to do it at the same time. With all the practice you have bossing your foster sisters around, it should be a breeze." He winked to make sure I knew he was kidding, though I was sure Halla would agree.

Except right now I didn't care what he said. I wanted to run around the café shouting and waving my arms in the air, "*Turn Up the Heat* with Sylvia Blakely! *Turn Up the Heat* with Sylvia Blakely! I might get to meet Sylvia Blakely and cook on her show!" over and over until I fell down with exhaustion. I loved Sylvia's show. In fact, I'd watched her religiously for the past four years. She'd taught me to braise beef, to make the best croissants, and her soups were going to be a regular feature in my café.

With effort, I managed to keep some semblance of dignity. But I still launched myself at Zane, kissing his face all over. "She is amazing! I love that show." Then after two heartbeats. "Why on earth does she want a novice like me?" If she did, I owed it all to Zane.

"It's just a matter of being in the right place at the right time. Come on."

This time I let him pull me to the door. I wished I could see if the dust was out of my hair, but a quick hand pulled through my ringlets told me it wasn't. *Great, just great.*

"One more thing," Zane said. "Let me do any negotiating and don't sign a contract without reading it carefully. Mason likes to cut any corners he can, but I know how to call his bluffs." With that, Zane led me outside.

Mason came toward us, a smile on his face. For the first time, it struck me as odd that Zane should have such a white cousin, but given my own sister situation, I decided not to mention it. Mason shook my hand as Zane made the introductions. I recognized Mason now. He was the producer who sometimes stepped onto the set to try Sylvia's food. He was suavely good-looking, if you like pasty white skin, but shorter than I'd envisioned—about my own height.

"Nice to meet you," I said. Forget butterflies—a whole flock of birds were playing some kind of weird game in my stomach, and I was grateful Zane didn't let go of my hand.

"I take it Zane's filled you in?"

"Yes, thank you for the opportunity."

"It was your pastries that did the trick."

Fleetingly I wondered what kind of pastries he'd been eating if old ones had impressed him. "I have some fresh ones inside, if you'd like to try more. I mean, not the same ones, but others."

"Well, maybe—no, I shouldn't. Another time. And let's talk details after the test run. I've been able to get the studio on Monday at three in the afternoon or Tuesday at five in the morning. Any preference?"

"Three." I would have to get off early or find someone to take my shift at the hospital. The trainee might be able to handle a couple hours. I hoped.

"Three it is. Good thing, too. The crew would hate getting up any earlier than they already do. Let's make those Napoleon things. Give Zane an ingredients list so we'll have everything there. It was nice to meet you." Mason offered his hand again before turning sharply on his heel and striding down the street.

Zane watched him go, laughing. "My cousin likes to put on the appearance of a no-nonsense producer, but he's an okay guy when you get to know him. Little high strung, though."

"He is nice." I put my hand to my burning cheeks. "I can't believe this is happening. Pinch me?"

"Really?" He held up his thumb and pointer finger.

"No." I grabbed his hand. "You said I could wear anything I wanted?"

"Within reason."

"Then I'm wearing my pink apron."

He laughed. "Well you can certainly try to get it past wardrobe." His arms slipped around me. "Now why don't you take a little walk, clear your head, clear your lungs, and make a list of what you need."

"But the café—"

"Will wait. I'll go in and pound nails for a while. You look exhausted. Beautiful, but exhausted."

Funny, because I no longer felt exhausted. I felt invigorated, alive, and hopeful. "Thank you."

He gave me a slow, foot-popping kiss before releasing

me and going back inside. I watched him go, pondering my good fortune as my racing heartbeat settled into a more normal pattern. He was right—this was a miracle. I only hoped I could pass the test run.

I took out my phone. I had to call Halla and Lily and everyone else right this minute. They would be as excited as I was.

Zane

As Ruth arrived at the studio in black slacks and a blue blouse, looking better than she had on the day of my photo shoot, I could tell she was nervous. Her back was stiff, and her smile just a little too bright. It was no surprise that Halla and Elsie were with her.

I kissed her in greeting. "All ready?"

"As ready as I'll ever get."

"What's that?" I pointed at the small cooler Halla carried.

"That's my extra dough," Ruth said. "No way can we wait as long as we need to between folds, so I'll switch out with these."

"It's going to be fine. And we'll all be there, so just talk to us like you're at home."

"Is Sylvia here?"

"Not today. You'll meet her soon." I hoped. I wasn't going to add to Ruth's nervousness by telling her Sylvia might never show up again. Besides, I still believed Sylvia would come around.

Mason greeted us inside and introduced the cameramen.

While Halla and Elsie put the dough in the fridge, Mason and I took Ruth backstage for makeup.

"She doesn't need much," the makeup artist said. "Just some blush and a bit more eye shadow. You have wonderful coloring, dear."

I stayed with Ruth through the discussion about the pink apron, which the wardrobe mistress finally agreed to. "It only works because she's so young," she said.

Ruth either didn't hear or ignored the condescension in her voice. "Thank you," she said. Then she winked at me.

She seemed to be taking it all very well. Frankly, being on camera with food and posing for photos didn't seem all that much different to me, but I hadn't lived Ruth's past.

I'd seen more of Sylvia's shows than I cared to, but the experiences had come in handy when prepping Ruth for the test. I'd recommended that she write out the recipe and whatever she wanted to be sure to say. There was a teleprompter in case she needed it.

"Okay, let's do this thing!" Mason called. "Everyone on the set!"

I walked Ruth into the set kitchen, and as I passed Mason, I whispered, "Notch it down a bit, okay? Turn on that charm of yours and get her talking."

He rolled his eyes. "I think you're more nervous than she is."

"It doesn't matter what you think," I countered. "Just be gentle on my girl."

"Your girl?"

Well, I wanted her to be, but maybe it was too soon to know. "You owe me," I reminded him.

"Fine. Now go sit down."

After three false starts, Ruth found her stride. She seemed to forget about the cameras as she mixed and rolled out the dough. Little jokes and side information about where she'd learned the tricks and what had inspired this version of the recipe evoked real laughter from all of us. She seamlessly worked in the pastry dough she'd brought, so in less than thirty minutes she had the perfect mil folhas ready for us to eat.

Mason was the first up there to taste the pastries, with one of the cameramen and her sisters not far behind. Her eyes met mine as I walked up the few stairs and onto the set. "Well, how did I do?" she asked.

"Amazing."

Mason came toward us, his mouth full. "These are better than I remember."

Ruth laughed. "They are always better fresh."

After Mason finished eating, he got down to business. "Look, here's what happens next. For the next day or two I'll be busy viewing the tape and showing it to those who make the final decisions. I'll get back to you by Wednesday. We'll want to see you and Sylvia together for another run before the live show on Friday."

"Live?" asked Ruth, her fingers rubbing at the base of her throat.

"Didn't Zane tell you? But that's only if Sylvia's here. Otherwise, we'll go with the canned show, and that'll be fine. In that case, we'll need to redo a few sections. Not much tweaking. Some of it would just be voice-overs. It's amazing what they can do with three cameras going."

That Mason wanted to use Ruth's show if Sylvia didn't return said a lot about what he thought of Ruth's performance. But none of that mattered right now. Ruth appeared to be struggling for breath and not hearing a word Mason said.

"Thanks, Mason." I put my arm around Ruth and led her off the stage. "If you'll excuse us. We'll just be a minute." I needed to give her time to process the idea of a live show.

"Live?" she asked as I led her through a door and into a deserted corridor. "Why didn't you tell me it might be live?"

"Would it have made a difference? Would you have backed out?"

She thought for a moment. "No. But maybe I would have been a lot more nervous."

"Exactly."

"Oh, right." A smile teased the corner of her mouth.

"So are you okay with it?" I asked. "You were wonderful."

Her chin lifted. "Not something I'd want to do every day, but it was mostly fun, and it means a lot to the café. Plus, the kitchen here is really great."

I loved her determination, her strength, the way she didn't let her natural shyness overcome her goals. Bending, I kissed her raised chin, but somehow that led to her mouth. Though I hadn't planned on kissing her this way when I'd brought her into the hall, I pulled her tightly against me, deepening the kiss. Her mouth opened under mine. She tasted of sugar and heat.

I was drowning, drowning, sinking so far out of my depths that I didn't know if I would ever come up for air. She was like the one perfect shot that was so incredible

I didn't dare take out my camera for fear of missing the moment. The chest-achingly beautiful scene that made me scream with frustration because no matter how good a photographer I was, I could never, ever capture it perfectly.

This was that perfect.

I didn't believe in love at first sight. But I had been attracted—compelled, even—by Ruth from the moment I'd seen her in that D-backs cap and jeans. Yes, I was fascinated with how she translated to film, and during our second meeting, it was her beauty I'd noticed and what it might do for my career.

After having spent this past week with her, none of that mattered. I knew she would never be the model I'd envisioned. She was much better. She was the kind of girl I could take camping, the kind of girl who wouldn't care if I took pictures of her in the morning before she did her hair and makeup. A woman I could envision playing ball and cooking in the kitchen with my kids.

Most of all, the perfection of this moment didn't have to be recorded on film, because it was recorded in the one place it really mattered: my heart.

Later during the night, as I tried to make up for lost hours of sleep, Mason woke me with a phone call. "We did some quick edits on Ruth's show, and I sent it to Sylvia and the other producers. No word from the producers yet, but guess what? Sylvia's coming back."

"Really?" I clutched the phone, wondering what that

meant for Ruth. There was always the chance that Sylvia would convince Mason to cut her out completely. "So what's the verdict?"

"Oh, Sylvia absolutely loves Ruth and her pastries. She agrees that Ruth should be the guest for the first live show." Mason paused, and I could hear talking and giggling on his end. Then, "Sylvia says she'd like to arrange a double date sometime with the four of us." Another pause. "Okay, okay," he said. "Zane, Sylvia wants me to ask you right now to be my best man."

"You're getting married? Are you serious? You're not just pranking me, are you?"

"We sure are. You gotta do the best man honors, buddy. I don't have a brother and you're my favorite cousin."

"Wow, okay. If you're sure."

"Oh, I am. I've been fighting it, but I don't want to live without her."

He sounded happy, so who was I to object? And maybe now with their relationship settled, Sylvia would go back to being her nicer self.

"Just remember to take care of Ruth, all right?" I added. "This means a lot to her."

"The check's as good as in the bank. Gotta go now. We have some celebrating to do."

I didn't remind him it was already two o'clock in the morning. He'd realize that soon enough when he tried to get out of bed in a few hours.

I couldn't wait until morning to call Ruth, so I texted her the good news about Sylvia loving the show. Maybe it would be the first thing Ruth saw when she woke up. I hoped so. *Call me when you can,* I added.

Ten minutes later, a too-loud buzzing pulled me from the brink of oblivion. "What is it now?" I moaned into my phone.

"You asked me to call?" came Ruth's voice, soft and sleepy, bringing to mind a vision of her in bed, which made me feel suddenly wide awake and wishing I was with her.

"Hey, Ruth. Sorry, I thought it was Mason again. He woke me up to tell me he and Sylvia are getting married, and I'm going to be the best man."

"Today?"

"No. Maybe. I don't know when."

"I think they make a great couple."

Now that I was used to the idea of them being together, maybe she was right. "Well, I just wanted you to know about the show. And I think you should make that appointment with some ceiling guys for next week if you can."

She laughed. "Actually, I already did."

Ruth

At fifteen to seven, I was ready. Or, we were all ready. Halla had taken the week off from the college print shop and would be in the back cooking with me. Bianca would be at the cash register, and Elsie and two of the girls were at the counter to get drinks and clear tables if customers didn't do it themselves. Lily was also here, and her sister was babysitting, so she'd be in and out as needed. We were all wearing bright blue frilly aprons that made us laugh.

As yet, people weren't lining up at the door for the opening, though I'd had a second appearance on *Turn up the Heat,* where Sylvia had announced the opening twice and had posted on social media to hundreds of thousands of followers. She'd also reminded them that a drawing for ten free wildlife sanctuary tickets would be happening each day.

I had dozens of fresh pastries in the floor display case that Halla and the others had somehow gone in together to purchase. It wasn't refrigerated, but a smaller one next to the register was, and we'd found a drink display case for almost nothing that we set on the back counter next to the two latte machines.

My lunch soups simmered on the stove in the kitchen. The sandwich fillings and salads were prepped. Fresh bread and rolls from the best bakery in town sat in the new cupboards Mario's dad had rescued from the dump and refurbished. I'd thought about making my own breads, but the bakery's were as good as mine, and I knew my limits. For now, I'd stick to deserts, drinks, and a few main dishes.

The dining room looked much larger than I envisioned, and so amazing that every few minutes, I had to stop and stare. The walls were a beautiful sky blue. On one of them Zane had organized a grouping of framed pictures that told the story of the café from the first night of construction to now and included a photograph of me with Sylvia Blakely on the set of *Turn Up the Heat*. Bianca's paintings filled another wall. The mismatched chairs and tables had all been painted white. Overlooking it all was the new ceiling, also painted a bright white.

I sat down on the stool next to Bianca at the cash register. "What if no one shows up?" I said.

She looked over to one of the tables where Lily sat with the other girls. "They will. I heard Mario tell Lily he's bringing his colleagues and some of the kids from Teen Remake here to eat lunch."

I grinned. "That's something."

"Don't worry. It's early yet. We haven't even opened the door."

I chewed on my lip and craned my neck, staring out the window. "Maybe Tuesday's a weird day for an opening."

"I'm glad it's today, or I couldn't be a part of it." Bianca rubbed her arm where it had broken in the accident, as if it pained her, but she'd already assured me it was fine.

"You all ready for your big move?"

"Yep. I'm looking forward to spending more time with Zoey in Kingman. And I need to get back to work."

"What did you decide to do about that guy?" Last week, we had confronted the man who'd stolen her logo and designs, but he'd shown no willingness to back down.

"I have an appointment on Friday at a law firm." Bianca gave me a smile that might be forced but proved her determination. "I am going to fight. Now that I'm all healed, I'll win back my customers and send him packing. Somehow."

"That a girl." I'd been worried about her, but she appeared ready to take the next step, and she'd have the rest of us for support, just like I'd had. "But isn't Friday when you're moving to Kingman?"

She laughed. "Yes, in the afternoon. Plus Zoey has gone and set me up on a blind date for the same night. It's ridiculous. She and I have never had the same taste in men. I'm not expecting much."

"You never know."

"Yeah, we'll see. What I need is a hot attorney to fall in love with me and fight my battles so I can work." She leaned forward and whispered, "Someone like your Zane." She nudged my shoulder with hers and tilted her head in the direction of the entrance.

Zane stood outside the locked door, peering in through the glass. Excitement fluttered through my stomach. "I'll go let him in."

The bell on the door chimed as he came inside. Zane

leaned in to kiss me. "I take it by the locked door that I am your first customer?"

"You are."

"Good, I was worried I'd be too late." He strode over to the register and peered up at the large laminated poster with all the pricing. It was temporary until I had enough to buy a real menu board, but it looked classy enough, and Halla had done an excellent job matching it to the smaller menus we'd placed at each table.

I paused a moment to peer up and down the street. Still no customers in sight. I'd decided to open at seven instead of eight in the hopes that more people would stop by before work, but this wasn't Europe so maybe it hadn't been a bright idea. We still had ten minutes before opening, but I turned over the sign in the window and left the door unlocked.

"Hey," Zane said to Bianca. "I'm here to buy something."

"Oh, then welcome to the Eats and Treats," Bianca said with over-exaggerated brightness. "What can I get for you today, sir?"

"I'll have a Portuguese thousand leaves pastry—along with whatever is your favorite latte."

"Oh, wait, Ruth has to ring up the first customer." Bianca motioned me behind the register. "I'll get your latte while she rings you up."

Zane spread out a crisp five and a bunch of new-looking ones on the counter. He grabbed a permanent marker from one of Bianca's ceramic mugs and wrote *First Dollar Earned* across the face of one of the bills. He scooped up the bills and handed them to me. "Keep the change. I plan to become a regular here, and I know tipping is the best way to get good service." He winked, making me want to kiss him all over again.

Lily, Elsie, Halla, and the other girls gathered around as I rang up the purchase and placed the tip money in a blue-marbled bowl. "Thank you for coming, sir." Everyone cheered.

There was so much noise, I almost missed the ringing of the bell at the door. A man entered, looking around with interest. "Is this the place that was featured on *Turn Up the Heat*?"

Featured wasn't exactly right, but I knew what he meant. "Yes. Hi, I'm Ruth, the owner. What can I get for you?"

He ordered a dozen pastries and a dozen regular coffees to go. Before he'd left, two more people came in the door, and then a large group of ten. We all went to work.

"I'll check on you later," Zane whispered in my ear. "Call me if you need me."

"Oh. You'll help cook?"

"Not if I have to put on one of those aprons."

I pretended indignance. "Hey, Sylvia is going to wear one on her next show."

He laughed. "Now that is something I have to see. Anyway, I can chop in the back or run an errand, if you need me."

"Okay, but I think we have it covered."

"I think so too. I'll see you later."

Closing was at eight, and by the end of the day, it felt like an eternity had passed, but at last we locked the doors behind the last stragglers. I went to sit by Zane, who was doing some work on his laptop at a corner table. He'd been in and out through the day, once going to buy some more rolls from the bakery.

I sat down wearily beside him. "What a day."

He leaned forward and took my hand. "Did you get any breaks?"

"Oh, yeah. I even went to lie down for a few minutes on the cot in back, but I was too keyed up to rest."

"So, sales went well?"

"They did." I paused a moment before rushing on, "I used up all the supplies I thought would last for the next three days. I reordered, and Lily's helping me restock. I'm just glad I froze so much pastry dough. All it needs is a final turn before it's ready. I know we had so many customers because of Sylvia's show and the sanctuary tickets, but I'm hopeful after the initial rush dies down that enough people will keep coming."

"They will."

My eyes followed the firm lines of his face, the endless dark eyes, the curly hair. Lips more sensual than any man had a right to. "Thank you so much for your help. I couldn't have done it without you . . . without being on the show . . ."

He shook his head. "You would have found a way. Your *family* would have found a way." He said it with such confidence that I had to believe it was true.

Something banged in the kitchen where Halla was still cleaning up. "I should go help her."

We'd let everyone else go home already, so they could come back early in the morning. I planned to be here by four to start the pastries, and Elsie was coming with me to learn how to make the dough. I was sure after a few more days and enough prep during the lulls that I could carve that beginning time back to five.

"Just wait a moment." Zane's eyes didn't leave my face as he took my hand and held it in both of his. "I brought something to show you."

"Now?" I hoped my smile wasn't as weary as I felt.

"Yes, now. It's something I've been meaning to show you."

The serious tone of his voice triggered a warning bell inside my head. He hadn't asked me to model again, but I saw how proud he'd been of me at Sylvia's studio. Would he be satisfied with a woman whose hands might always be rough from dish washing and who worked all day in an apron? He was here now, but would he be for the long haul when I couldn't go out with him yet again because of the café?

"Zane," I said. "You know this place is going to be my life for a while."

"Probably a long while." He laughed and massaged my hand until the heat from his touch silenced the warnings in my head. "And that probably means you won't be able to go on any landscape photo shoots I'm planning this summer. And I'll probably have to come here every night to do this . . ." He scooted his chair closer and kissed me.

And kissed me some more. Tingles spread through my body, and I pushed even closer. His mouth slid to my cheek and my ear and down my neck before trailing up and capturing my lips again. My hands played in his hair.

It was almost painful to draw away. "That sounds about

right, although maybe I could carve out a few days to get away. It's just . . . I'm not the kind of girl you usually date. And I'm not ever going to be famous enough to have my own cooking show. I-I—" I wanted to ask him if he was disappointed that I wasn't comfortable modeling. Deep down, I still wondered if our worlds weren't too far apart.

"You are exactly the kind of woman I want to date." His eyes were half-lidded, his voice thick with desire, which drove me to kiss him again. The sights and sounds of the café faded until there was only this man and the feelings that pulsed to every tip of my body.

This time he was the one who pulled away. "Okay, I need you to see this now while I can still think straight." He pulled his laptop closer.

Somehow during our kissing, I'd ended up in his lap. I snuggled against him and gazed at the screen, shaking my head a little. What was so important that he'd interrupted the most amazing kiss I'd experienced in my entire life?

I laughed. "That sounds a little ominous."

"No, it's just . . . I want to prove something to you." He gave me a nervous smile.

Since he enhanced photographs on his computer, I suspected this demonstration had something to do with his work. The warning bell was back in my head. What had he done? Was he going to show me a stock photo site with my pictures plastered across the page? I bit my lip to stop it from trembling. I didn't want to lose him, but if he didn't understand who I was by now, maybe he never would.

He touched my face with his fingertips. "Don't look so worried. I think you'll like it. But first a little story." He took both my hands, interlacing our fingers. "You see,

I was out snapping candid shots like I do almost every day of the week. And then I saw this girl—woman—with a couple friends. They made such a great contrast in colors and races, and she in particular was so incredibly beautiful in her baseball cap and jeans."

I relaxed against him, unaware until that moment that I had stiffened. "Baseball cap?"

He nodded. "D-backs. I just knew she'd be perfect on film. Sometimes people only look good in person and pictures of them turn out awful, but I knew this woman would be fabulous . . ." He took a breath and let it out slowly. Why was he telling me this? Was it to say he was infatuated with a girl he didn't know and that our relationship was a mistake? But why would he be holding my hands so seductively and looking at me as if I were the only woman in the world?

He rubbed his fingers against mine, sending a delicious shudder up both my arms. Maybe I could trust him a bit longer.

"Before I could approach her and get a model release," he continued, "they got a phone call and hurried away. I would have chalked it up to yet another batch of pictures I've taken and couldn't use, but the pictures of her were stunning, so I put a couple of them in my portfolio. Then the manager of a resort saw them and wanted the woman to be in his booklet."

"The resort booklet I posed for?"

"The very one. Because the gig paid so well, and I wanted to make them happy, I looked for her for the next couple of weeks. That's what I was doing on that street where we met." He paused, nuzzling my ear. "It wasn't until you left that I realized I'd found the woman, and I'd missed getting her contact information twice."

He released my hand to bring the computer to life. My face appeared on the screen, complete with messy ringlets, D-backs cap, and oversized jeans.

"You gotta be kidding." I pushed the arrow to go to the next picture. Sure enough, it was Halla, Elsie, and me. I remembered that day, one of our many trips to see the music store. I looked happy. All of us appeared ordinary but somehow also beautiful.

"This is the girl I've fallen in love with," he said, kissing me again. "With you. And I don't care if I'm the only one who ever sees pictures like these, or that we spend most of our dates right here."

I turned on his lap enough to wrap my arms around him. I never thought I'd say it this soon, or that I'd ever trust someone enough to say it at all. But he deserved to hear it because he was kind and sweet and caring—and because it was true. "Good, because I love you too."

Then he kissed me.

BIANCA'S HOPE

Bianca

The fifteen minutes of waiting in the small conference room at the Phoenix law firm Eaton & Eddington made me feel claustrophobic, despite the wall of windows overlooking the wide corridor. I wished Stephen Carey would hurry. It was bad enough needing an attorney in the first place, and waiting had only increased my anxiety. I still didn't know how I was going to pay, but if I didn't act, the past eight years of work and everything I'd created could be ripped from me.

I pulled out the little white card and stared at the silver embossing. I didn't remember who'd given it to me, but it was in my purse with two others I'd gathered in the past month since I'd discovered someone was using my logo on pottery that closely resembled my signature designs. I'd chosen this appointment with Mr. Carey because his name sounded familiar, and because I like the artsy interlaced E's on the law firm's logo.

The door opened, surprising me with the suddenness of the motion. I straightened as a man in a dark brown suit entered the room, filling up the small space even more.

"Hi," he said with a smile. "You must be Bianca Mendez. I'm Stephen Carey. Sorry to keep you waiting—and sorry to startle you."

"No, it's fine." I stood and shook his extended hand, my eyes having to travel far up to reach his face. At five-foot-three, I had to look up at a lot of people, even in ultra-high heels. Our gazes connected as his fingers closed over my hand. His eyes were blue, the color of the sky on a brilliant summer afternoon, and framed with short brown hair that made them more prominent. For a moment I couldn't find my breath. He was handsome in a way that set my heart skipping beats. I had expected someone a lot more . . . stuffy.

His hand retracted quickly from mine as if touching fire. "Please have a seat." He indicated the conference table.

I tried not to be offended. "Thank you, Mr. Carey."

"Please, call me Stephen." He sat in the chair kitty-corner to mine.

I couldn't help noticing there wasn't a ring on any of his fingers. If we'd met under other conditions, I'd try to find out more about him. A man hadn't made my heart skip like this since my freshman year in college.

No, I warned myself. *Keep it professional.*

He took out a pen and laid it next to the pad of paper he'd set on the table. "Before we begin, I want to clarify that I'm an intern with Mr. Eddington. I'm currently in law school, and while I've been studying law for several years, I am not yet an attorney. What I can do today is discuss your case and let you know your options. If we proceed from here, I'll likely be working on your case. Which is good for you, because my involvement will cut down on attorney fees. But Mr. Eddington would be attorney of record."

"So you're not an attorney?" I'd just assumed he was, since someone had recommended him. "I thought they gave the first consultation here—with an attorney—for free."

"Oh, yes, absolutely. But since we're here, and Mr. Eddington's in court today, why don't we talk a little about your case? Afterwards, if you decide to continue, we'll set up a joint meeting with Mr. Eddington."

Something in his tone made me bristle, as if he didn't expect me to continue past our consult. Was he not taking me seriously? And why not? It wasn't as if I was wearing ratty jeans. And I was almost certain I'd gotten all the clay out of my hair from yesterday's attempt at my pottery wheel. I'd even slipped on fancy high heels before heading into the law firm.

"What do you mean *if* I decide to pursue the case? I don't have any choice."

"Maybe not. So, someone is using your logo?" He leaned forward, tenting his hands on the table. He suddenly felt too close.

I inched back in my chair. "Yes, his name's Kent Fletcher. He runs a pottery shop here in town. I first learned about him using my logo a month ago." Four weeks ago to be exact, while I was still recovering from surgery after the accident caused by the big storm. "Two days ago when I tracked him down, he practically admitted what he's been doing. But when I said I was going to seek legal help, he just laughed and said to have my attorney talk to his."

"Did he say who his attorney was?"

"He gave me a card, but I don't have it with me." It was crumpled on the floor of my truck. "He's also using my designs. But I know copycats are always out there.

I just want him to stop using my logo. It's my initials—very distinctive. A large B with an opening and M inside the bottom curve of the B. I've been using it for eight years. Since high school and all the way through college. Here, I'll show you."

From the pocket of my suit coat, I extracted a small blue-marbled, fluted candy dish I'd made, turning it over to show him my potter's mark. "I carve one into each of my pieces."

He examined the dish before placing it on the table. "It's unique. Did you file a trademark?"

"No." My mouth suddenly went dry. "Is that bad?"

His lips tugged downward into a slight frown. "It makes your claim more of a hurdle, especially if someone else has trademarked it in the meantime."

Frustration flared inside me. "You mean it doesn't matter if I've been using it for eight years? That can't be right! I'm finally starting to be noticed. I have regular orders from retailers, people are beginning to ask for my work—for quality handmade pieces. But last month when I contacted my clients to set up a time to show them my latest patterns, four of the shops I called had already bought dozens of new pieces from Fletcher. Pots that all had my logo on them."

Those orders represented half my potential quarterly income, and just thinking about the loss made me panicky. Maybe if I hadn't been injured two months ago, I'd have been able to contact the retailers sooner and Fletcher would have had less opportunity to step in. I breathed deeply and waited several heartbeats before adding, "And they weren't even good pieces."

"So, not like your work?"

What was he implying? "No. I mean, yes, they were copies, but bad copies. Uneven formation, ragged edges, poor artwork, improperly glazed." I dug in my purse for a second piece of pottery, a different color, but similar. "See? This dish isn't symmetrical. The glaze is spotty, and the logo is completely lopsided."

"But the owners of the shops felt this man's work was good enough to sell to their customers?"

"His pots are less expensive," I clarified. "I don't know how this Fletcher can afford to live off what he's charging—unless he's paying a bunch of kids next to nothing to make pots for him in his shop."

"Wouldn't be the first time." Stephen made a face. "Unfortunately, it happens."

"I'm not some big-time artist. Why would he target me?"

"I'd have to do some legwork to answer that definitively, but my bet is that you've cut into his market by offering quality pieces, so he's pushing back."

"How can I stop him from using my logo?" Was that desperation coming from me? "Shops are thinking it's my stuff—so are customers. He's going to ruin my name, my livelihood."

Stephen leaned back and folded his arms, his eyes intent on my face. What did he see? A strong, independent woman with a college art degree? Or a part Latina girl who was too stupid to trademark her own logo?

"We can send him a notice to cease and desist," he said, glancing at his watch, "and maybe file an injunction. But without a trademark backing us, and given his reaction when you confronted him, you may have to sue to get him to stop permanently. Even to file the lawsuit, we'd be talking in the range of seven thousand dollars. If he's trademarked the logo in the meantime, it'll be an uphill battle to prove you used the mark first."

Was he kidding? I couldn't breathe again, and this time it had nothing to do with his proximity. "There's no way I've taken that much business from him. Would he spend so much to defend himself?"

"It cost a lot less to respond to a lawsuit, at least in the beginning. His attorney may advise him to let you take sue him, hoping you'll give it up because of the expense."

"Then what can I do?" To my utter mortification, tears threatened behind my eyes.

"Well," Stephen said, "you have a case for common trademark and copyright violations, but speaking from experience, the expense of proving it would likely be far more than what you'd want to spend. A lawsuit could cost one hundred to three hundred thousand dollars, depending on how willing this guy is to keep your logo. And damages are almost impossible to obtain without a registered trademark. There are attorneys who will take cases like yours on contingency—receiving money only if they win the case—but that's usually when it's a corporation or wealthy individual who has infringed on a trademark."

"I see." No, I would not give into tears. Not in front of him. He'd barely heard a few details and already he'd made a judgment. He had no idea what this meant to me.

"Miss Mendez, I know this isn't what you want to hear, but perhaps you should consider redesigning your logo and filing a trademark for it instead."

As if that would be so easy. "And what's to stop him from stealing the new one?"

"In that event, you'd have proof, and it would be easier for a judge to order him to stop. You'd also have a better chance of winning statutory damages."

I surged to my feet. "I don't want to design a new logo. This one is mine! And by using it, he's cut my clients by half!" Or more.

Slowly, Stephen rose too, and I lost my height advantage. "I understand that he's in the wrong. I just want to be clear about expectations before you pursue any legal options." His voice became placating. "Aside from the money, a lawsuit takes a huge emotional toll on people."

"Having my life's work stolen is already emotional." In fact, since returning to work in the past two weeks, I hadn't created a single piece that was worth selling. "You know what, you said it yourself—you're not even a real attorney. I think I'll find someone who is." I turned and strode the four steps to the door.

"Miss Mendez," he called. "If you want to meet with Mr. Eddington . . ."

I continued out the door and down the corridor without a backward glance. That negative intern was not getting me down. I would find a way to fight this with a *real* attorney at a better law firm who would believe in me and my work. There had to be some justice in the world.

There had better be, or I'd be starving soon.

Stephen

Bianca Mendez stalked from the conference room with all the grace and taut energy of an angry tiger. I couldn't help stepping to the door and watching her petite figure until she rounded the turn. I didn't blame her for the emotion; many people were frustrated when they realized how hopeless a case could be. How costly. Three times I tried to call her back, but the words caught in my throat.

I didn't know what I'd expected when the scheduling assistant returned Ms. Mendez's call and set up our appointment, but it hadn't been this thin firebomb dressed to kill in a form-fitting suit that set off her slender curves and especially those gorgeous legs. From the moment I'd walked into the room, she'd brought out every bit of protective desire inside me. Especially because what she'd told the assistant about her personal situation led me to believe there was no way she could afford to pursue this lawsuit.

That was the reason I hadn't scheduled her to meet with Eddington. He was one of the best attorneys I knew, but he wasn't averse to letting a client pay out whatever life savings she had before urging them to drop the case and go on with their lives. In the past two months, I'd seen too many clients regret filing lawsuits, even though they were clearly in the right.

Eddington also wasn't one to take on pro bono work that didn't boost his career, and Mendez's case had nothing to entice him. Well, except for Mendez herself—but Eddington was happily married.

I looked back at the conference table, replaying the scene in my mind. I should have taken it more slowly and let her talk through her anger. If I had explained her situation more gently, more tactfully, maybe I could have convinced her that she'd only victimize herself further if she pursued the matter. Instead, I'd been distracted by those golden brown eyes and the touch of her hand.

Well, I'd never see her again. Even if I called and asked for another meeting, she would probably ignore me. I just hoped the next attorney she sought out had the guts to tell her the truth like I had instead of immediately taking her money.

Alternatively, I could track down some of the shop owners she sold wholesale to, and find out what they knew. But what was the point?

My phone gave a soft chime, alerting me that it was time to prepare for my meeting with Eddington about my own case—or rather, my uncle's. Then I had to drive three hours to a blind date that would probably end in disaster. Despite that thought, some part of me hoped that this evening would somehow turn out to be exactly what I needed. I'd been too busy these past months to bother with women.

After the date I'd be close enough to my aunt and uncle's place to drop in for an overnight visit. They'd supported my decision to stop managing their exotic wildlife sanctuary, but in the six weeks since I'd come to Phoenix to intern at Eaton & Eddington, things between us had been slightly awkward. The strain in our relationship bothered me. They were the only parents I'd ever known.

My eyes fell on the candy dishes that our almost-client had left on the table. Ms. Mendez would probably return for them. Too bad, because the blue-marble one that she'd made was really quite good, and I would love to use it in my office. Maybe I could buy it from her to assuage the guilt I shouldn't be feeling after speaking honestly with her about her legal standing.

Eddington was right. I'd better grow some backbone, or I was going to be the poorest attorney in the history of the world.

I picked up the candy dishes and took them to my office. The blue dish felt smooth in my hand, still warm the woman's pocket.

A feeling settled on my shoulder, one that felt a lot like regret.

Maybe during Monday's lunch hour I'd call around to a few pottery shops. It couldn't hurt, even if Bianca Mendez never knew I'd tried.

3

Bianca

I hefted my last bag, threw it into the passenger seat of my pickup, and stared up at Lily's House one final time. It was silly, the nostalgia that filled me at once again leaving, because I'd be coming back to visit often. This weathered, sprawling house had been the first real home I'd ever known, and it represented everything Lily, my foster mother, had been to me and so many other girls over the years. Most of my happy memories were tucked into the nooks and crannies of the house, except a few of my early ones with my older sister, Zoey, and our mother before her death.

With all the changes in my life, I felt myself clinging to my memories of Lily's House. I still didn't know what I was going to do about my logo—or winning back my customers.

"You're always welcome to come home whenever you want."

I lowered my gaze to see Lily on the front porch, her creamy white skin, blond hair, and blue eyes a decided contrast to the darker features of the baby in her arms. After dozens of foster girls and two sons, Lily finally had her own daughter, one who looked just like the baby's European daddy.

I went to hug Lily. "Thank you for taking care of me."

"You sure you're ready to leave?"

"I don't mean just after the accident. I mean since I was a kid."

"Aw, sweetie." Lily pulled me tighter into her one-armed embrace. "You're welcome. I've enjoyed every minute."

I knew that couldn't be exactly true. I was ashamed to admit that I'd gone through a period of time when I'd made Lily cry and stay up late worrying—something Zoey still didn't let me forget.

I couldn't resist taking the baby from Lily's arms. Cherie owned a heaping handful of my heart, like she did with all the foster girls. "It's been two months. The cast is off my arm, the scar on my stomach is practically invisible, and that annoying boot is no longer dragging me down." I pounded on the cement with my foot, now comfortably clad in a flat sandal. "Ankle barely twinges, unless I try to put on heels. The doctor says I only have to wear that smaller brace if I'm hiking or swelling too much. So I'm good to go."

"I guess you're excited to get back to your pottery full-time."

I wished that were completely true, that the panic hadn't removed so much of my joy and the desire to create beautiful things. "I do need to concentrate on working. Plus, Zoey needs me in Kingman. It's not good for her to live alone in a strange city." I'd been driving to Zoey's to move in with her on the day of the accident. Today, I'd finally complete that trip.

"Doesn't Zoey have a new boyfriend there? He's probably keeping her busy."

"That's exactly why she needs me. They've only known each other, what, three months? Dating for only two. I know they work together, but she's already hinting at marriage and about changing her whole life. I need to make sure it's the real thing."

"I thought you said she was happy."

"Zoey's happy working with the animals, yes. But suddenly thinking about grad school to become a vet because of them? It's crazy. He might be pushing her."

Lily laughed. "It's crazy to you because you're an artist. Your sister loves science. Whether or not she marries her boyfriend, she'll make a perfect vet."

"Well, you're right about that." I kissed Cherie's dark hair and reluctantly handed her to Lily. "It will be a few weeks before I can visit—or pick up the rest of my things." The three-hour drive to Kingman wasn't that long, but one I dreaded. "Once I get my pottery wheel set up at Zoey's, I have to concentrate on making up lost time." Or try to.

My eyes strayed to where the wheel sat in the back of my truck with the rest of the equipment Lily and her husband had helped me move from their shed this morning before I'd driven their car to the attorney's office. Once the wheel had been my best friend; now I almost dreaded seeing it. But the move to Zoey's should help.

Lily hugged me again. "Have a safe trip. Promise me you won't take that road."

She meant Hackberry Road, the unpaved one where I'd had the accident—though the cause had been a terrible storm, not the road. "I'll be fine. Isn't that what my new pickup is all about?"

New to me, I meant. The compact Ford had four-wheel drive and a bed big enough to carry a lot of inventory. It would be a lot better for my line of work than my old car had ever been. "Anyway, I'm taking the I-40 right to Kingman. Don't worry. I'll call when I get there."

I didn't add that I still had nightmares about the hours I'd sat huddled in the trees by Hackberry Road, hoping my car didn't wash away in the sudden storm.

No, I didn't plan to go anywhere near Hackberry Road ever again.

What I would do is move to Kingman, somehow resolve the problem with my logo, and create wonderful designs again so I could help Zoey pay our rent.

As I pulled out of Lily's driveway, my thoughts wandered to Mr. Carey from the law firm. I'd been thinking almost continuously about our conversation while I finished getting ready for my trip. Strangely, it wasn't the impossibility of my situation that came to mind so much as the blue color of his eyes.

"You're serious?" I stared agape at my sister, Zoey. "You bought that cabin off Hackberry Road, the abandoned one we broke into the night of the storm? That's where we're going for our double date tonight? To that dump? You've *got* to be kidding."

Zoey pulled a heavy box of tools from my pickup, getting ready to carry it into her garage in Kingman where we were setting up my new studio. "Not me, exactly," she said. "Declan bought it. He's been fixing it up." She stared dreamily into space.

My sister, who had double-majored in biology and chemistry and was now thinking about veterinary school, was acting like any young woman in love. I had only met her new boyfriend briefly when she and Declan had found me after the accident, but I was already impressed at the changes in Zoey. For too long she'd been taking care of everyone—especially me—and any man who could put that expression on my sister's face was probably in our lives to stay.

"Do you love him?" I asked as she put down the box. I was sure it certainly didn't hurt that he was a biologist who worked at the same wildlife sanctuary Zoey did and shared her interests.

She laughed. "Yeah. I do. I never thought I'd find someone like Declan, and now . . . it's just so right. That's why I set up this date tonight. I want you to be as happy as I am."

"About that." I set down my own box, looking away from her. "I've had a pretty rotten day. I don't know that I'll be much company, and blind dates are always so awkward."

Immediately, she was concerned. "What happened?"

There was no use in trying to hide anything; my sister would get it out of me one way or the other. I stopped trying to avoid her gaze.

"Okay, so that's why I didn't come yesterday like we planned. I went to see a guy at a law firm about my logo earlier this afternoon before driving here, and he pretty much told me it was a waste of time. He wasn't exactly tactful about it, either. I kind of felt like . . ." Like an orphan no one cared about. But I wasn't going to tell Zoey that because we'd come too far from those days to dwell upon my inadequacies. "I'm not sure what I'm going to do now. Probably get a second opinion."

Zoey smiled. "Then tonight's going to be perfect, because my friend can help. I told you all about him when I visited you in Phoenix—he has connections."

"The last time you visited me at Lily's, I was still on narcotics." I touched my stomach where they'd opened me to fix the internal bleeding after the accident.

"There is that. Well, I'll forgive you then for not following through on his business card."

"You gave me his card?" I didn't remember getting one from her.

"Never mind. Anyway, like I told you then, you're going to love this guy. Seriously, I'd be dating him myself if I hadn't already fallen for Declan. Stephen is smart, gorgeous, and super nice."

Before I had time to wonder why the name sounded familiar, her gaze slid past me. "Oh, look, there's Declan now—just in time to help us get your pottery wheel off the pickup. That thing weighs a ton."

"The kiln's even heavier," I muttered. It was a small, second-hand portable machine, nothing like the brick kiln I'd built at Lily's House, but it would do for now with all the work I wasn't getting done.

No response from Zoey, who was already sprinting across her driveway to throw herself into Declan's arms. They made a striking contrast: Declan so fair, curly-haired, and freckled by the sun, while Zoey's even, light-brown skin and straight dark hair linked her to our mother's heritage. I'd always envied Zoey her skin. We had the same parents, but I felt pale beside her.

When Zoey finished kissing Declan with a passion that left me jealous, we moved my pottery wheel and the kiln into the tiny garage of Zoey's rental house. Declan started unloading the substantial boxes of clay.

"Don't you think you'd better change?" Zoey asked suddenly, turning a critical eye over my shorts and T-shirt that was showing wet in the front and under my arms after moving an hour of unpacking the truck. I didn't know how she did it, but Zoey still looked fresh.

She handed me a suitcase from the passenger seat of my truck. "We'll get the rest. Hurry, he'll be here any minute."

Declan laughed. "There's time."

"I just want it to be perfect." Zoey grinned at me as though she was doing me a huge favor. "If it hadn't been for that stupid accident, they would have already met."

I stifled an internal sigh. Zoey and I had never been attracted to the same kind of men, so this night, even if I hadn't been preoccupied, was already doomed. Unless the guy really could help me with my case—though he probably wouldn't want to, once we inevitably didn't hit it off. I'd never hit it off with a blind date.

Then again, maybe Zoey knew something about me that I didn't know myself. She said he was smart and nice *and* gorgeous. Maybe he wasn't like other men who bored me to tears. Maybe once he found out I made pottery, he wouldn't suggest that we reenact the sensual scene from the old movie *Ghost*. Not that it playing in clay with the right man wouldn't be fun. Yes, the right guy could make a huge difference.

What were the chances? Not high, but somehow I found myself humming with anticipation as I stepped into the shower.

Ten minutes later, I was wearing hot pink cotton dress that set off my hair and skin but could still be worn with sandals. I wasn't about to endanger my ankle by putting on heels again today—especially since we were going to that horrid cabin. Avoiding the temptation of alleviating some of the heat with a ponytail, I made my way to the living room toward the voices I heard. Zoey was with Declan and another man discussing something about a tiger and a habitat. Probably related to the sanctuary where Zoey and Declan worked. The stranger's face was turned away, and for an instant I registered an impression of lean strength. Then he turned and I gasped.

"You!" There was no mistaking that square jaw and those sky blue eyes: Stephen Carey. The anger and helplessness I'd felt at his office that afternoon returned in force.

He stared at me, looking every bit as shocked as I felt.

"You're Zoey's sister?" He glanced from me to Zoey. "Well, that explains why you seemed familiar this afternoon. I, uh, you have a different last name."

"I use my mother's maiden name." By the time I'd been born, our father had split so my mother had put Mendez instead of Morgan on my birth certificate. I'd always loved having that piece of her all to myself.

"Wait." Zoey's forehead furrowed with worry. "You two know each other?"

I tore my gaze away from Stephen. "He's the attorney I saw today—or rather, the *intern* I saw."

"I thought you didn't use the card I gave you," Zoey said.

"Narcotics," I reminded her. No wonder Stephen Carey's name had sounded familiar, both at his office and when I'd arrived at Zoey's today. She'd probably told me all about him.

"Narcotics?" asked Stephen.

Zoey turned on him. "Never mind. So you're the jerk who told my sister she was wasting her time she came to you for help today? Really?"

"Well, not exactly." He took a step back. "I thought I was—"

"What? What could you have possibly been thinking?" Zoey's eyes flashed, and her color deepened. "When I encouraged you to leave the sanctuary and follow your dream of being an attorney, I thought you'd be helping people. Oo! I'm so mad at you right now. I bet you never guessed the person you would end up *not* helping would be the girl you asked me to set you up with."

Stephen winced. "I asked you to set us up?"

Great, just great. This was getting better and better. Zoey had probably twisted his arm to get him to go out with her poor dateless younger sister.

Declan nodded. "You did ask—that night of the storm. I was there. But to be fair, you had a broken leg, and we really haven't seen you much since."

I backed away from the group. "Look, this is clearly not a good idea." Stephen didn't want to go out with me, and I certainly didn't want to go out with him. It wasn't like I was a hermit or anything. I went out plenty—or I did before the accident. "Let's just call it off."

An abrupt silence fell over the small living room as everyone stared at me.

"I didn't say I didn't want to go out," Stephen said. The flush covering his face was almost amusing. "I do. I was, uh . . . just giving you a way out."

Zoey elbowed him. "Lame."

I laughed at that despite all the awkwardness. "Honestly, I have no desire to go back to Hackberry Road. I still have nightmares of that place."

"She's afraid of the dark," Zoey explain to the men.

Later, I'd kill her. "Thanks," I said with a false sweetness I didn't feel. "But I do sleep without the light on."

Well, sometimes. Okay, never, but Stephen and Declan didn't need to know that.

"Let's get going," Declan suggested. "We can talk about it on the way. I was there yesterday, and the road repair is finally complete. I can't wait to show you the cabin."

"I'm game." Stephen flashed me a sudden grin that did crazy things to my stomach,

Probably because I disliked the idea of this date so much. Yeah, that had to be it.

Zoey turned puppy dog eyes on me. "Let's just start over, okay?"

"Okay," I said, caving. I could make it through one lousy evening, and then I'd come home and pound clay in the garage until I released the anger.

Stephen stepped forward and offered his hand. "Hi, Bianca. I'm Stephen Carey, and I'm really pleased to meet you."

When I stared up into his eyes, I could see only sincerity. "You learn to bluff like that in law school?" I asked.

"No, at Safe Haven Exotic Wildlife Sanctuary. My aunt and uncle own the place, and I used to manage it—Declan's job now. Zoey started with us about a month before I took off to Phoenix. Anyway, you learn to stare down the big cats. You know, pretend they don't scare you."

A smile somehow found its way to my lips. At least he was comparing me to a tiger or a lion instead of a cranky tourist. Okay, so maybe this evening wouldn't be pure torture. I stuck out my hand and shook.

His touch sent current rippling up my arm, and for that instant we might have been alone for all I cared about the others.

Oh, no.

I might be in trouble.

Stephen

Despite her smile, Bianca seemed to pull away from my touch faster than necessary. Nothing I could do about it now. We'd both have to endure this evening for Zoey's sake.

Declan was driving with Zoey riding beside him, which put me with Bianca in the back seat of the car. I wasn't surprised that she hugged the door, but instead of remaining silent, as I expected, she and Zoey began to chat about the baby raccoons at the sanctuary.

"They're still all perfectly happy in a special habitat with their mother and the other raccoons," Zoey told her.

"The videos you posted online are so adorable," Bianca said. "If you hadn't told me how terrible being domesticated was for them, I might have tried to buy one for a pet."

Zoey laughed. "Never a good thing with a wild animal."

"I can't wait to see them in person—to see all the animals again." Bianca's smile included me, and an unexpected heat stirred in my belly.

Bianca had come to the sanctuary? Up until two months

ago, I'd spent most of my days there. Why hadn't I seen her? But then Zoey and I had only worked together a month, and I was often traveling on sanctuary business. Zoey had said her sister had recently finished college, so it was entirely possible Bianca had come on a weekend—which I never worked.

"Looks like they did fix the road." Bianca craned her neck to peer out the front window. Her long hair cascaded over her shoulder, blocking her face. I stifled the urge to feel the silkiness of it between my fingers. "Or at least there aren't any huge ruts."

Her voice was strangled, and I looked at her more intently. Was she actually nervous about being on this road? Her accident had been frightening, I knew, and I couldn't help wishing I'd been with Zoey and Declan when they'd found her instead of being stuck at the sanctuary with a broken leg caused by the same storm.

Zoey turned in the front seat. "You're going to love what we've done to the cabin." Her abrupt change of conversation suggested she'd also heard the anxiety in her sister's voice.

"Can't wait." Bianca gave her sister a grin that fell flat.

I'd studied body language too much to miss the sign of how very much Bianca didn't want to go to the cabin. Or maybe she just wasn't excited about going there with me.

I leaned over and said quietly. "Look, about this afternoon. I know it stinks, what I told you, but please understand I wasn't trying to be a jerk. I've just seen too many people lose too much in the search for justice. One advantage you have is that you're a creative person, and you can create something else that's just as amazing. The guy who stole your logo and designs is a leach and probably doesn't have a creative bone in his entire body. He won't excel at anything."

For a few seconds Bianca studied me without replying, her gaze briefly straying to Zoey and Declan in the front seat. "I guess I'll take that as a compliment. I'm glad you're being honest with me."

"It *was* a compliment. I've seen your work—at least a little bit of it." I remembered her candy dish, still on my desk where I'd left it. "In fact, I'd like to see more. Maybe buy a few pieces?"

In the front seat Zoey snorted. "Since when are *you* interested in pottery?"

"You don't have to," Bianca said in a rush.

She thought I was trying to placate her. "Well, I need decorations for my office, and clients love candy."

Bianca nodded, but made no attempt to sell me anything. Either she was a lousy saleswoman, or she didn't want to interact with me after tonight.

"So how'd your boss like the write-ups for your uncle's case?" Zoey asked. "For your summary-whatever thing."

"Motion for summary judgment." I stole a glance at Bianca, and for a moment, something caught in my throat. "He loved them. But apparently our opponent is threatening to file a lawsuit saying Cuddles was outside her pen when he was attacked."

"What?" Declan and Zoey exclaimed together. Zoey whipped around in her seat to stare at me, and Declan's gaze met mine in the rearview mirror.

"As if we'd let a full-grown Bengal tiger walk around,

ready to bite any dumb trespasser," Zoey muttered darkly. "Although in the case of this guy, it might be tempting."

"Wait, is this about that guy who used the text and videos from the sanctuary's website to steal donations from people, pretending the money he collected was being used to care for the animals?" Bianca looked at me with one brow arched.

I nodded. "Yeah, he raked in over a million dollars before we discovered it. We couldn't figure out why donations plunged so drastically. At some point he snuck into the sanctuary to get a video of himself with one of our Bengals and got himself bitten."

"Just a nibble," Zoey protested. "Cuddles has a right to protect her turf."

"He was lucky it wasn't fasting day," Declan added.

"Yeah, exactly," I agreed. "Unfortunately, the new lawsuit would include a motion to put Cuddles down as a danger to society. But the man's attorney came right out and said he won't file if we drop our lawsuit."

"That's crazy—all of it," Bianca said. "People like that are a danger to themselves and everyone. If that man is willing to lie and threaten to kill an innocent animal to save himself for being prosecuted for fraud, what else will he do?"

"I wonder the same thing." I met her curious stare, the car suddenly feeling too warm. Maybe because my heart was pounding in my chest. What was it about her that made me feel so self-conscious? "Anyway, this means I'll have to add information to my motion so that the judge rule on our behalf."

"You really love the law, don't you?" Bianca said quietly.

"Yeah, I do." My voice was just as low as hers, and I couldn't tell if the others were still listening. I could only stare at Bianca and wonder if the skin of her cheek felt as soft as it looked.

"I can tell."

Her smile made me break out in a light sweat. Why did it suddenly seem like a good idea to lean over and kiss her?

"It's good to find what you were meant to do," she added.

Did she feel that way about her work? Of course she did. But asking about that now seemed a bit like throwing what happened with her logo in her face. The irony of that I was pursuing my uncle's case when I had advised her to cut her losses didn't escape me. It wasn't the same thing, though, and I hoped she'd understand.

"What if the judge doesn't decide for summary judgment?" she asked. "You go to court and battle it out, right?"

"Right. And everyone loses more money—except the attorneys. I'm doing as much as I can to limit my uncle's legal expenses. But the idea that Ross is benefitting so much from this whole thing burns me up."

"Ross?"

"Baxter Ross. The counsel for the defendant." In fact, Baxter had been a major pain in my side for the past fifteen months. The more I learned about the law, the more irresponsible I found him.

Bianca's brow furrowed slightly. "His name sounds familiar."

"He does an annoying commercial," Zoey put in from the front seat.

"I haven't watched commercials in years," Bianca said. "Not since I got Netflix."

Zoey shrugged. "He's the kind that gives all attorneys a bad name. Not like the kind Stephen's going to be."

I knew this wasn't so much a compliment as a little jab at me at how she thought I'd treated Bianca in my office, but I didn't take the bait.

"Well this Ross guy will probably settle as soon as he's spent all the money his client stole," Bianca said, her laugh smoothing over Zoey's remark.

Bianca might even have moved away from her door a few inches, which I shouldn't care about but did.

"Well, here we are." Declan pulled off the road and started up a short hill.

So we were, and there had barely been an awkward moment the entire thirty-minute drive.

As Bianca hopped from the car, I wished more than anything that our meeting this afternoon had been scheduled for next week. I'd blown it big time, because from what I could see, Bianca was everything Zoey had promised—fun, witty, smart, and talented. I wondered if she could ever see me as anything but the guy who told her to give up years of work without a fight.

Maybe.

Regardless, Zoey was right that I'd gotten into this business to help people, and as hopeless as Bianca's case seemed, I was somehow going to help her.

Bianca

Walking across the new porch, I stepped into the cabin, whistling in appreciation. "Nice. This doesn't look like the same place we broke into during the storm. New windows, wood floor, paint. Even a cool couch."

"The best thing is that there are no more mice." Declan shivered dramatically.

That made me laugh. "Seriously? A big guy like you, afraid of mice?"

"Only animals I can't stand. Them and rats."

I smirked. "Remind me not to show you my new pets, then. And I hope you don't plan to spend much time at our place. Rats are sensitive creatures."

Only Stephen laughed. He got my humor, or at least pretended to.

"Wait until you see the kitchen," Stephen said. "I helped Declan lay the tile."

I was surprised that a wildlife guy turned law student knew anything about home repairs. "Lead the way."

The new tile turned out to be a marbled tan, adding an unexpected elegance to the rough little cabin. Wasn't the remodel a bit overkill for a place Declan used only on the weekends?

Zoey began setting the kitchen table with dishes from a new-looking cabinet while Declan unpacked a heated container with heavenly-smelling chili and corn muffins.

I examined the old black stove, running a finger along the cool surface. "I seem to remember this was already here?"

Declan laughed. "It's a classic. Heats the entire place—and you can cook on it. But don't worry. I'll put in a microwave for you."

I pivoted on my heel. "For me?"

Zoey set down the last plate and turned in my direction. "Declan's going to move here permanently after I begin school, because it's closer to the sanctuary than his place in Kingman."

I blinked at her. "So you've decided for sure to go to veterinary school?" School meant her leaving Kingman, and I'd only just arrived.

"Yeah, but I can't get into any veterinary school until a year from this fall, so I'll just be doing a few online classes until then." She smiled at me. "Don't worry. You're not getting rid of me that fast."

Relief waved through me.

"Anyway, we've been spending a lot of time here, and now that you're living with me, you probably will be too." Zoey shrugged and gave Declan a glance full of hidden meaning I couldn't interpret.

I was happy for her, despite having the odd sense of being left out—which was silly. "This place is a little out of the way," I commented.

Zoey laughed. "Bianca likes the city," she explained. "Not sure that even Kingman will have enough people for her."

"Actually, no people is exactly what I need." I hooked my purse over the back edge of a chair. "I've spent too much time streaming movies lately. I need to focus on work."

I'd only worked a few times on my wheel at Lily's since the accident—and that wasn't only because my right arm wasn't strong enough to throw a decent pot without pain. The biggest issue was the shutdown of my creativity.

But I wasn't going to let it take over my life. That was why I'd pushed myself to track down Fletcher and had made the appointment with Stephen—and part of why I'd moved to Zoey's. I needed my sister and a change of scenery. I needed to regain control.

"Ready to eat?" Declan asked, indicating the pot of chili.

"I am." Habit had me checking my fingernails for clay. To my chagrin, I found a little bit under my thumbnail that must have become lodged there when we'd hauled my stuff into the garage. Not even my vigorous shower had worked it loose. I headed to the sink.

Apparently Stephen had the same idea about washing, and our hands brushed as we collided. At least with the prolonged absence from work, my hands didn't have their normal texture of sandpaper.

I looked up to see Stephen watching me. My heart began doing odd things in my chest and heat filled my face.

I dove for the water and flipped it on. But there was no bar soap, and in my hurry I put too much dish detergent on my hands. The water didn't seem to want to wash it off.

As Stephen waited his turn, he glanced back at Zoey and

Declan, and I followed his gaze. They were wrapped in each other's arms, ignoring us completely, which for some reason made my heart do even more gymnastics.

Forgetting the bit of clay, I abandoned the sink and hurried back to the table. "I'm starving."

For the next half hour, I let the others talk while I busied myself eating. I'd lost weight after the accident and hadn't much appetite in the past weeks, and now was as good a time as any to start making up those calories. Plus, it meant I didn't have to participate in the conversation.

When everyone did finally look at me during a lull in the discussion, all I said was, "These corn muffins are fabulous."

I used the rest of the muffin to sop up the dregs of my chili, but when I put it into my mouth, my fingers tasted like dish soap.

"Something wrong?" Zoey asked me.

I forced myself to swallow. "No. It's great. Really."

I popped up from the table to rinse again at the sink, knocking my bag off the chair and spilling its contents. I bent to collect everything, and Stephen stood to help. Why hadn't I thought to remove the two oversized Ghirardelli chocolate bars I'd shoved in there before my drive? At least I'd eaten the other two on the way, or I'd really look greedy.

He scarcely glanced at the chocolate. Instead, he stared at the crumpled business card I'd retrieved from the floor of my truck after our meeting this afternoon. "Did you go see this guy?" He thrust the card at me, but when I reached for it, he didn't let go.

"Actually, that's the card Kent Fletcher gave me when I confronted him about stealing my logo." I could still see Fletcher's smirking face, the unruly salt-and-pepper growth on his chin reminding me of the bum who foraged for food in the garbage bins outside my old apartment in Phoenix. "After I called him to ask for a meeting, he must have wasted no time tracking down a sleazy ambulance chaser to represent him."

"It's Baxter Ross."

I looked at him blankly. "And?"

"You mean the attorney defending that jerk who wants to kill Cuddles?" Zoey glared at us, and for an instant it was difficult to remember her emotion was for the "jerk" and not us.

"Oh." No I understood. "That must be why his name sounded familiar when you were talking about it in the car. I only just read it the once."

Stephen finally relinquished the card, and I shoved it with the chocolate bars back into my purse. "I should have figured Fletcher would have an attorney with the moral fiber of a"—I glanced at Declan—"rat."

Zoey laughed. "Fletcher probably saw his commercials. But don't let them ruin our evening. Anyone want more chili before the chocolate cake?"

"Sure," I said at the same time Stephen muttered, "No, thanks."

Wait, maybe he had the right idea. The faster we ate dessert, the faster we could finish this mockery of a date. "Actually, cake is a better idea."

"Good. Declan, would you get out the games while I cut the cake?"

Games. Seriously? I opened my mouth to protest, but my sister looked so content that I shut it again. She deserved to be happy, and even if I had to bite my tongue all night and pretend I wasn't annoyed at being here with Stephen Smartypants Lawyer-in-training, it was worth it to see her smile like that.

We ended up playing Monopoly of all things, which surprised me because Zoey hated the game. When we lived at Lily's House as teens, I'd always beaten her and anyone of the other foster kids who dared played. However, this time I wasn't the only one taking the game seriously. After Zoey and Declan surrendered, Stephen and I battled head-to-head—until he landed twice on my Pennsylvania Avenue hotel and went bankrupt while I spent a happy three turns hiding out in jail.

I smirked at him.

"Nice game," he offered.

"Are you this agreeable when you lose in court?"

He laughed. "I don't know. We haven't actually lost any of the cases I've worked on. But I'm sure there'll be a first time."

His eyes went to my bag, still hanging off the chair, and his smile vanished. I wished I'd kept my mouth shut. He was actually fun to be around when we both forgot about my logo and the way we'd met.

The game had lasted long enough that Declan and Zoey called it a night. Even though it was Saturday tomorrow, they'd both be going into the sanctuary to make sure feeding time for the big cats went smoothly.

"Bianca," Stephen called as I tried to follow Declan and Zoey to the car.

I turned, gazing at him where he stood on the porch. "Yeah?"

He came down the steps to stand beside me. Moonlight

bathed the path in a soft, romantic light, and I was all too aware of his closeness. His hair seemed almost black in the darkness, and his eyes navy. He was taller than me by at least a foot, so I had to look up to see his expression. But there was no indication of his thoughts—until his gaze lowered to my lips.

My mouth watered suddenly. He wasn't going to try to kiss me, was he? That would be ridiculous. Yet I didn't back away. What would I do if he tried? All at once, I very much wanted to find out.

"About your case," he said, redirecting his attention to my eyes.

I arched a brow. "I thought you said I didn't have a case."

"You know what I mean." He paused and then rushed on. "Look, there are a few things I can do. I know this guy Ross, and sometimes with clients like his, sending a cease and desist and showing intention to pursue can make a big difference."

"That's not what you said before. Why the sudden change of heart? You said it probably wouldn't make a difference."

"It might not. But like I said, I'm familiar with Ross, and if he really is representing this Fletcher guy, Ross knows I don't back down easily. I'll just remind him how hard I've pushed in my father's case."

"You mean, threaten him?"

He nodded. "If you want to call it that."

"I don't care what you call it. I am serious about fighting for my rights. My designs and my logo are mine, and Fletcher deserves a lot more than threats." I swallowed hard, trying to control my emotions. I wanted to scream at the injustice of it all. I wanted to hurt Fletcher for upsetting my life, but most of all I wanted to yell at Stephen for making me feel so hopeless this afternoon and now suddenly changing his mind. I had enough anxiety without this roller coaster ride.

"Then why not take my offer?" He scrubbed a hand through his short hair, making it stand up in front, which I found oddly appealing. "You seem upset at the suggestion, and I don't understand why. Legal work can be very expensive; I can cut those costs."

"You're right—I am upset. Because this afternoon you told me to give up, and then tonight when you learn who Fletcher's attorney is, suddenly you're willing to help me. *That's* what bothers me. My case hasn't changed, but apparently you hate this Ross guy so much that you're ready to do anything you can to fight him. It's not my case that's important, is it? It's beating him and proving yourself that you care about."

Stephen's jaw clenched and unclenched, but when he spoke, his voice was still calm. "Look, I admit I dislike Ross, and maybe I do want to push back at him. But you're Zoey's sister, and she asked me to help you. That's what's important."

So on top of everything else, I was a charity case, just as I'd been since my mother died. He didn't want to help me because he was attracted to me, or because I had rights. He would help because Zoey forced him and because he hated Fletcher's attorney.

"I appreciate the offer," I told him, "but I think it's best if you forget the whole thing. We made it through tonight for my sister. Let's leave it at that, okay?"

Turning on my heel, I hurried after my sister, but a pebble caught in my sandal, and I had to stopped and finger it out. When I glanced back at Stephen, he was still standing where I'd left him, a sorrowful expression on his face.

A tiny bit of guilt crept into my mind, but I pushed it away. I didn't need Stephen's help. I'd find another way. Maybe going public with my story on social media would open some avenues.

The drive home was subdued, but somehow Stephen and I made it without exchanging more words. Zoey and Declan were so caught up in each other, they didn't appear to notice.

When Declan and Stephen walked us to the door, Stephen pushed a card into my hand. "If you change your mind, call me."

I wouldn't, but I nodded and watched from the window as he climbed into his own car. I wondered if he was driving all the way back to Phoenix tonight, or if he was crashing at Declan's. I told myself I didn't care, but as he drove away, my determination to carry on my fight alone faded. He knew the legal process, and maybe I'd been hasty rejecting his offer. His reasons might not be important. After all, how far was social media really going to take me?

I wouldn't be honest if I didn't admit that I had enjoyed the game part of the evening. Stephen had stolen my breath away more than once, but somehow my pride had gotten in the way. Maybe I'd even been a little rude.

What was I going to do now?

Stephen

Though it was after eleven when I arrived, my aunt and uncle, Lena and Josh Carey, were waiting up for me in the house they'd built on Safe Haven Exotic Wildlife Sanctuary property. They both hugged me and invited me in for some of my aunt's special sleep potion: warm milk blended with melted chocolate, cream, and vanilla, then topped with whipped cream and chocolate shavings.

Lena poured me a mug. "So how did the date with Zoey's sister go?"

I nodded. "She's nice. Not to mention beautiful."

"I figured as much with a sister like Zoey," Josh said. "Declan spends far too much time at work staring at her."

Lena dug her elbow into his side. "It's good he does that. They're perfect together. And it's not like he doesn't work far more hours than he should." To me she added, "So, you going out with her again?"

Not if Bianca had her way. But I didn't want to kill the hope in Lena's eyes. "Maybe. We'll see. She's an artist."

"That's good," Lena said. "She can keep you from burying yourself too much in all that legal stuff."

I searched for another topic that would catch their attention. "So how's the new tiger adjusting?"

"He's doing great!" Josh launched into a detailed story about his beloved tigers.

My guilt at leaving their dream—the sanctuary—to pursue my own was a burden I might never fully overcome. They'd been everything to me after my parents died in a car crash when I was three, and I wanted to be as much to them. Or at least everything their estranged biological daughter hadn't been. I would never stop owing them for giving me a happy, contented childhood.

The truth was that if Zoey hadn't pushed, and Declan hadn't been so ready to take over as manager at the sanctuary, I'd still be working there—making my uncle happy, but dying a little bit inside each day. In a big way I owed Zoey and Declan for the direction my life had taken. But the first time Zoey had asked for help, I'd made a mess of it.

Then there was Bianca . . . it was hard to even think about her, standing there so beautiful in the moonlight with disdain in her eyes, accusing me of only caring about beating Ross. I didn't know what made me angrier, the allegation or the fact that maybe there was some truth to her claim.

Whatever my motives, I *had* decided to help her before I'd learned about Ross being Fletcher's attorney. Even before I knew she was Zoey's sister, I'd been thinking about calling the local pottery shops.

Not that Bianca would believe me.

When Josh had finished his story about the new tiger, my aunt gave an exaggerated yawn. "You're probably tired, aren't you? If you're going to the sanctuary with your uncle in the morning, you'd better get to bed. I have your room all ready. Don't worry about the cup. I'll clean up."

"Thanks." I kissed her cheek, nodded at my uncle, and headed to my room, grabbing my overnight bag where I'd left it in the hallway.

Once in my room and ready for bed, I couldn't sleep. Monday was too far away to sate my growing curiosity about Bianca and her case. I spent the next few hours researching common law trademark cases on my laptop and drawing up the rough draft of a cease and desist letter that would make even Ross think twice about using Bianca's logo. If Eddington wouldn't let me officially take the case and back me up with his degree, I'd be on my own as a non-attorney helping Bianca, but I was willing to try.

If only I had something to up the stakes.

Usually, if someone stole something and got caught, it wasn't the first time. Maybe with a little research, I could find out more about Kent Fletcher and other scams he might be running.

Around two in the morning I found it. I laughed out loud. "This is it!" Hurriedly, I began taking screenshots.

Tomorrow after visiting the sanctuary and catching up with the staff and the animals, I was going to see Bianca—whether she liked it or not.

I couldn't help but hope that she'd like it, because no matter the awkwardness between us, I wanted to see her again.

Bianca

The slanted light of the sun through the window danced on my face, waking me. It had to be at least ten. I should have been up hours ago, arranging my equipment in the garage and maybe throwing a simple pot or at least doing something productive, like searching the Internet for a new attorney.

Instead, my hand reached for the remote to the TV sitting on the dresser against the wall.

No! What was wrong with me?

Not so long ago, the idea of spending the entire day making my ideas come to life in clay had been my idea of paradise. Now the thought of going to the garage and putting my hands in clay filled me with panic. My heartbeat pulsed in my ears, and I wanted more than anything to pull the covers over my head, squeeze my pillow to my aching chest, and stay there until Zoey returned from work.

I recognized the anxiety for what it was. After becoming our foster mother, Lily had taken me to a psychologist because of my fear of the dark. It had been years since

I'd had to deal with the anxiety, but the symptoms had crept back since the accident—at first so slowly I hadn't recognized it, but increasing after I learned about my logo. I could no longer ignore the problem.

"I can do this," I told myself after several deep breaths.

The first step was the hardest. It always was.

I forced myself from the bed and down the hall to the only bathroom. A warm shower, clean clothes, and a good breakfast with plenty of protein went a long way toward helping me feel normal.

I washed the dishes by hand, though we had a dishwasher, and started sweeping the floor before I caught a glimpse of my wide eyes in the shiny reflection of Zoey's microwave. What was I doing?

"Stop stalling." Dropping the broom, I headed to the garage. Already, the place smelled familiar, with my tools and bags of clay, half-finished pots, and jars of paint filling up the space. For now, the unpacked boxes could wait. All I needed was my wheel and the extra bats.

Using a cutting wire, I sliced off a good chunk of porcelain clay from a new rectangular block, and an equal lump of ball clay. Slowly and methodically, I began wedging the relatively soft masses together, like my grandmother used to knead bread. Not even a twinge from my arm. So far, so good.

The wheel was next, and for that I needed to fill a small bucket with water from the kitchen sink. Finally, I slammed the clay onto the wheel and begin centering it. Yes, this was nice. The clay was much smoother and more malleable than the castoff bits I always kept and reworked. I couldn't afford to waste clay. I dipped my hand in the water before working the mass up and down, shaping it first taller and then shorter and wider.

What should I make?

For no reason at all, the memory of Stephen saying he needed a candy dish came to mind. The one I had brought to his office had been a simple bowl-like design, with hand-fluted edges added after throwing. But for a law office, something more dramatic would be in order. A larger, vase-like piece with intricate designs, a fancy lid, and vibrant glaze.

Like coming home after being away far too long, the piece formed under my fingers, the act of creation a breath of magic. The first two pots were halfway decent, but not as good as my usual. I left each on a removable bat as I set them on the worktable before slipping a new bat in place and starting again. More pots formed under my hands. The minutes became hours. My right arm began to ache where it had been broken.

And there it was—maybe the most perfect dish I'd ever made. Far from finished, of course, because it would have to dry a day before I could trim it and bring out the details, but the bones were there. The lid would be the crowning piece, and I bet my suppliers would be eager to get their hands on similar ones.

Then a week after they showed up on store shelves, Fletcher would probably use my logo on inferior copies.

My breath caught in my throat, and for a long minute, I felt like drowning. My heart pounded and panic blackened my vision. My hand came down on the piece, crushing it.

Tears leaking down my face, I pushed back from my

wheel and curled in on myself. Flashes of memories flooded me. Of nights huddled in bed, listening to Zoey cry. I hadn't known then what my uncle was doing to her, but I knew he was hurting her even more than she hurt herself with the knife she'd used on her arms to release her pain. There had been nothing I could do, nothing but shiver in the dark and wet my pillow with tears.

"Bianca!" Zoey's voice came from the kitchen doorway. The next minute her arms were around me. "Sweetie, what happened? What's wrong?"

I buried my face in her shoulder and let myself cry.

"Is something wrong? Are you hurt?"

My sister's anguish drove me to my feet. "No! I just have to get rid of these. They're no good!" I reached for one of the five other completed pots, crumpling it and throwing it into the five-gallon bucket I used to store scraps. The lid and another pot followed. I was reaching for a third when Zoey grabbed my hands.

"Stop it! Bianca, tell me what's wrong." Tears shone in her eyes, and the worry in her face made me feel ashamed.

"What's the use?" I said. "I haven't been able to work at all, and now that I finally can again, it's not the same. That man's just going to steal my designs and fool the shop owners. He'll make horrible copies with my name on them. Better that it all end up in the garbage!"

"That's not true! Your work is good, and those shop owners will see the difference. Your work is nothing like his."

"He sells his stuff too cheap. I can't compete."

"I know it seems that way now, but that's the panic talking. You know that, right? We're going to make this work out. I promise." She hugged me tightly.

I clenched my eyes against the light, willing myself to be calm. This wasn't Zoey's problem, it was mine. I wasn't a child anymore that she had to take care of. I needed to find control. I could overcome this. *I would.* "I'm sorry," I murmured.

"No, *I'm* sorry." Zoey paused for a moment. When she spoke again, there was a hint of the old pain in her voice. "I didn't realize how this was for you. Not until right now. It's like . . . being violated."

I pulled back from her then and opened my eyes. "No, not like y—"

But she was right. It wasn't exactly like the kind of physical violation my sister had suffered as a child, but it was still an attack. Fletcher's mocking laugh as he'd handed me his attorney's card had made me feel utterly violated.

"It's going to be okay." Zoey put her face close to mine. "You will deal with the panic—you did it before. And you'll regain all the business you've lost."

I nodded because I believed in her, even if I sometimes didn't believe in myself. "Okay. But I'm not sure where to begin."

"First, we're going to get some food in you. It's past three, and I bet you haven't eaten. Then you're going to talk to Stephen Carey."

I stared at her. "What?"

Her eyes narrowed. "Don't play stupid with me. He was at the sanctuary today, and he told me he offered to help you last night. Said you shot him down."

"He only offered after he found out who was representing Fletcher. He has it out for that attorney, and I don't want my chances of winning to dwindle even more because two attorneys hate each other."

Zoey shook her head. "Nope, think again. Stephen told me he'd decided to help before he learned about the attorney."

I scowled. "Anyway, it's only because I'm your sister."

"So?" Zoey rolled her eyes. "How many wall plates or vases have you made for friends of friends? You wouldn't just do that for anyone off the street because you couldn't make a living. Neither would Stephen."

"Are you forgetting he told me to give up yesterday?"

"Look, I'm not saying you have to date him, but you can't throw out the idea of him helping just because he didn't offer to burn through your life savings when first you went to see him yesterday."

My mind churned at her words. She was right. Obviously, my perception of Stephen had been colored by my emotions—both the panic about my logo and my attraction to him.

"Well?" Zoey said.

"I'll think about it."

"Good. Now let's get something to eat."

Two hours later, Zoey left somewhere with Declan, and I faced the garage and the mess I'd made earlier. The garage was over-heated now, after soaking up the afternoon sun, and I opened the automatic door to ventilate the stuffiness. There was a breeze, at least.

First, I moved the three undamaged pots to the wall of shelves Zoey had installed for me along one entire side of the garage. The pots were nearly ready to put plastic over to stop them from drying too quickly. My heart sped up a little as I thought about actually finishing the candy dishes and sending them out into public. I could do this.

I put a cover over the bucket of water, now mixed with clay scraps after my work this morning. Together it made "slip" and was silky smooth, exactly the way I liked it. Next, I had to deal with the rest of the scraps and the ruined pot still on the wheel. Once I threw them into my scrap bucket with a little water, everything would soon be ready to form into something new.

A clearing throat startled me into nearly dropping the scraps of clay onto the ground instead. I turned to see Stephen Carey standing just outside the garage, his figure framed by the light of the late-afternoon sun.

The little jump my heart gave wasn't at all related to panic. He looked good in snug jeans and a T-shirt that hinted at the muscle beneath. He might be currently working in an office, but he was obviously accustomed to physical work. His hair was slightly tousled, as though he'd been running his hands through it.

Zoey had given me his number, and I'd promised to call, but I hadn't worked up the courage. I realized I owed him an apology. I hadn't meant to be so awful to him.

"Hi," he said, shuffling one foot like a nervous boy. "Can we talk?"

I opened my mouth and hoped this time the words would come out right.

Stephen

I took it as a good sign when Bianca didn't immediately throw me out.

She wore clay-spattered jeans and an equally messy yellow T-shirt. Her skin glistened with moisture, and her shirt look partially damp. Pieces of dark hair had escaped her ponytail. Her tongue wet her lips, and my eyes wandered there and stayed, even as I reminded myself that this was a business call.

I stood in the opening of the garage, feeling awkward as I awaited her response. Zoey had texted me that Bianca was going to call me about her case, but I wasn't leaving things to chance. Zoey was an eternal optimist these days.

"Been working?" I surveyed the open boxes of unpacked tools and the three fresh-looking pots on a shelf against the wall. A collapsed pot lay abandoned on her pottery wheel.

"Something like that." She indicated the ruined piece with a delicate snort. "That one's yours." There was a lightness in her voice that hinted she was teasing.

I grinned. "Uh, can I pick another one? That looks

too much like my efforts all those years ago back in high school." Though now that I thought about it, if my teacher had resembled Bianca, I might have paid more attention in art class.

"Sorry, only one per customer." She brushed her hands together before wiping them on a rag. Then she folded her left arm across her chest, rubbing the biceps of her right arm, as if it pained her.

"Look," I began. "I know you're upset with about yesterday, but I've been doing some research, and I think there's something I can do to help you." I hesitated a moment before adding, "I probably should have done some checking before I advised you to give it up. Your case is stronger than I thought."

Her lips parted as if I'd surprised her. "What did you find out?"

"Last night I came across a blog by another local artist. He claims Kent Fletcher stole his logo and designs four years ago. He filed a lawsuit but later had to drop it for lack of funds."

"Really?" Arms unfolding, she took a few steps toward me, and a pleasant, earthy smell reached my nose, probably from the clay on her hands and clothing. "That's great. I mean, sad for the other artist. But to know I'm not the only one . . ." Her eyes glowed. "I should contact this man."

"I talked to him this afternoon."

Her eyes flew to mine. "You were up late finding him, and you already talked to him? You've been busy."

"I couldn't sleep. Anyway, this artist—name's Chad Peterson—ended up creating a new business logo and filing a trademark for it. He says he's barely returned to the level of business he had before. He lost all his savings in the lawsuit."

She looked down, rubbing a tiny bit of clay between her fingers. "Poor guy. It's not fair that Fletcher could do that to him. It shouldn't cost so much to defend what's already yours."

She took a deep breath, her gaze going to the three new pots on the shelf, and then wandering over her equipment and the unpacked boxes. Her teeth bit down on her lower lip, as if holding something back. Finally, with a little shake of her head, she turned to me.

"I don't want to lose everything I've worked for. I'm creative. I can design something new . . . eventually."

Her voice was strained but determined. I could almost swear her skin had paled significantly. How had I not seen yesterday at my office how much this meant to her? I wanted to wipe that sadness off her face.

"Maybe you won't have to," I said. "You said you've been using the logo for eight years. We'll find people who have your work and get them to testify, if it comes to that. But with the other artist on our side, I think we can resolve this before it gets anywhere near a court. Fletcher lost money too when he hired Ross, and he only won the other case because the real artist couldn't afford to continue. If Ross and Fletcher see me backing you, even if I can't get my firm to sign on, both of them will think twice."

"Why? Wouldn't they just think I'd run out of money to pay you?"

"No. Because you'd be a *pro se* litigant—which means

representing yourself. Any citizen has a right to act in their own behalf. Usually, it's a terrible idea because too much depends upon knowing how to navigate the system, but with my experience, you'd still have the advantages of legal representation. You can push this all the way. Or make them think you'll push it all the way."

Her gaze held mine, and I had the gentle sensation of drowning in them. "How much will it cost?"

"I won't charge you anything for my time, and if my firm agrees to help, it'd only be the time I take to report to them about it. They might even write that off. There would be incidental fees if we have to go further, but we can discuss that if we get there." I didn't think telling her that I'd cover any fees would convince her to agree. I'd already seen evidence that she was as stubborn as Zoey about taking care of herself.

"Okay." Bianca's arms dropped, and the smile she gave me now was real, as if she'd been faking all the others before. "Thank you. And I'm sorry about being a jerk last night."

"Does that mean I get a new pot?" I nodded at the misshapen piece on her wheel.

She laughed. "Yeah, I think so."

"One of those?" I waved at the others on the shelf.

She scooped up the ruined attempt and tossed it into a large white bucket of scraps. "Maybe. Depends on how they turn out."

I hoped that meant she wanted to give me a good one and not something she'd normally discard.

"Tell you what," I said, looking around the garage once more. There were still numerous boxes scattered over the floor and a second worktable by the opening of the garage that should be moved to wherever she wanted it. "I'm not heading back to Phoenix until tomorrow night, so I have time to help you set up here, if you want a hand. I'm thinking you could move that wheel closer to that little window. With a small air conditioning unit there, you should be able to work here even during the hottest summer days. Might need some insulation along the walls, though. It's easy to install. Declan and I could help."

"First tile and now this. You're full of surprises."

Why did that make me feel ridiculously proud? "I get it from growing up with my uncle. He's the quintessential do-it-yourselfer."

"Zoey mentioned you'd lived with them since very young. How was it practically growing up at the sanctuary?"

"Best life a boy could have."

I wondered she knew how my parents had died, and I wanted to tell her. Maybe sometime soon. We were both orphans, though from what little I got from Zoey, the sisters had experienced more hardship than I had. Maybe someday Bianca would tell me about her childhood, about why she was afraid of the dark. Her dreams for the future.

Because I wanted to know all of it. There was something here between us, something I'd felt if not from the moment I'd seen her at the office, then for sure at the cabin last night. It wasn't only the way she looked but had a lot to do with her determination and personality.

And maybe just a little bit because of the way she'd obliterated me at Monopoly.

"That reminds me," I said as Bianca opened a box of unglazed pottery and started arranging the pieces on a shelf. "I demand a replay. You would never have won last night if you hadn't convinced Zoey to sell you Pennsylvania Avenue."

Her eyes glinted. "She had to sell it to me or go bankrupt. I won fair and square."

"Maybe so. I still demand a rematch."

"Okay, you're on."

By the time the garage was completely organized and Bianca's air conditioner and insulation ordered, it was dark.

"I have to admit you know how to get things done," she said. "If you're even half as good at law stuff, my logo will be the only one carved into any pot."

"Can I see that? You carving it?"

Her eyes went wide, and she seemed to hold her breath.

"If that's okay," I added.

She nodded sharply. "Yeah, I just haven't . . . since I found out about Fletcher." She glanced around. "I don't have a leather-hard pot to carve—that one that's still wet but dried enough to handle without deformation—but I can show you on a block of fresh clay."

She grabbed a tool from a plastic organizer while I brought up the video feature on my phone. It took less than three minutes for her to make a perfect logo.

"Amazing," I said. "Looks like a stamp."

"I had a stamp made, but I only use it on pieces that are too thin to carve well."

"Do you have a receipt for the stamp?"

That was only one of a million questions I'd asked during the afternoon and evening, typing her answers into my phone. She was wary around me still, like a wild animal new to the sanctuary. Talking while we worked had made getting information easier.

"I probably have a copy of the receipt online," she said. "I'll email it to you with the names of my high school and college teachers. Come on, let's go wash up." She led me inside to the kitchen sink, where the remains of the pizza we'd shared for dinner still sat in the delivery box.

"Thanks for all your help today," Bianca said.

I leaned back against the counter as I dried my hands. "Actually, I had fun. I haven't taken too much time off lately."

"What do you mean, time off? You were working on my case all day."

I grinned. "And here I thought I'd been discrete with my grilling."

"I'm really grateful."

I tossed her the towel. "Look, just leave Fletcher and Ross to me. You go back to doing what you do best."

"And you'll let me know when I need to worry?" The irony in her voice was unmistakable.

"Something like that." Keeping my eyes on her face, I stepped toward her. My pulse raced. I wanted to kiss her, maybe as much as I'd ever wanted anything.

She held my gaze and didn't move away.

"Bianca." My voice came out hoarse.

"Yeah?"

"I think I'm going to kiss you."

"Well, then do it already."

I closed the space between us, leaning down and pressing my lips against hers, one of my hands behind her neck. So soft, so good, so right. I'd meant it to be a simple kiss, something just to let her know I was interested. But a shudder went through me as she kissed me back. Heat effused my body, and I lost it a little as her arms slid around my neck, bringing us closer. Before I realized what I was doing, I picked her up and placed her on the counter. She tasted so good. My arms went around her, pulling her against me. I might never stop kissing her.

When we did come up for air, Bianca's eyes were huge, and again I felt myself drowning in them. I didn't mind in the least.

"I'm sorry," I said, feeling suddenly embarrassed at my lack of control.

"Don't be," she whispered. "I've been wondering what that would be like since last night."

"Last night? That explains why you were so cranky."

She laughed and started to kiss me again.

"Uh, sorry to interrupt," said a voice.

I jerked my head over to see Zoey standing in the door between the kitchen and the living room.

"Zoey!" Bianca said. "We didn't hear you."

"Obviously." She gave us a wide, knowing smile. "You two must be making headway on the case."

"Really? Bianca's hands pushed on my chest as she jumped off the counter. "You had to say that?"

"And I have something more to say." Zoey held out her left hand where a ring glinted on her third finger. "Look, Declan just proposed! We're getting married!"

"Oh, Zoey!" Bianca launched herself at her sister, and the two hugged and squealed in excitement.

"Congratulations," I said as the women gushed over the

ring and began discussing dates. They looked prepared to discuss wedding details all night, and I had a cease and desist to revise and more research to conduct. "Uh, I'm sure you two have a lot to talk about. I'll see you both later."

"I'll walk you out." Bianca grabbed my hand, pulling me through the living room to the front door.

For a moment we stood on the cement porch in the moonlight. "Thanks again," she said.

"Can I see you tomorrow?"

She grinned. "Only if you'll let me beat you at Monopoly."

"Never."

"Okay, then you can come over. I hate it when people let me win."

I kissed her one last time. A simple kiss, the way I should have kissed her before. But the passion still burned beneath, promising much more.

She watched from the porch as I drove away, and I had an overwhelming sense of rightness. I was falling—maybe too fast. And I didn't care.

To think I'd almost missed this, getting to know Bianca, earning her trust, helping her. Even if nothing more ever developed between us, I was glad to be in a position now to do the right thing.

"I won't let you down," I told the absent Bianca. "I promise."

Bianca

Early Sunday afternoon when I'd barely awoken from a brief afternoon nap, Stephen appeared on my doorstep, his eyes bright. My face was probably flushed as I recalled our kiss from the night before. I hoped he attributed it to the heat of the day.

"Here." He handed me a paper, his face bright with anticipation. "Read this."

"What is it?" After Stephen's kiss and Zoey's excitement about her wedding, I hadn't fallen asleep until around five a.m. Then Zoey had awakened me early for church. So despite my nap, I still felt fuzzy.

"A cease and desist letter that I intend to deliver to Fletcher in the morning."

I began scanning the letter: a no-nonsense accusation of copyright and trademark infringement, a request for Fletcher to account for his use of my logo and designs, and a demand to cease all usage. Included were the names of people who could verify my use of the logo and designs.

"This would scare me to death," I said. "But that list of people is only from the beginning of my college years."

"Yep," he said. "I'll call Ross in the morning and tell him we have additional proof for earlier use that we'll use when we ask for a court order. And I'll mention that we know about the other artist. No doubt Ross and Fletcher can find people to say he's been using the logo for years, but if he doesn't know the exact year we're claiming . . ."

"Then he won't know when to say he began."

"There are ways he can get around that, so we're more posturing than anything for now. But Ross understands that sort of thing. I'm banking on Chad Peterson's involvement to be the determining factor. If not, we can request a court order to stop him temporarily."

"Thank you so much." I couldn't help hugging him. The minute we touched, the tension between us increased. His eyes went to my lips, and then away just as fast. Ah, so he was thinking about last night too. That seemed a good sign.

"I'll let you know how it goes tomorrow, though we probably won't hear anything for a couple of weeks."

"That long?"

He grimaced. "That fast."

"I see."

"Try to focus on work. Leave the rest to me. Try not to worry."

I found it impossible not to believe him. "Okay, I'll try."

"Now how about that game of Monopoly you promised me?"

"Zoey and Declan should be here any minute. They had an appointment this afternoon to talk to the pastor about their wedding plans. We might be able to twist their arms to get them to play."

"This time, I'm going to win."

"No way."

Turned out he did win, but only because Declan sold him Park Avenue.

That night before Stephen left, he placed a soft kiss on my mouth. "I like you, Bianca Mendez. I like you a lot."

I liked him too.

The next week slipped by as I divided my time between working and helping plan Zoey's September wedding. Three months suddenly seemed like nothing when we were talking the rest of her life.

"How's it going with you and Stephen?" she asked, looking up from the eggs we'd made for Friday morning breakfast. "He's been calling every night."

I forked up a piece of egg. "We only talk about the case."

Her eyes took on a mocking glint. "No, you don't. I'm not deaf, you know. I hear you laughing and flirting in your room. You really like him."

"Maybe a little."

I'd have thought with my artistic background and his love of the law that we wouldn't have much in common, but he loved music and art, and his research on past court cases fascinated me. We talked about everything and anything.

"Any news on the cease and desist letter?" Zoey asked, rising from the table with her empty plate.

"Not yet. They have ten days to respond. It's a waiting game."

At least with Stephen taking on my battle, it was easier

for me to focus on work, or pretend to focus, and to stave off the panic. I now had forty of the new candy dishes in different stages of drying or painting. Still, on some days I became so angry at Fletcher and so hopeless about the future of my pottery that creating was impossible. I felt vulnerable, as if Fletcher had stolen a little piece of my soul.

So far, I'd put my logo on only three of the new pots. Because the more I thought about it, the more unsure I was that going through a lawsuit, if Fletcher didn't back down, would benefit me in the long run. Clinging to the old logo and being unable to work because of the emotions surrounding the case would only be self-defeating. But the few clients who preferred my superior pots would likely support me through a logo change. I could build again.

Except I hadn't yet designed a new logo I felt good about. Zoey suggested it was because I hadn't given up hope on the current one, and she was probably right.

"I'll see you after work," Zoey said, gathering her purse and keys. "Do you know if Stephen's coming up this weekend?"

"He hasn't said anything." My heart did a funny little jump at the idea of seeing him again.

Zoey paused at the door. "Bianca, if things between you two . . . With Declan and I getting married . . . What I'm trying to say is, if you decide to move back to Phoenix, I'll understand."

"Because of Stephen? I barely know him."

"Sometimes a week is all it takes."

Several hours later found me taking the three candy dishes I'd made on Saturday from my kiln. They'd turned out better than I'd imagined, especially the intricate lids. The shape of each dish and the patterns I'd carved on them were the same, and each had vibrant glazes, but each hand-painted design was unique. I'd send pictures to my distributors, and if I was lucky, I'd have pre-orders for hundreds more over the next month. Fletcher would have nothing like them yet. I was back in the game.

A knock at the rear door leading from the garage drew my attention. The air conditioner was already installed, and Declan was putting in the insulation tomorrow, so I wasn't expecting anyone.

I opened the door, a grin spreading on my face. "Stephen?" How different I felt seeing him compared to our first meeting a week ago. "Come on in. You must be dying in that suit. It's already hot out there."

He stepped inside, his attention zeroing in on the new candy dishes. "Now that's something I'd like to put on my desk. It's big and in your face, but still . . . elegant."

"Glad you like them, because one is for you."

He examined a dish, opening the lid and peering inside. "Very nice. Much better than when I saw them last." He ran a finger over the surface of the glaze, and a shiver ran through me, as if he'd touched me instead. He set the dish on my worktable.

"So what brings you all the way here?" I asked. "Shouldn't you be at work?"

"Yeah, I was driving there but somehow ended up here. I have news—I guess I couldn't wait to tell you."

"What news?" My stomach clenched. He didn't look

upset, but who drove three and a half hours to give the sister of a friend good news he could share easily over the phone?

"Ross emailed me late last night. His client has agreed to stop using your logo. He claims the similarity was unintentional, and that his client will pull your mark immediately from his future designs."

I stared at Stephen, unable to stop my smile from widening. "That's wonderful!"

"Well, he's still claiming the designs are his, and that he won't stop using them, but I've seen his stuff, and it's obviously inferior. The buyers will notice eventually, if they haven't already."

"The logo is the important thing, because it means quality—my quality. Oh, Stephen, thank you!"

The next minute I was in his arms, and his lips met mine. Passion flared, but there was also tenderness and hope and, somehow, a hint of the future. He pulled away after only a few minutes.

"I have to go to work," he said. "But I'm driving back out tonight. Late, since I'll have to make up for this morning. Can I see you tomorrow?"

Excitement curled in my stomach. "I'd like that. A lot."

And then, even though we both knew he had to leave, he didn't. Not right away. Instead, he kissed me again.

Rachel Branton has worked in publishing for over twenty years. She loves writing women's fiction and traveling, and she hopes to write and travel a lot more. As a mother of seven, it's not easy to find time to write, but the semi-ordered chaos gives her a constant source of writing material. She's been known to wear pajamas all day when working on a deadline, and is often distracted enough to burn dinner. (Okay, pretty much 90% of the time.) A sign on her office door reads: Danger. Enter at Your Own Risk. Writer at Work. Under the name Rachel Branton, she writes romance, romantic suspense, and women's fiction. Rachel also writes urban fantasy, paranormal romance, and science fiction under the name Teyla Branton. For more information or to sign up to hear about new releases, please visit www.RachelBranton.com.